"The funny thing is, you know, I do trust you.

"I trust you to behave exactly as you have been, with honor and integrity. The problem is, you and I are on opposite sides of the fence, C.J."

"I don't think that's true." His denial was automatic and held no conviction at all.

Caitlyn shook her head. "You still plan on being a lawyer?"

"Yes, I sure do."

"Well, then? As a lawyer, you are bound as an officer of the court to uphold the law. And there's no getting around the fact that I—" her smile wavered "—for the best of all possible reasons, am often...shall we say...*forced* to circumvent it." She shrugged as if to say, *That's the way it is. What can you do?*

What *could* he do? What could he say? The answer to that: Not a damn thing.

Dear Reader,

The days are hot and the reading is hotter here at Silhouette Intimate Moments. Linda Turner is back with the next of THOSE MARRYING McBRIDES! in *Always a McBride*. Taylor Bishop has only just found out about his familial connection—and he has no idea it's going to lead him straight to love.

In *Shooting Starr,* Kathleen Creighton ratchets up both the suspense and the romance in a story of torn loyalties you'll long remember. Carla Cassidy returns to CHEROKEE CORNERS in *Last Seen...,* a novel about two people whose circumstances ought to prevent them from falling in love but don't. *On Dean's Watch* is the latest from reader favorite Linda Winstead Jones, and it will keep you turning the pages as her federal marshal hero falls hard for the woman he's supposed to be keeping an undercover watch over. *Roses After Midnight,* by Linda Randall Wisdom, is a suspenseful look at the hunt for a serial rapist—and the blossoming of an unexpected romance. Finally, take a look at Debra Cowan's *Burning Love* and watch passion flare to life between a female arson investigator and the handsome cop who may be her prime suspect.

Enjoy them all—and come back next month for more of the best and most exciting romance reading around.

Yours,

Leslie J. Wainger
Executive Editor

Please address questions and book requests to:
Silhouette Reader Service
U.S.: 3010 Walden Ave., P.O. Box 1325, Buffalo, NY 14269
Canadian: P.O. Box 609, Fort Erie, Ont. L2A 5X3

Shooting Starr

KATHLEEN CREIGHTON

Published by Silhouette Books

America's Publisher of Contemporary Romance

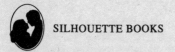 **SILHOUETTE BOOKS**

ISBN 0-373-27302-9

SHOOTING STARR

Books by Kathleen Creighton

KATHLEEN CREIGHTON

has roots deep in the California soil but has relocated to South Carolina. As a child, she enjoyed listening to old timers' tales, and her fascination with the past only deepened as she grew older. Today, she says she is interested in everything—art, music, gardening, zoology, anthropology and history—but people are at the top of her list. She also has a lifelong passion for writing, and now combines her two loves in romance novels.

Chapter 1

South Carolina, Early Autumn

Even with the bruises it was the most beautiful face he'd ever seen. Stark against the pillow, it needed no adornment. Framed in white bandages, the features were pristine, elegant, exquisite. It was a face that belonged in dreams, or fairy tales. Sleeping Beauty, maybe, or Snow White...the enchanted princess waiting for her hero's kiss.

If only, he thought, it could be so easy.

The woman in the bed stirred. Eyes the pale gray-blue of sunlit water swept over him, and his breath caught, then fluttered in uneven breaths.

Hearing it, she murmured a soft and slurred, "Who's there?"

He cleared his throat. "It's me." He leaned forward and touched her hand. "C. J. Starr."

She closed her eyes and turned her face away. After what seemed a long time, she whispered, "Why are you here?"

He sat and stared at his hands, loosely clasped between his knees, and tried to think how he could answer that without laying the burden of his guilt on her. Finally he shrugged and mumbled simply, "I wanted to be."

"I don't blame you, you know." Though still groggy, her voice took on a raspy edge. He looked up and saw that her eyes were wide-open again and gazing at him. *Silver eyes.* "You did what you had to do. I knew the risks."

He shifted restlessly. There was a heaviness in his chest that wouldn't go away. "If I hadn't been there—"

"—I'd have picked somebody else to hijack. I guess that's true." There was a pause and then, to his surprise, he heard a whisper of a laugh, soft and ironic. "Of all the truckstops on all the interstates, why'd you have to pull into that one?"

He angled his gaze toward the window, where the sky was the clear, translucent blue it takes on only in autumn, when the early trees are turning and the goldenrod is in bloom. Yellow-flower season, his momma called it—her favorite time of year.

He sighed and settled back in the chair. "I guess I'd have to blame it on the thunderstorm," he said.

Five Months Earlier—Springtime

It wasn't a bad one, as storms go, even if the rain was coming down in sheets the way it can in the South in the springtime, and visibility was about zero. But it was the third time a four-wheeler had stopped dead in front of him and he'd had to hit his air brakes while he prayed and swore loud enough to outroar the rain on the roof of his big blue Kenworth.

It was in view of the fact that—despite his momma's ⸱ᵗ efforts—he hadn't been keeping up on his praying the ⸱ should, and had probably used up a goodly portion ⸱ᵢme's allotment of Divine Intervention, that the next time he saw a sign for a rest stop swimming toward him through the rain, C.J. put on his blinker and pulled off the interstate.

A number of other drivers had had the same good sense, it seemed, because the rest stop was full and he just did find a place to pull in well up along the on-ramp, the last available spot big enough to wedge an eighteen-wheeler into. Once he'd got the Kenworth buttoned down to his satisfaction, he put on his slicker and jogged back up the sloping drive to the buildings.

It looked to him as if the rain was letting up some, though that could have been because he wasn't on the interstate, where the truck spray always made things seem worse than they were. A chilly wind had sprung up and was blowing what rain there was in nasty gusts under the roofed shelter areas, so with the exception of a couple of women trying to use a cell phone, most people had taken to staying in their vehicles.

C.J. meant to do the same himself, once he'd made use of the rest room and vending machines. He planned on getting himself an assortment of junk goodies to help pass the time, which was something truckers did a lot of and was one of the reasons why some of them got so big-bellied and heavy, or so he'd been warned by his brother, Jimmy Joe, who was also his boss.

C.J. had noticed, though, that after near twenty years driving big trucks, Jimmy Joe himself was as lean and lanky as ever, leading C.J. to conclude that leanness pretty much ran in the Starr family, along with chocolate-brown eyes and dimples.

He wasn't worried much about health and fitness as he fed coins and dollar bills into the vending machines and filled up the pockets of his slicker with tortilla chips and Little Debbie's. What concerned him more was making it back to Georgia in time to take the exam he had scheduled for three days from now. After that one there was just the

final and then he was through with law school after ten
long years; that is, if you counted college and before that
the time it had taken him to pass his high school equiva-
lencies, since he'd had the bad sense to drop out of school
a month into his senior year.

Not a single minute of it had been easy. A whole lot of
folks were bound to be surprised he'd made it this far, C.J.
included.

Juggling a soda can and a package of cheese puffs, he
stuffed the leftover change into the pocket of his jeans,
hunched his shoulders inside his slicker and headed back
to his truck. A little farther along the breezeway he had to
pass by the two women who were still trying to get through
to somebody on a cell phone—without much luck, it
seemed evident to him.

The one with the phone looked about fourteen. Tall but
slender and small-boned, she was wearing jeans and a
hooded sweatshirt with the hood pushed back, and she had
short blond hair cut in that spiky, messed-up way younger
women seem to favor. She had her finger stuck in her un-
occupied ear and kept turning this way and that, looking
up into the mist or down at her feet, the way people do
when they're trying to get something besides static on a
wireless phone. The other woman was older—maybe early
thirties—but pretty, with reddish brown hair worn long,
thick and curly, what C.J.'s sister Jess would call "big
hair." She seemed edgy, the big-haired woman did. She
kept hugging herself as she watched the girl with the phone,
throwing glances over her shoulder into the rainy dusk.

And now C.J. could see a third person there, snugged up
against the older woman's legs. A child, a little bit of a girl
with dark hair cut to chin length and straight across her
forehead, and the biggest, blackest eyes he'd ever seen.
Since those eyes were gazing straight at C.J., he did what
came naturally to him. He smiled. The eyes kept on staring

at him, not blinking, just kind of shimmering, like deep, dark pools.

C.J.'s heart gave a peculiar quiver, and all at once it seemed like the most important thing in the world to him to see that child smile. So he smiled even bigger, showing those famous Starr dimples, and said, ''Hey, hon', how're you doin'?'' Since it struck him that the eyes had kind of a hungry look, and that it might have been seeing him tucking those goodies away that was making her stare at him that way, he held out the bag of cheese puffs and added, ''Here you go, darlin'—you want some of these?''

C.J. would have been the first to admit there was a lot he didn't know about kids, but even so it set him back some when the child cringed away from him and tried to hide behind her momma's legs, as if there'd been a dead rat in that cellophane package instead of cheese puffs. It wasn't the reaction C. J. Starr was used to getting from people when he turned on that smile—put it that way.

He transferred the smile to the child's mother and ruefully explained, ''Sorry, ma'am, I sure didn't mean to scare her.''

The woman gave him a tight little smile in return and muttered something politely vague, along the lines of, ''That's okay, but we're fine.''

Not friendly types, these people. With a mental shrug, C.J. was about to go on his way when for some reason he glanced over at the girl with the cell phone, and it happened to be just as she pivoted and looked right at him. His heart gave another one of those odd little shivers. She wasn't as young as he'd thought; young enough, but definitely not a kid. Her eyes were searching, soul-piercing sharp, and…it might have been something about the artificial lighting in that rest stop, but he'd have sworn they were *silver*.

He didn't know what it was about her, but whatever flirty comment he'd planned on making went right out of his head. Instead he gave her a polite nod and a mumbled,

"Ma'am..." and added on the trucker's benediction: "Y'all have a safe trip, now," as he hunched inside his slicker and plunged out into the mist. A few steps farther on he broke into a jog.

Back in his truck, he put the two women and the little girl out of his head while he stashed his goodies in the usual places and popped open the can of soda. Then he turned on the cab lights and reached for the pile of law books he kept handy on the passenger seat beside him. The way he saw it, with that exam coming up and his entire future riding on the outcome, every little minute he could squeeze in some studying was a plus.

The roaring of the wind brought C.J. out of his doze. *Damn,* he thought, that storm must be moving back in again.

No, wait—that wasn't wind. *Trucks.* It came to him that what he'd been listening to for a while now was the sound of big diesel engines and a whole lot of tires churning past him down the on-ramp, one after the other. The rest stop was clearing out fast. A check of his mirrors showed him an empty parking lot, but for one nondescript gray late-model four-wheeler in the back row, over by the doggy-john. Somebody else having a nap forgot to leave a wake-up call, he thought.

He had himself a stretch to get rid of the kinks and cob-webs, then gathered up his junk-food wrappers and soda can and climbed out of his truck—one last stop at the rest room, he told himself, and he'd be headin' back out on the road himself.

The air was warm and soupy, but he was a Southern boy, and to him warm and soupy was the way it was supposed to be in the springtime. Wet dogwood petals dotted the grass and sidewalks and the roof and hood of the parked car, and the air smelled of crushed leaves and mud, with a sweetness from some sort of plant he couldn't identify, and maybe a hint of something rotting off in the woods somewhere. Smelled just right to him. Like spring.

Spring wasn't C.J.'s favorite season of the year, though. "Spring can break your heart," was the way his momma, Betty Starr, put it, stoic after a late freeze had wiped out her saucer magnolias and flowering crab apple trees for the umpteenth time. C.J. preferred fall, with sky so blue it made your eyes ache, and that indefinable touch of melancholy in the air.

Then he had to laugh at himself like any Southern-raised boy would at such thoughts—even though he knew the momma who'd raised him wouldn't have laughed. Betty Starr was a schoolteacher who'd brought up her three daughters and four sons to enjoy books and reading as much as they did hunting and cars, and to have an appreciation for the softer aspects of nature that was at least on a par with a fine deer rifle or the inner workings of a gasoline engine.

In spite of that, given the circles in which he'd grown up and spent most of his life, C.J. had gotten in the habit of keeping poetic notions to himself.

"Excuse me, sir..."

Lost in his musings and shaking water from his hands as he emerged from the restroom, C.J. damn near jumped out of his skin when the slender form stepped out from behind the wall that screened the entrance, blocking his way. She had both hands tucked in the front pocket of her sweatshirt, and her neck looked fragile as the stem of a flower rising out of the folds of the laid-back hood.

"Whoa!" he said, rocking back and putting out his hands in the exaggerated way people do when they almost collide with somebody, but at the same time turning on his smile, full wattage, to let her know he wasn't put out about it. "Ma'am, I believe you've got the wrong door. The ladies' is around there."

He would have gone on his way, but she seemed inclined to stay where she was. Though she didn't return his smile.

"I'm sorry to bother you—"

"Hey, no bother—what can I do for you?" C.J. was radiating charm from every pore. And that didn't have anything to do with the discovery he'd just made that the woman was a whole lot prettier than he'd first thought she was, in a strange, almost fairy-tale sort of way, with a ballerina's neck, little delicate chin, soft lips and skin so fine it seemed lit from the inside. But he'd have turned on the charm in equal measures for a freckle-nosed kid or a ninety-year-old with a face like a road map. That was just his way.

"I need to ask you a favor. A really...big favor." A smile flickered briefly, as if some distant voice had prompted her to mind her manners. It struck him how tense she was, like a deer in that last instant before she figures out you're watching her and bolts for the bushes.

"I'll be glad to do what I can, ma'am," C.J. responded automatically. But he was beginning to feel uneasy now, too, just a faint "Uh-oh..." whispered in the back of his mind. The last thing he needed right now was more delays.

"My car won't start. I'm afraid it might be the alternator. I was wondering if you—"

"Be glad to take a look for you." Relieved that what she wanted was something he could give her without taking up too awfully much of his time, he was feeling confident and was already walking off toward the only remaining vehicle in the parking lot. "That it over there?" He spun back and held out his hand. "Got the keys? Won't take me but a minute—"

"No. There wouldn't be any point in you looking at it." She was standing where he'd left her with her hands stuffed deep in the pocket of her sweatshirt. She was shaking her head, and her voice was a hard, flat monotone. "I'm sure it's dead. What I wanted to ask you was—"

"Did you call Triple A?" Really uneasy, now, he was

remembering the cell phone, and the anxious way her big-haired friend had watched her make the call. Not wanting to, he also remembered the little girl with the haunting eyes.

"They're backed up—a lot of accidents, they said. Because of the storm, I guess. Those get priority, so they said there'd be at least a two-hour wait. That was an hour ago."

"Well then—"

"I just called again. Now they tell me it's going to be another two hours. We can't stay here that long. We can't."

It occurred to C.J. that her voice might be easy on the ears without that edge of tension in it. As it was, its very quietness gave her words an urgency that set his teeth on edge and raised the volume of the warnings in his head to a holler.

He scratched his head and mumbled, "Well, ma'am, I don't know what to tell you...." Truth was, he was stalling, because he was pretty sure he knew where this was heading and what she was about to ask of him and wanted to hold off disappointing her and her friend—especially that little girl—as long as he could.

At the same time he was beginning to resent the hell out of her for putting him in a position where he'd have to.

"If you could just give us a ride to the nearest—"

Damn it. He elaborated on the swearing under his breath while he shook his head and rubbed unhappily at the back of his neck. "Ma'am, I wish I could do that—I do. I'm not allowed to pick up passengers, okay? I could lose my job." Which was sort of a lie—the part about losing his job, anyway. His brother might chew him out good, but he wasn't going to fire him. On the other hand, the no-hitchhikers rule was something all the Blue Starr drivers understood and agreed on, mainly because it made basic good sense. Picking up strangers was dangerous, especially the female variety. Those could complicate a driver's life in ways C.J. didn't even like to think about.

But because he was softhearted by nature and hated to

let anybody down, he looked at this particular female and tried on his best smile, dimples and all. "Unless it's a matter of a life-or-death emergency, I suppose that'd be different."

"It is."

C.J. narrowed his eyes and didn't say anything for a minute or two; she'd caught him off guard with that, with the quiet tension in her voice and those silvery eyes never leaving his face. He felt a prickling under his skin, a kind of itchy-all-over, shivery feeling that made him think of the way an animal's fur lifts up when he's feeling threatened. He couldn't have said why he should feel danger connected with such a fragile-looking woman, but right then he was pretty certain if he'd had fur it would have been standing on end.

"Are you in some kind of trouble?" he growled without stopping to clear his throat.

She made a sound he'd have sworn was a laugh, except her face didn't look like she thought anything was funny. She spoke slowly and deliberately, as if to a not-very-bright child. "I thought I'd made that clear. My car is broken down. I need you to take me—us—to the nearest town. Right now. As in, immediately. *Do you understand?*"

The urgency in her was so palpable C.J. actually stepped backward. His mind was racing, looking for explanations that would make sense to him. "Wait— How…is somebody—"

She didn't wait for him to work his way through it. Closing her eyes, she gave a regretful sigh and withdrew her hands from the front pocket of her sweatshirt.

Momentum carried C.J. through. "—hurt or someth—" Then his hands shot up in the air without his brain even telling them to. A natural response to the gun in her hand. "Aw, *jeez.*"

"I'm sorry," she was saying in that same quiet but urgent way, "I don't have time to explain. I said we have to leave here immediately. This—'' she gave the gun a little wave, a *very* little one, she wasn't being careless with it ''—is to let you know how serious I am about that. I will shoot if you—''

She interrupted herself with an exasperated sound and a hissed, ''Oh, for heaven's sake, will you *please* put your hands down? You look silly with them up in the air like that.''

Not to mention what it's gonna look like to anybody who happens to pull into the parking lot right about now, was C.J.'s thought—his first coherent one since she'd pulled the snub-nosed pistol out of her sweatshirt pocket.

He snorted and muttered crossly, ''Yeah, well, it seemed like the thing to do when somebody's pointin' a gun at me. Sorry—guess I just don't know how to act.'' He did lower his hands, though…slowly. Now that the first shock was fading, he was starting to get good and mad, and he ground out the rest of it between gritted teeth. ''I've never had anybody threaten to kill me before.''

She made a grimace, the first sign of honest-to-God emotion he'd seen in that fairy-princess face. ''I did not threaten to kill you. I said shoot—I meant in some nonlethal place, of course. A leg or a foot, maybe. Anyway, I promise you won't like it. Plus, although I'm a fairly good shot, there's always a chance you'll move and make me nick something important, like an artery, or…you know. So I suggest you don't start weighing your chances.'' She paused, then added, ''And I can really do without the sarcasm. I don't do this sort of thing every day, you know.''

''Coulda fooled me,'' C.J. muttered. ''You're pretty damn good at it.'' His heart was pounding and he felt sweat beginning to trickle between his shoulder blades.

''Look—I said I'm sorry. I just don't have time to stand here and argue with you. Or justify myself.'' She turned her head enough so she could call over her shoulder without taking her eyes off him, "Mary Kelly, it's okay, I've got us a ride."

After a moment, C.J. saw the big-haired woman edge out from behind the ladies' room entry screen farther down the back side of the building. The little girl was still snugged up against her side, and he knew now what she reminded him of. It was those pictures he'd seen on the news of refugee kids in Bosnia or Afghanistan—big-eyed and scared, but stoic.

"Turn around, please, and start walking toward your truck." The low, almost whispered command jerked his attention back to the woman with the gun, and he saw that it and her hands had disappeared back inside the pocket of her sweatshirt. "I don't want to upset Emma," she explained, speaking rapidly now. "I hope I won't have to. Trust me—the gun's still right here, pointed at your belt buckle. Now, go on—*move*."

What could he do? What *did* he do? Something brave and heroic? Hell, no, he did what anybody with a lick of sense would have done—he turned around and started walking. His spine was stiff as a poker and his back felt exposed, as if his clothes had been split open down the back and an icy cold wind was blowing in the gap. He had the good sense to be a little bit scared and wobble-legged, too, but mostly what he was, was madder'n hell. Madder than he could remember being in his life.

Behind him he could hear the scuffle of footsteps on pavement…a murmur of conversation between the two women. He didn't turn to look, but he kept seeing the little girl hugging her momma's legs, and her big scared refugee eyes. That was what made him the maddest. At least he thought it was. The truth was, C.J.'s feelings were pretty complicated right then.

When he was even with the back end of his trailer, he stuck a hand in his pocket and hauled out his keys, making a big deal out of holding them out to show his hijacker what he was doing. He unlocked the passenger-side door and held it wide open, and in a PO'd, sarcastically polite way waved his "passengers" in.

He felt mean and childish when the big-haired woman looked at him as she was lifting her little girl into the cab and murmured a breathless and sincere, "We really do appreciate this, mister—thank you." Her accent was thick Southern—not Georgia, someplace farther west. Arkansas, maybe, or Oklahoma.

"Get back in the sleeper and shut the curtain," the hijacker ordered the woman, just as if it had been her truck. When C.J. waved her in ahead of him she gave him a tight little smile and murmured, "After *you*."

So he had no choice but to get in on the passenger side of his own rig and climb across the seat and the center console, dumping his law books on the floor in the process. By this time his anger was a buzzing inside his head, incessant as a horsefly trapped against a windowpane, and if there were any calm and reasoning voices left in there, he couldn't hear them.

A gun. She'd pulled a *gun* on him!

What he wanted was to lash out and knock that damned gun into next week. He considered trying it. There'd be a moment—maybe when she was hauling herself into the cab and her hands were otherwise occupied.

Jeez. He was being hijacked by a *woman,* for God's sake. And one who looked like something out of a book of fairy tales!

Well, shoot, he couldn't very well knock *her* into next week. Reluctantly C.J. allowed that one inescapable fact into his consciousness, where it had the effect of pouring oil on boiling water. He'd never struck a woman before in his life and wasn't about to start now, not even for this. His stomach turned queasy and his right arm went numb just thinking about it. Plus, there was that little girl. What if he put up a fight and hurt her by accident?

C.J. put his anger on slow simmer and settled into the driver's seat. The hijacker lifted herself up to the cab, light as a butterfly landing on a blossom—and all the time managing to keep one hand, he noticed, on that gun in her sweatshirt pocket. She took her eyes off him only once, and that was when she was hauling the door shut and she glanced out at the mirror.

She gave a hiss of alarm and instead of settling into the passenger's seat, crouched down in the space in front of it. "Pull out," she said in a croaking whisper. "*Now. Go…go!*"

It was on the tip of his tongue to remind her in a withering tone that it wasn't a dragster he was driving, that eighteen-wheelers don't *do* jackrabbit starts, but what he did instead was take a look in his mirrors to see what it was that had got her so spooked. All he saw was a dark-gray sedan with tinted windows cruising slowly through the rest stop behind him. As he watched, the sedan pulled up behind the lone car parked in the lot and stopped. Two men got out of the passenger side.

"They lookin' for you?" C.J. inquired, keeping his eyes on the mirror.

"Can we just go? Please…?" For once it was a plea, not an order.

Glancing over at his hijacker, he saw her face gazing at him from out of the shadows, pale as a daytime moon. Without another word he turned on his running lights, shifted gears and pulled the Kenworth slowly onto the ramp, accelerating on the downslope to the interstate. His heart was pounding and he had a peculiar, hollow feeling all through his insides, even his head, and he wondered if that was what people meant when they said something "didn't seem real."

He'd just about gotten up to cruising speed and was still keeping a close watch on his mirrors when he saw the gray sedan with the dark-tinted windows come barreling up behind him. His heart leaped into overdrive, but the sedan had already zipped into the fast lane and was shooting on past him. C.J. figured it had to be doing at least ninety.

He waited until the sedan had disappeared over a rise in the road ahead before he spoke to the hijacker in his quiet new voice, what he thought of as his unwilling coconspirator's undertone, muttered out the side of his mouth. "You can come up now, if you want to. They're long gone."

She hesitated, then came up slowly in kind of an elongating process, first swiveling her head like a periscope to take in the road ahead and alongside as well as her mirror before easing into the seat with an exhalation that was almost a sigh. After giving C.J. a look to make sure he understood he was still under cover of that pistol of hers, she set about fastening her seat belt and settling in.

"Those guys were looking for you," he said again, only this time it wasn't a question. "Why in hell—"

She stopped him with a frown and a warning shake of her head, then jerked it toward the sleeper compartment behind them.

Exasperated, he turned on his radio, already set to a country music station, and flipped the speakers to the sleeper so they'd provide some cover noise. Then he said, "You could have just told me if you're in some kind of trouble, you know. You didn't have to go and pull a gun on me."

"I thought I'd made that pretty clear."

"Something besides car trouble, for Pete's sake!"

When she didn't answer right away, he looked over at her. She was staring straight ahead, and he could see the pale, slender arch of her throat move with her swallow. Her lips tightened. "I didn't have time to explain. How could I know what you'd do? I knew they had to have caught up with us by now—"

"Who's *they?* What do *they* want to catch up with you

for?'' *What in the hell have you gotten me into, lady?* was
what he really wanted to ask.

He could feel her look at him. ''They're not cops,'' she
said in a cold hard voice. ''If that's what you're thinking.''

It wasn't. In fact, he realized it was about the farthest
thing from his mind. Those guys had looked like a couple
of serious thugs to him, but now that she'd mentioned it…
He chewed on it in silence for a minute, then said in what
he thought was a friendly sort of way, ''Okay, you want to
give me an idea *now* what kind of trouble you're in? Maybe
I can help.''

She gave the kind of laugh without any humor in it.
''You're helping the only way you can. And the less you
know about anything, the better. Believe me.'' She turned
her face toward the window then, but out of the corner of
his eye he could see her hand flex inside the pocket of her
sweatshirt, and he knew that gun was still pointing in his
direction.

Chapter 2

"Hey. You hungry?"

The hijacker jumped, as if she'd forgotten—for a few minutes, at least—that C.J. was there. She looked over at him but didn't reply.

"There's all kinds of snacks and things," he went on, thinking now about the little girl with the hungry eyes. "You know, if anybody wants anything to eat, just help yourself."

Those silvery eyes held steady on him for a heartbeat or two. Then she softly said, "Thank you," and unbuckled her seat belt so she could hitch around and slide back the curtain that closed off the sleeper. After a moment she eased it shut again, settled back in her seat and rebuckled the belt. "Asleep," she murmured, then added on an exhalation, "Thank God. They were both exhausted."

And you? he thought, gratified to feel his brain shifting into work mode again. He was getting the glimmer of an idea.

Aloud, he asked, "How long've y'all been on the road?"

"Since yesterday." Was it wishful thinking, or were her words a little slurred? He figured if anybody ought to be exhausted it was her, since she'd been doing the driving. He hoped so, anyway.

"Whereabouts you come from?" he persisted, growing braver.

She hesitated. "Miami."

C.J. gave a low whistle and nodded. He was starting to have an idea what this might be about, and after a moment he asked the question that had popped into his head when she'd first mentioned the word *cops.* "Have you thought about going to the police?" Which maybe seemed like such a natural thing to do because his own family was lousy with lawyers and law enforcement, including one in-law who was with the FBI.

His hijacker shook her head. "That's not an option," she said in a flat, dull voice. He could feel her head swivel his way as she added impatiently, "Look, believe it or not, I know what I'm doing. Okay? Just…keep driving and don't ask questions. Please," she added, as a polite afterthought, then scrooched down on her tailbone and put her head back against the seat. She didn't close her eyes, though, and again he could see the telltale shape inside her sweatshirt pocket, of her delicate little hand clenched around the butt of a snub-nosed pistol.

He went back to driving and keeping his mouth shut the way he'd been told, but he was starting to get angry again. Not the burning-all-over rage that had overwhelmed him before, but a slow simmer of resentment. First of all he wasn't one to take kindly to being bossed around, never had been, and being bossed around by somebody holding a gun on him was even harder to take. Add to that the fact that the person holding the gun and doing the bossing was a *woman,* and a pretty one… It surprised him that that particular aspect bothered him, given the way he'd been raised, but dammit, it *did.* He couldn't help but feel it reflected

badly on his courage that he'd let such a thing happen—
and even, in some foggy way, on his manhood.

Adding a whole other layer to his resentment was a thin
veneer of guilt, which came over him whenever he thought
about that little girl with the refugee eyes. Dammit, the
woman was right; he ought to have known those people
were in trouble when he'd first set eyes on them, there in
that rest stop. He *had* known, if he'd let himself think about
it, but he hadn't wanted to think about it. He hadn't wanted
to be bothered, afraid their trouble might interfere with his
tight schedule. Truth was, if he'd offered his help right off
the bat, the woman wouldn't have had to pull a gun on
him.

Not that that excused what she'd done. No way. And he
wasn't about to stand for it any longer than he could help.

It was quiet in the cab of the Kenworth in spite of the
sweet rumble of the big diesel engine up there in front of
him, the steady rush of highway noise and the muted thump
of rockabilly music coming from the speakers back in the
sleeper. The last of the storm had moved on east, and the
late-afternoon sun had dropped down out of the clouds and
was pouring liquid gold over his left shoulder. The interstate was straight and monotonous, traffic was light, and
normally C.J. would have been fighting drowsiness pretty
hard. But not this time. Right now he was wound up tight
with all his senses honed.

It reminded him of the way he'd felt as a kid when his
oldest brother, Troy, had taken him out hunting the first
time, sitting up in that deer blind in the first light of a cold
autumn dawn…wide-awake and shivering with excitement,
waiting for his quarry to tiptoe into the clear.

Out of the corner of his eye he could see his passenger's
head make little jerking motions from time to time. He
knew what that meant. The hijacker was fighting sleep.

C.J. drove in silence, as smooth and steady as he knew
how. He'd timed it to hit Atlanta during dinner hour and

was lucky enough to sail around the beltway without any major stalls. By the time he'd got sorted out and was heading northeast out of the city, twilight had given way to darkness and traffic had thinned out the way it usually did at that hour. It was mostly just big trucks, now. Long-haul drivers, like him.

And the hijacker was sound asleep.

C.J. had had plenty of time to think about what he was going to do and how he was going to do it. He'd rehearsed it over and over in his mind, visualizing the movements, preparing himself. Even so, when it came time to put his plan into action, and he saw the first signs for the exit he had in mind, his heart was thumping so loud he was afraid it was going to wake her up and spoil everything.

It was one of those exits to nowhere, common in that part of the Southern foothills, nice wide straight on- and off-ramps that fizzled out quickly into little two-lane roads that wandered off into woods and cow pastures. Before it did, though, there was a cleared turnaround space off to the right where a failed gas station and minimart had once stood, where a tired driver could park his rig and catch a quick nap when he was in dire need. C.J. had done so himself there, more than once.

He slowed gradually, with care not to make any jerks or grinds that might jolt his sleeping passenger, and took the exit a bit faster than he normally would. He could see the stop sign looming dead ahead at the bottom of the ramp. There was no cross traffic, and the few vehicles that had been sharing the interstate with him had zipped on by the exit, oblivious. He took a breath and held it, trying without any success at all to calm his runaway pulse.

Now! No, not yet…not yet.

It was now or never. Choosing what he hoped was exactly the right moment, with his truck going neither too fast nor too slow, C.J. braced himself and hit his air brakes.

At the same moment he reached over with his right hand and released his passenger's seatbelt.

It went exactly the way he'd hoped it would, which was a gratifying surprise to him. With a giant hiss the Kenworth bucked like a mule and came well nigh to a stop. Having no seat belt to stop her, the woman beside him kept right on going, with just enough momentum so she would have ended up on the floor without hitting the windshield or too much damage being done to her person on the way down. The only thing that could have kept her from doing that were her reflexes, and she had good ones, he'd have to give her that. She came awake with a gasp, and did just what he'd hoped she would—she threw out her hands to catch herself. Both hands.

By that time, C.J. had the emergency brake on and his own belt undone, and was stretched across the center console and getting a firm grip on those slender-strong wrists with both *his* hands. Making sure to keep the captured hands a safe distance from that gun in her sweatshirt pocket, he quickly overcame her silent struggles—she was stronger than she looked, but he was a good bit bigger— and got her pinned down on her back across the console. A second or two later he had that snub-nose pistol in his own hand, and was scooting back into his seat, breathing like a racehorse and drunk with triumph.

The adrenaline high he was on didn't let him think about, then, the intimate female body warmth inside that pocket, or the glimpses of struggle-bared torso, of delicate muscle and cream-pale skin.

He twisted around to face his erstwhile hijacker and, keeping one eye on her while she eased herself slowly back into her seat, quickly examined the gun. He'd been thinking maybe it wasn't loaded, but he was wrong.

"This thing's *loaded*," he said in an outraged tone, the skin on the back of his neck crawling.

She gave a faint snort. "I told you it was. I don't tell

lies.'' He noticed she didn't rub at her wrists, or anything
like that, although he could see the red marks his fingers
had made on her skin. She simply sat with her hands relaxed in her lap, momentarily thwarted, maybe, but—he
had a feeling—not defeated.

He gave a start when the curtain across the sleeper
twitched back and the big-haired woman put her head out,
looking mussed-up and scared to death. ''Caitlyn?
What—''

''It's okay, Mary Kelly,'' the hijacker quietly said, while
C.J. was stuffing the gun down in the pocket alongside his
seat where she'd have to go through him to get at it.
''We're just stopping for a minute. Everything's okay.''

''Sorry 'bout that, ma'am,'' C.J. muttered. *Caitlyn,* he
was thinking. So that was her name. Nice to be able to
think of her as something besides ''the hijacker.''

He tensed when she turned in her seat, but it was only
to inquire softly of the woman named Mary Kelly, ''How's
Emma?''

''Still sleepin','' Mary Kelly replied in her heavy Mid-
dle-South accent. ''I think she's 'bout wore out.''

''Why don't you see if you can get some more sleep,
too?'' Caitlyn said. ''We'll be on our way in a minute—
oh, and Mr. um…''

''Starr. C.J.''

''Nice to meet you,'' Mary Kelly said, sticking out a
hand for C.J. to shake, and as he muttered the polite ac-
knowledgments, he was thinking how weird it felt to be
doing that with that loaded gun sitting there in his side
pocket.

''Mr. Starr says to help yourself to something to eat, if
you're hungry.''

''Yeah, you take anything back there you want,'' C.J.
said. He was already putting the Kenworth in gear, creeping
onto the crossroad pavement, and feeling shaken but much

more in control of the situation and a lot better about things in general.

He pulled into the abandoned gas station and parked. Then he looked over at his passenger. Hijacker. Caitlyn. She looked back at him, not saying anything. "Let's you and me have a talk," he said grimly, jerking his head toward the darkness beyond the windows.

She nodded and reached for the door handle. C.J. considered the gun in the seat pocket, decided it was safer where it was than anyplace else, and did the same. They met in front of the Kenworth, between the headlight beams. He hesitated, then touched her elbow to tell her to walk with him, and they strolled side by side toward the abandoned minimart, across a concrete apron awash in unnatural twilight from the perimeter yard lights nobody had bothered to take down. The night was noisy with spring sounds, frogs and crickets and some kind of bird—a whippoorwill, maybe?—singing its head off out in the dark woods. The air was cool and sweet, and he thought how nice it might have been to be out in it, walking in the company of a beautiful woman.

Out in the open on that bare slab of gravelly concrete, a reasonable distance from his truck, he stopped and she did, too.

"About time you told me what's going on," he said.

It struck him, as he was waiting for her to say something, how hard it was to look at her now. No, not *hard,* exactly—she had the kind of looks that makes a person want to look and look and keep on looking. But strange. Disturbing. Like looking at one of those pictures with something hidden in them, something you're supposed to be able to see if you look at it a certain way, only he'd never figured out how to do it right. She was a puzzle to him. A woman who didn't look like what she was. What she was, was somebody who'd hijacked him and his truck at the point of a gun, for God's sake. What she looked like was somebody fragile, somebody he wanted to protect and defend.

"Okay. How 'bout if I tell you what I *think* is going on?" he said when it became apparent she wasn't going to. He was fighting anger again, or maybe just frustration, and his voice was harsh with it. "It's pretty obvious to me you're helping those people in there—that woman and her little girl—run away from somebody they're scared of, my guess is the husband. Right?" Her eyes, which had been focused intently on the empty parking lot behind him, slid toward him for the first time. He sucked in a breath. "Okay, I'm right. What I want to know is, if the guy's abusive or whatever, why don't you go to the cops?"

Why didn't you just tell *me* that? he wanted to ask her. Wife beaters were way high up on his personal list of people he had no use for.

"I told you," she said flatly. "The police weren't—aren't—an option."

He let out a breath with a sound like the Kenworth's air brakes. "Come on, don't give me that. There're laws—"

"Which in this case are all on his side." She rapped it out, then abruptly closed her eyes and held up an appeasing hand, palm toward him. "Look—I told you, the less you know the better. I never would have involved you if I'd had any other choice. If you'll take us someplace so we can rent another car—"

"What do you mean, the law is on his side?" C.J. was getting a heavy feeling in his stomach.

She closed her eyes again, briefly. When she opened them they had that silvery shine, which he recognized now as anger. Or maybe frustration. "I mean that Mary Kelly's husband is a rich, powerful—*very* powerful—man." She almost spat the words. "He is also a charming and intelligent, violent and dangerous—*very* dangerous—man. He terrorized his wife for years, but she only got up the courage to leave him when the violence began to affect her child. Unfortunately, as is often the case, when that happened is when her husband turned from merely violent to deadly. First, he took all the legal steps to ensure he'd get full custody of Emma—a parade of witnesses to testify to Mary Kelly's unfitness as a mother, 'proof' of infidelity, drug abuse—the whole thing. She knew she didn't have a prayer of winning against him in court, and that once he had custody of Emma, he would kill her. Mary, I mean. That was when she called us. We had to act quickly—''

"What do you mean, 'us'?" Then he forgot that question as the rest of what she'd said sank in. "*Kill* her? Come on. Who *is* this guy? Sounds like a TV movie of the week, for God's sake." But the heavy feeling in his belly was squeezing into his chest.

She pivoted away, moving in that weightless way she had, and raked fingers through her hair in a gesture of helpless frustration. "Please—don't ask any more questions, okay?" And she was back before him, her hands light as butterflies on his stubbornly folded arms. "Look—I'm sorry I ever dragged you into this. But I—*we*—really do need your help right now. There's no one else we can turn to. Please."

It took a lot of willpower with those eyes gazing into his, liquid and shimmering with held-back tears, but he held himself aloof, gruff and immobile. "Just tell me one thing. Who has custody of that little girl? Right now. You said they'd been to court. Did the judge make a ruling?"

She nodded, not looking at him, not answering. She didn't have to. Her silence only confirmed his worst fear.

Furious now, he jerked his arms away from that featherlight touch and slapped one hand to his forehead. "Oh, *man*. The judge gave the father full custody, didn't he? And you two took her, anyway. In direct violation of a judge's order. *Jeez*. That's *kidnapping,* don't you know that? *Jeez*."

He paced off across the concrete slab, trying to think his way through the disaster. His boots made loud scraping, crunching noises on the gravelly surface, and to him it sounded like his whole life, all his hopes and dreams, ten years of hard work and struggle, slip-sliding away into an abyss of failure.

He stopped, turned and looked back. She was standing where he'd left her, in a pool of light from the yard lamp, arms folded across her waist, head bowed, looking nothing at all like a hijacker or kidnapper. Looking like a lost traveler.

His heart lurched, then sank into his stomach. "I can't do it," he said, walking back to her, his voice echoing the harsh sound of his boots on that gritty slab. "I'm sorry. I can't help you commit a felony. That'd make me guilty, too. I can't do that. I just can't. I'm sorry...."

He expected her to argue with him. What she did was worse. She waited until he'd run out of words and then, still staring at the ground, lifted a hand to brush at something on her cheeks. After a moment she hitched her shoulders in a resigned sort of way and said in a muffled voice, "I saw the law books in your truck. You studying to become a lawyer?"

C.J. let out the breath he'd been holding, and all his anger went with it. "Yeah. Trying to. I'm almost done— on my last semester of law school, in fact. Then all I have left to do is pass the bar." *And meanwhile keep from committing any felonies.*

He wasn't all that surprised when she seemed to understand.

They'd begun walking back toward the truck, her with her head down and her arms still folded across her middle, him with his fingertips poked into the tops of his hip pockets, feeling guilty and mean. When they reached the place between the headlights where they'd have to part company and go to their respective sides of the truck, for some reason he felt reluctant to let her go. Then she angled a look up toward him, and to his surprise there was a ghost of a smile on her lips.

"I sure picked the wrong truck to hijack," she said.

He managed a ghost of a laugh. Then, about to turn away, he stopped and jerked back to her. "Out of curiosity, why did you? Pick me, I mean."

Her eyes came to rest on his face and her smile lingered a wistful moment before fading. "You were the last," she said with a shrug. "I couldn't very well have witnesses. Even if I hadn't had to use the gun, somebody might remember seeing us get in a truck, might even remember which truck we'd gotten into. So I waited until everyone else had gone. You were the last to leave." After a pause she softly added, with a brief reprise of her smile—ironically tilted now, "And you were kind to Emma."

C.J. grunted, the way he might if he'd been socked in the stomach. Obeying some compulsion he didn't understand, he put his hands on her arms, up near her shoulders. He was shocked at how *real* she felt—and that was how he thought it, while at the same time acknowledging how ridiculous it was to think that way. *Real?* He knew she was no fantasy, in spite of ethereal grace and fairy-tale beauty—he'd felt the weight of that pistol of hers in his own hands—but it jolted the healthy red-blooded male part of him anyway, the tactile proof that there was a flesh-and-blood woman underneath that sweatshirt, a body warm and pulsing with vitality, slender and supple and wiry strong. He felt the jolt in his own muscles and nerves, all the way down to the pit of his stomach.

"Look, I'll help you turn yourselves in," he said, rushing the words because it had become gravely important to him that she see how right he was about this. "Okay? I'll take you to the police station, see you get a lawyer. Hey—" he flashed her his dimples "—my family's lousy with lawyers. My brother Troy's wife, Charlie—this is right up her alley. I'll give her a call as soon as we get back on the road, have her meet us—''

"Thanks, but that's not necessary." Her voice was remote.

"It's the best way," he said. "Trust me. You can't keep running forever, not with both the law and—" He stopped for a moment, remembering the gray sedan, and the dark and purposeful men he'd watched in his rearview mirrors. "If this guy, this…"

"Vasily," she grimly supplied. "Ari Vasily."

C.J. nodded. "If this Vasily guy is a killer, and he has the kind of resources you say he does, what makes you think you—or your friend and her little girl, rather—would ever be safe as long as he's after you?" He paused to listen to himself, liking his own reasoning more and more. "No— the best thing, I'm telling you, is to turn yourselves in. Tell your story to the police. They can protect you. Then, we get you a good lawyer—''

"Thanks, but you've done enough." Her sardonic little smile reproached him. He let go of her and stuck his hands underneath his arms, then stood there feeling vaguely embarrassed while she hitched up her sweatshirt and took her cell phone from its holster. "I would like to make a couple of phone calls, though. If you, uh, don't mind?" she added when he didn't get the hint she was asking for privacy.

"Oh…oh, yeah, sure," he said, catching on, and was about to leave her there when she stalled him with a questioning gesture.

"Where are you taking us? To turn ourselves in."

So, at least it looked like she was calling her lawyer. He thought about it, then told her the name of the next major stop on up the interstate in South Carolina, which he knew to be a town big enough to have its own courthouse and police department but small enough not to be too overwhelmed with bureaucracy.

She repeated the name under her breath, then said very

softly, "Don't...say anything, okay? Let me tell them... please?"

He nodded and went around to his side of the truck.

When he climbed into the cab he saw the sleeper curtain was pulled wide open. The woman, Mary Kelly, was sitting in the middle of it, rocking her daughter back and forth while the little girl sobbed and shivered and tried to hide her face against her momma's neck.

C.J. felt a stab of pain in his heart. "Well, hey there, sweetheart...what's wrong?" He reached across the back of his seat to pat the kid's back, and again felt awful when she flinched.

Her momma tried halfheartedly to come up with a smile. "Oh, it's nothin', she just had a nightmare—she gets them sometimes. She thinks the bad men are comin' to hurt me." Her smile quivered and went out, and C.J. felt another twist of pain, this one in his guts.

Armoring himself with his own smile, he said, "No bad men here, darlin', just me, ol' C.J."

He looked around for something—anything—that might put a stop to those tears, and his eye lit on a little flat package tucked behind his sunshade. It was a toy, one of those action figures based on the latest cartoon-character craze, which apparently involved a bunch of little bitty girls with super powers and great big black eyes. He'd bought it in the last truck stop he'd hit for his niece Amy Jo— Jimmy Joe's little girl—who happened to be nuts about the cartoons, and he figured one little girl probably wasn't all that different from another, right? Anyway, it seemed worth a try.

Plucking it from behind the sunshade, he tapped the kid's arm with it. "Look here what I found, darlin', just for you."

Her momma picked up her cue and sang out, "Oh, Emma, looka here—it's your favorite! What do you say? You tell Mr. Starr thank you, now."

So, like any child above the age of two being raised in

the South, Emma had to sit up straight and sniffle out a "Thank you, sir." She could have been dying, and she'd have pulled herself together and managed it somehow.

It broke the ice, though, and by the time Caitlyn joined them in the cab he and Emma were good buddies, and she was telling him all about which particular supergirl this action figure was and the names of all her friends, and all the cool things they could do. She hadn't quite got so far as to sit on his lap, but she was leaning against his knees and drowning him with her eyes, which, it struck him, bore a fair resemblance to those little cartoon supergirls' eyes.

It made his heart hurt to think how sweet and little she was and how badly she wanted to trust somebody, and what a lousy hand life had dealt her so far. And how he was just about to make it worse for her, maybe, at least for a while.

In the long run, though, he knew he was doing the right thing, what was best for her *and* her momma. He'd had close brushes with some bad apples like this Ari Vasily, and if there was one thing he'd learned from the experience it was that dangerous people like that were best left to the professionals to deal with. And as for the courts, well…sure, they got it wrong sometimes, but they generally straightened things out sooner or later. The thing to do was get a good lawyer.…

Yeah, and that got him thinking again about the pile of law books under his passenger's feet, and the exam waiting for him back in Georgia, and the hard work and tough years it had taken him to get to this point and what it would mean to the rest of his life if he blew it now. That gave him the resolve to put the Kenworth in gear and do a turn-around through the abandoned gas station's parking lot, and a few minutes later he was back on the interstate, growling his way toward South Carolina.

Anderson's Main Street, which ran straight down through the town and past the courthouse square on one side and the police station on the other, had been landscaped and refurbished in the old downtown section and was closed to big-truck traffic. Following the truck route signs, C.J. found a place to park one street over, with a well-lit and mostly empty parking lot between him and the police station's back door. With the big diesel engine throbbing and the air-conditioning blowing cold, he looked over at Caitlyn and tried to think of something to say that would justify what he was doing to her. She looked reproachfully back at him, not making it any easier for him.

As he tried to read her eyes, it struck him how tangled up with one another two strangers could get in a short period of time, under the right circumstances. He felt again that strange reluctance to let her go, a dragging weight of denial at the realization that she was going to walk out of his life forever.

It was Mary Kelly who broke the edgy silence, hitching herself forward in the sleeper so she could look out the window. "Why're we stoppin' here? What is this place? Caitlyn?"

But she already knew. C.J. opened his mouth to explain, but before he could get a word out, her head was swiveling toward him, her mouth a big round *O* of dawning realization, and panic and denial in her eyes.

Caitlyn reached around and put a gentling hand on her arm. "It's okay," she murmured, as if she were soothing a child after a nightmare. "It's going to be okay."

Mary Kelly wasn't buying it. She shook off Caitlyn's hand, looking like a hunted animal. Her eyes darted back and forth between Caitlyn and C.J., and her voice was high and scared. "No—I—we can't go in there! We can't go to the police—they'll send us back, you know they will! They'll lock us up and take Emma. He'll take her away, you know he—"

"Shh," Caitlyn hushed her, with a warning tip of her

head toward Emma, who was waking up and looking scared by all the commotion. "It's going to be okay. I promise—"

"It's the best way," C.J. broke in, meaning again to explain himself but only sounding harsh and angry with his gravel-filled voice. "You couldn't keep on running like that, not with…" He, too, tipped his head toward the little girl, not daring to meet those big dark eyes peering at him over her momma's shoulder. "Sooner or later either the cops are going to catch up with you, or somebody worse will. And *then* what're you gonna do? Somebody might get hurt, for sure it's going to be traumatic for *her*. You want her to see her momma arrested? Shot? Hauled away by force? Remember what happened to that little Cuban kid?" He was shouting by this time, and Mary Kelly just kept staring at him until finally a tear pillowed up on her lashes and slipped away down her cheek.

Well, that did it. He said, "Aw, hell," under his breath and turned around in his seat so he was facing forward and didn't have to look at her *or* her kid anymore. Instead, he stared squinty-eyed at the windshield while his heart thumped in shallow, trip-hammer beats.

Beside him, Caitlyn unhooked her seat belt and got turned around and up on her knees on the seat so she could look Mary Kelly eye to eye. "It's going to be okay," he heard her say in the kind of firm, confident way parents do when they talk to their kids. "I promise. Okay? Come on— let's go inside. Emma, you first—give me your hand, honey. Come here to me." She opened up the door and started backing out, showing the little girl how to climb out of the sleeper.

C.J. cleared his throat. "Uh, you want— Maybe I should go in with you," he said, not happily.

Caitlyn shook her head, and that ghost of a smile, the ironic one, hovered around her lips. "That won't be necessary."

"You sure you don't want me to call my sister-in-law?

She's in Atlanta—could probably be here in a couple hours."

Her eyes zeroed in on his, flared silver for one incredible moment. Then the shutters came down and she looked away. "Thanks—we'll be fine."

Emma was standing beside C.J.'s seat, peeking at him past his shoulder. He felt something nudge him there, and looking down, saw the supergirl action-figure toy he'd given her, clutched tightly in her hand. She waggled it at him, both a shy and silent thank-you and a wave goodbye. Then she scrambled across the seat and dropped down out of his sight.

Mary Kelly followed, brushing at her cheek and moving like somebody going to her own execution. At the last minute, framed in the doorway of his truck and her face a mask of shadows, she paused. "I'm not blamin' you, Mr. Starr, and I want to thank you for all you done for Emma and me. I truly do believe you just don't know what it is you've done." She sniffed, tried hard to smile one more time, and then she, too, dropped to the ground. The door closed with a flat and final *thunk*.

C.J. sat and watched them cross the mostly empty parking lot, bathed in light that turned everything a washed-out bluish gray, like death. Caitlyn had her arm around Mary Kelly's shoulders, and Emma was clinging to her momma's hand and sort of hop-skipping the way little kids do to keep up. He didn't know whether he expected them to bolt and scatter for the shadows like flushed mice before they got to the entrance or not, but he didn't take his eyes off them until they'd disappeared inside the police station.

He felt wrung out...drained. He couldn't seem to talk his muscles into moving, not even enough to do what needed to be done to put his truck in gear and pull off down the street.

Which, C.J. told himself, was maybe a good thing. Because it was probably the only thing keeping him from going after them and bringing them back. And that, he knew, would be the biggest mistake of his life.

Chapter 3

What else could I have done?

C.J. had spent the last twenty-four hours asking himself that question and still hadn't come up with an answer. His mind played and replayed it for him while he was churning up the interstate, like a piece of music sung to the rhythm of his eighteen tires. It was there in the background noise of his thoughts while he dropped off his load in Jersey, got new marching orders from his dispatcher, made his way down to Wilmington. Now, with an overnight to kill waiting for his load to be ready, he was holed up in a motel room with nothing but his thoughts, and he'd never been in worse company.

What the hell was I supposed to do? I didn't have any choice. I didn't! Stretched out on the bed in his undershorts and T-shirt, he stared up at the ceiling and argued with his conscience. *What would it have cost you to drop them off at the airport? They could have at least rented a car there. Most likely nobody would ever have known you were involved.*

Most likely...

C.J. wasn't all that comfortable with "most likelys."

The TV program he'd been watching without really see-ing had ended and the eleven-o'clock news was coming on. He reached for the remote. Maybe he'd have better luck on HBO; nothing like gratuitous violence to numb the mind and quiet a restless soul.

While he was feeling around for the remote amongst the tumble of bedspread and yesterday's newspaper he heard the anchorman begin his intro. And then...

"Topping the news this evening: a niece of former pres-ident Rhett Brown is in jail tonight in South Carolina on contempt charges, after refusing to comply with a judge's order to reveal what she knows about the whereabouts of a Florida millionaire's missing daughter. For more on this breaking story we go to..."

With remote in hand and scalp prickling, C.J. jerked around and squinted at the TV screen. *Too late.* He caught only the barest glimpse of a file-photo head shot before the scene shifted to a young, slightly windblown woman cor-respondent standing in a nighttime courthouse square lit by old-fashioned-style street lamps, the wide empty courthouse steps behind her.

"Yes, Tim... it's quiet here now, but this was the scene earlier this evening, when Caitlyn Brown, niece of former President Rhett Brown, was taken from this South Carolina courthouse in handcuffs...."

The scene was pushing, shoving crowds of reporters, grim-faced men in uniforms and suits surrounding a slender figure wearing a sweatshirt with the hood pulled up to hide her face.

"Ms. Brown was ordered to spend the night in jail after she refused to obey Judge Wesley Calhoun's order to di-vulge the whereabouts of five-year-old Emma Vasily, who is the daughter of Florida billionaire, Ari Vasily. The little

*girl had been missing since Tuesday, and is the object of
a nationwide hunt...."*

On the television screen, the knot of law enforcement
bodies loosened to reveal glimpses of the lone hooded figure sitting in the back seat of a police car. She turned her
head and looked straight into the camera, and for one heart-
stopping moment her eyes flared silver.

*"The child's mother, Mary Kelly Vasily, allegedly took
her daughter from her school in Miami Beach only hours
after a Florida judge had granted sole custody of the little
girl to Mr. Vasily, also granting Mr. Vasily's request that
the mother be denied visitation...."*

The young reporter stood alone once more in front of
the deserted courthouse. A windblown strand of hair teased
her cheek as she earnestly continued.

*"Details are still sketchy at this time, but according to
police sources, around 9 p.m. yesterday Mrs. Vasily, ac-
companied by Ms. Brown, walked into the police station
here and gave herself up. The little girl was with the two
women at that time, that much is certain, but what happened after that is unclear. As nearly as we can ascertain,
the child apparently left police headquarters in the custody
of a woman who identified herself as a representative of
family services, but it now appears that woman may have
been an impostor. Here's what we do know—more than
twenty-four hours later police and social service agencies
still have no idea where the child is. Little Emma Vasily
seems to have vanished into thin air.*

*"Just what Ms. Brown's involvement is in the case is
also unclear, but police investigators must have strong reason to believe the president's niece has some knowledge of
Emma's whereabouts, because this morning they asked a
judge to order Ms. Brown to tell what she knows. She was
given until the close of court this afternoon to comply, and
when she refused, Judge Calhoun ordered her to jail.*

"Mr. Vasily, who arrived this morning from Miami ex-

*pecting to be reunited with his daughter, has been un-
available for comment, but at a press conference just before
noon a visibly angry chief of police promised a full inves-
tigation into his department's handling of the whole affair,
and vowed to remain personally committed to finding the
little girl and returning her safely to her father. Back to
you, Tim.''*

A sharp pain in his chest reminded C.J. of the breath
he'd taken in some time back and hadn't gotten around to
letting go. He released it in a gust of swearing and mashed
the power button on the remote, cutting off the anchorman
as he was launching into news of the latest statehouse scan-
dal. He hitched himself around on the bed till he'd got his
feet on the floor and reached for his cell phone. His heart
tapped hard against his ribs as he punched a number pro-
grammed in the autodial.

"Hey, bro," he said to the groggy voice who answered.
"Wha'd I do, wake you?"

"What? Who's that—C.J.? Naw, you didn't wake me. I
just dozed off watching the news. What's up?" There was
an audible yawn. "Where in the hell are you? Everything
all right?"

"I'm okay." Well, it wasn't *much* of a lie. "Hey, is
Charly around?"

"She's right here. Aw, hell—you're not in jail, are
you?"

C.J. shrugged off that conclusion and the low opinion of
his own character it reflected. Where his brothers were concerned, he'd accepted the fact that it was going to take a
while to live down certain escapades of his misspent youth.
"Just let me talk to her, okay?"

There was a pause, and then in a molasses-thick Alabama
drawl, "Hey, C.J.—honey, how're you? What's up?"

"Hey, Charly. You see tonight's news?"

"I'm watchin' it right now. What part in particular?"

"The president's niece getting jailed for contempt."

"Oh, yeah. I did catch that. What about it?"

"Well, I'm...I think I'm sort of involved. Or...I might be."

"*What?* Lord's sake, how?"

He told her the whole story, then waited through a thinking silence. A quickly drawn breath.

"You did exactly the right thing, if that's what you're askin'. I don't think you have anything to worry about. The police are probably gonna want to ask you some questions—that's to be expected. If you want me—"

"That's not..." C.J. rubbed at his temples with his free hand. "It's not me I'm worried about. What I was wondering...I was thinking, you know, maybe you could go up there, see if she needs anything..."

"She? You mean the mother—what's her name—Mary Kelly? Hon', you know she's probably lookin' at kid—"

"Well, her, and...uh, Caitlyn."

"*Caitlyn?*"

He said a bad word under his breath. "*Miz Brown*, then—the president's niece. Whoever." He paused, but his sister-in-law didn't say anything, so he added in self-defense, "I didn't see any sign of a lawyer on that news footage, did you? Aren't they usually right there, shielding their client from the buzzards? I offered, you know—to get her one. Well, hell, I'm the one turned 'em over to the cops, it seemed like the least I could do." He'd about rubbed a burned spot on the skin of his forehead, but it hadn't done a thing to help the pounding inside his skull.

"Don't you go blamin' yourself," Charly scolded. "Those women are grown-ups, they made their choices, one of which was to involve you in their mess. It's not your fault their choice of getaway driver turned out to be a law-abidin' citizen."

C.J.'s face stretched into a grimace nobody was there to see. "Yeah, well...I'd feel a whole lot better about that if I knew she had somebody in her corner, is all. I know she made at least one call after I told her I was turning her in, and I just assumed… But I'm thinking that must've been how she arranged for somebody to pick up the little girl. If she did, maybe—''

''C.J., she's the ex-president's niece, for Lord's sake. Do you seriously think they won't have the best lawyers money can buy?'' C.J. didn't say anything, and after a moment she let out an exasperated breath. ''Okay, look, do you want me to see what I can find out for you?''

It was his turn to let a breath out in a rush of relief. ''If you wouldn't mind? I'd go myself, but I'm stuck up here in Wilmington waiting for my load. Soonest I can get there is—''

''Best you stay out of it,'' Charly said in a warning tone. ''If she gives you up as the person who gave her a lift and the cops come lookin' for you to ask you questions, that's one thing. Otherwise, speakin' as your lawyer and as your brother's lovin' wife and therefore *family,* I'm advising you to keep your distance. For all kinds of reasons, startin' with the fact that if this Ari Vasily is as dangerous as these gals make him out to be, you don't want to mess with him. And like I said, it's not like she hasn't got resources. She's the president's *niece.*''

''Yeah…'' His laugh was dry and bitter. ''She neglected to tell me that little bit of information.''

Charly snorted. ''What did you expect her to do? Say, 'Hi, I'm hijacking you, and by the way I'm the president's niece'?''

''She had plenty of time later on to tell me anything she wanted to,'' he said, feeling sullen and put-upon. ''She never told me a damn thing about herself. Not even her name. I only got the Caitlyn part when the other woman called her that.''

''She was probably just tryin' to keep you out of it as best she could.'' Charly's tone was uncharacteristically sympathetic. "I doubt she was happy about havin' to do what she did."

"Spoken like a defense attorney."

"Which is what I am, and the whole reason you called me, sugar. And by the way, if you're so PO'd at the woman, why are you tryin' to help her?"

Damned if he knew. He closed his eyes, thinking how much he wished he had a beer right now. Or something stronger. Which was just about unheard of, for him; he'd spent his teenage years watching his brother Roy battle the booze and it had left a lasting impression on him. He heaved a big sigh and said, "Just see what you can do, okay? I'm gonna be home probably late tomorrow night, but you can reach me on my cell."

"I'll make some calls, but I'm not promising anything."

"That's fine. And Charly...thanks."

He disconnected but sat where he was for a long time, fidgety and keyed-up, slapping the cell phone against the palm of his hand. He'd done the right thing, turning them in, he knew he had. It wasn't his affair, and Charly was right, he ought to stay the hell out of it. So why was it he couldn't get her out of his mind? *Her.* All three of them, really. Except, it wasn't Mary Kelly's scared brown eyes or even little Emma Vasily's big black ones he saw whenever he shut his eyes, as if the backs of his eyelids had been tiny TV screens. Uh-uh. No, it was *her* face that haunted him, pale and frozen in the shadows of the back seat of a police cruiser, the silvery slash of her eyes zeroing in on *him,* seeming to look right into his soul with mute and desperate appeal.

He was on I-95 somewhere south of Richmond when his cell phone tweedled at him from the no-hands holster mounted on the dash. He reached over and mashed the Receive button and hollered, "Yeah?" over the roar of highway noise.

"C.J., honey, that you?" Charly's voice was distant and tinny.

His heart gave a little kick. He turned up the volume and yelled, "Yeah, Charly. What'd you find out?"

"Couple things. First thing is, she's still not talking. Neither one of 'em is—the mother, either. So they're both back in the pokey, and it looks like they might be there for a while. Judge Calhoun seems determined to keep 'em where they are until they give up the little girl." She paused.

"And?" C.J. prompted. He kept his hands easy on the wheel, but a pulse was tapping hard against his belt buckle.

"She doesn't want any help, C.J.—at least, not from you."

"Did she say that?" He squinted at the ribbon of interstate rolling out ahead of him, though there wasn't a speck of glare. "You got that straight from *her?* Not some other lawyer? You talked to her?"

He heard the gust of an exhalation. "In a word, C.J., yeah. What she actually said was that you'd done enough." There was a long pause before Charly added gently, "She's right, you know. Give it up, honey. It's not your trouble, so don't go spendin' any more time stewin' about it. You got other things to worry about—which reminds me, how's that law degree comin'? When are you plannin' on tackin' up your shingle here with Troy and me?"

C.J. managed a grin, his first in quite a while. "Why would I want to do that? I'd have to live in Atlanta. Hell, might as well just shoot me now."

Charly laughed. "Wait'll you pass the bar, and then we'll see about that. Atlanta's where the action is, sugar."

"Yeah, yeah—just don't hold your breath." His grin lasted about a second longer than it took him to disconnect. Then he took in air and huffed it out, waggled his shoulders like somebody'd just relieved him of a burdensome load.

Charly was right; it wasn't any of his affair. He had a

load to deliver, an exam to take. A semester to finish. A final to pass. A law degree to earn. A life to get on with.

As for a hijacker with a fairy-tale face and unforgettable eyes…well, he'd find a way to forget her. Somehow.

During the next five months or so C.J. concentrated hard on doing that, which, if nothing else, had a beneficial effect on his study habits. He got his law degree in June and spent the summer cramming for the bar exams, which he was scheduled to take the last week in September and as a matter of principle was determined to pass on the first try. He still had a lot to prove, mainly to himself.

What he mostly learned during that long, hot summer, in addition to a whole lot of law stuff, was that it was one thing to *try* to forget somebody and another to actually succeed.

His task wasn't helped any by the fact that hardly a day went by he didn't hear the name Caitlyn Brown or see her face on the nightly news—that same file footage of a hand-cuffed prisoner in a hooded sweatshirt being hustled into a police cruiser. It seemed to be one of those stories the media had sunk its teeth into and wouldn't let go, and why not? It had everything: a mysterious billionaire, his ex-stripper wife, a beautiful young woman with connections to one of the most famous families on the planet, and, of course, a missing child.

Everyone with any connection at all to the case, no matter how dubious, had been interviewed over and over and *over* again, on the network morning shows and the prime-time news magazines as well as the major network and cable news. *Biography* had done a two-hour piece on the former president, featuring his entire family and making a big deal of their Iowa farm beginnings. The tabloids trumpeted wild and improbable theories from their racks beside the grocery store checkout lines.

And night after night reporters stood in front of file photos of the red brick courthouse in South Carolina, faced the cameras and told the same story: Caitlyn Brown still wasn't talking. The *Today Show* reported that office pools had sprung up around the country, and that betting on how long the holdout would continue was more popular than playing the lottery.

C.J. had taken to avoiding television sets the way certain celebrities and mob bosses avoided cameras.

That particular afternoon, though, he was a captive audience. He was in a truck stop in Virginia, having his usual truck-stop lunch—a club sandwich on white bread with potato salad and sweet tea—and no matter which way he turned there was a wall-mounted TV set looking down at him. Normally they'd be tuned to the Weather Channel or some sporting event or other, but today for some reason they all seemed to be set on CNN. And sure enough, there was the same reporter standing in front of the same damn red brick courthouse he'd been looking at for months, no doubt saying the same damn thing. At least the sound was turned off, and he didn't have to read the closed-captioning if he didn't want to. Stubbornly he pulled his eyes from the screen and scanned the dining room instead.

When he noticed every set of eyes in the room except his was riveted on those television sets, a chill ran down his spine. It reminded him of another bright and beautiful September morning not so long ago. The bite of club sandwich he'd just swallowed made a lump in his throat as he forced his eyes back to the television screen, dreading what he was about to see, preparing himself for unthinkable disaster.

The familiar white-on-black letters of the closed captioning darted across the bottom third of the picture:

''...*the scene earlier today, as Caitlyn Brown and Mary Kelly Vasily left the courthouse to return to their jail cells under heavy police guard. It was the same scenario that has played out so many times before during the last months, only this time something went terribly, terribly wrong. As the two women, flanked by police officers, made their way down the courthouse steps, shots rang out...."*

The words ticked on across the screen, but C.J. wasn't watching them now. His eyes were riveted instead on the pictures behind them, jerky and incoherent pictures of unexpected violence captured live on videotape. Pictures of pushing and shoving and falling bodies, of horror-stricken faces, of arms waving and fingers pointing and mouths opened in silent shouts. The chill in his spine ran into his very bones. Around him the clatter of dining room sounds retreated to a humming silence.

The melee on the screen gave way to the reporter's face, mouthing words. C.J. jerked his eyes back to the closed captioning.

"...on the exact number or condition of the injured at this time. We do have information that at least four people have been taken to a local hospital, but that has not been officially confirmed. Police and hospital personnel have refused to comment on reports from eyewitnesses. Repeat, these are unconfirmed reports, that at least one of the prisoners—one of the women—has been killed in this brutal attack."

"Do police have any idea who might be responsible for the attack, Vicky?"

"As you can imagine, things are still pretty chaotic here, Tim. It does appear the shots were fired from the bell tower of a church across the street from the courthouse—that's about half a block down from the police station—but as far as we know no traces of the gunman or a weapon have been found."

"Any indication as to whether this was a random shooting? Or if it was deliberate, who the intended target might have been?"

"No, Tim, and police are refusing to speculate—"

"'Scuse me, hon', were you needin' your check?"

"What?" C.J. looked down at the waitress, frowning in confusion; he didn't know when or how he'd come to be standing up. He blinked what was left of his club sandwich into focus and mumbled, "Yeah, that'd be great...thanks."

His skin felt clammy. Barely aware of what he was doing, he dug his wallet out of his hip pocket and randomly selected some bills, which he thrust at the waitress with a muttered "Keep the change." Next thing he knew he was outside, gulping air like a netted fish and soaking the September heat into his chilled body. Ninety degrees, it had to be, and it wasn't warm enough. He felt he was never going to be warm enough again.

You just don't know what it is you've gone and done.

He felt as though he might throw up but made it to his truck before the shakes hit him. He climbed into his seat and spent the next five minutes or so fighting for control the way most men of his acquaintance did, those that weren't smokers: he swore. And swore. And swore some more. When he ran out of cusswords, some of which he'd never used before in his life, he ran a hand over his face and reached for his cell phone.

"Charly?" he croaked when he heard his sister-in-law's voice. His own was probably unrecognizable, so he added for good measure, "It's me, C.J. You heard?"

"Yeah, I did, sugar, just a little while ago. Troy called me." Charly's voice was low and urgent, like a conspirator's.

"They said somebody'd been killed, some more injured, but they aren't saying who. You don't—"

"No. I don't know any more than that, either. I've been in court all morning, I just got back in the office a little while ago. There's supposed to be a press conference at the hospital any minute now." Her voice turned sharp. "C.J., honey, don't you go and blame yourself for this."

I'm not blamin' you, Mr. Starr....

"I didn't believe her," he muttered, shaking his head

like a dazed boxer. "She told me he'd do it and I didn't— I thought she was just—"

"She, who? He, who? Do what?"

"She told me he was going to kill his wife, but I just thought she was…you know—"

"Who, you mean *Vasily?*" Charly lowered her voice even further, as if she thought somebody was going to overhear. "You think that's who did this? My God, C.J.—"

"Who the hell else?" He spat the words into the phone.

There was a pause before she said, cautiously at first, "I know the husband is always the first suspect, but that's assuming Mrs. Vasily was the target, and even if she was—" she was arguing, now, with herself as much as him "—my God, C.J., the man's a billionaire. A friend of the governor. He's had dinner at the White House. He's—"

He is also a charming and intelligent, violent and dangerous—very dangerous—man.

"I don't care who he is, Vasily set it up." C.J.'s voice was stony. "You can bet on it."

"Even if he did, there's no way on God's green earth they're ever gonna prove—"

"I know." He cut her off, calmer now, his brain beginning to function again. "Hey, look, Charly—I gotta go. Do me one favor, would you? I'm going to try and find me a news station on the radio, but if you find out anything, could you let me know? Call me on my cell."

"What are you going to do? You're not fixin' to go down there now, are you?"

There was a long pause, and then: "I have to, Charly. I need to find out what's going on."

He heard a sigh. "C.J., you're just gonna insist on blamin' yourself for this, aren't you?"

The only reply he could manage was a sharp and painful laugh as he disconnected.

He called his dispatcher and told her she'd need to find another driver to pick up his load, then fiddled with the radio for a few minutes trying to find an all-news station. Antsy and impatient to be on the road, he gave it up and settled for a golden oldies station he knew would have up-dates on the hour, then rolled his Kenworth out of the truck stop and back onto the interstate, heading south.

A long hour later his cell phone tweedled, interrupting tumultuous and totally useless thoughts. He mashed the connect button and barked, "Yeah!"

"C.J., I thought you'd want to know—they're having that press conference at the hospital. It's still going on, with all the questions and such, but they've made their state-ments. The official toll is, three injured, two critically, one dead...."

"Yeah?" He stared at the road ahead, flexed his fingers on the steering wheel. Preparing himself. As if he could.

"C.J., honey, it was Mrs. Vasily who was killed. The mother. Mary Kelly Vasily..."

A cool rush of feeling blew through him, like a breeze through a stuffy house. He nodded, though there wasn't anybody to see, and his mind filled with images: Mary Kelly's face, Southern magnolia-type pretty, almost lost in billows of fluffy red-brown hair...a tentative smile as she shook his hand and murmured polite phrases like a well-brought-up child...lips forming *No!* as she shook her head in fear and rejection...then quiet eyes, accepting smile. *I'm not blamin' you, Mr. Starr.*

But the feeling, that cool, lightening wind in his soul—he knew what it was, and it shamed him so that he slammed the doors of his mind to it, tried every way he could to deny it. Shaken, he tried to explain to himself why he should feel relieved when a good woman had just been killed. But he was. Relieved it wasn't Caitlyn Brown who'd died.

"C.J., are you there?"

"Yeah."

"Honey, I'm sorry—I know how you must be feelin'. I just feel so bad for that little girl...."

"What about the others?" He made his voice hard and clipped off the words, leaving no room for emotions. "You said two were critical?"

"One of the guards was shot in the arm—he's not serious. The other took a bullet in the chest and is still in surgery.

His chest tightened; he forced a deep breath. "Caitlyn?"

"They just said her condition is critical. No details. C.J., there's no point in you going down there. There's not a thing you can do except get yourself into trouble."

His vision shimmered. He blinked the highway back into focus and mumbled, "I just want to talk to her."

"How? They're never gonna let you in there, you know that, don't you? I mean, seriously—a stranger? After somebody just tried to kill her? The president's niece? I wouldn't be surprised if they've got the Secret Service, the FBI—"

She broke off, then was silent for so long C.J. prompted, "Charly?" and was ready to start mashing buttons on his cell phone, thinking maybe they'd got disconnected the way cell phone calls do sometimes.

"C.J., I'm gonna have to call you back, okay?" She sounded rushed and distracted. "Just...don't do anything until you hear from me. Promise? This is your lawyer speakin' now."

"Yeah," he grunted, "I promise." He disconnected and settled back, trying hard to concentrate on driving and on not letting himself think about what *critical condition* might mean. Trying not to think about a fairy-tale face, silvery eyes, a light-as-a-feather touch. One thing he didn't have to try very hard to avoid was thoughts of that exquisite face and graceful body bloody and torn...ruined by violence. His mind cowered and protected itself from those images, like eyes avoiding the sun.

Though it seemed longer, it was barely half an hour later when his phone chirped at him again.

"C.J., it's me." Charly sounded out of breath and in a hurry. "Hey, I'm gonna meet you there, okay? If you get there—"

"Meet me there…"

"The hospital. If you get there before I do, sit tight. Okay? Don't do anything until you hear from me, you hear?"

"Charly, what're you up to? I don't think I'm gonna be needing a lawyer for this."

"Maybe, maybe not. But I've got somebody who can get you in to see Caitlyn Brown."

The woman in the hospital bed stirred. Her fingers plucked at the sheets, rearranging them needlessly across her chest.

"The thunderstorm…" Caitlyn murmured, and closed her eyes. After a moment she asked in a slow, drug-thickened voice, "What is it you want? Absolution? You have it, okay? I told you, I don't blame you for anything. In fact, I suppose it was bound to happen…someday. When you go against violent people… I just…" Her voice cracked and dropped to a whisper; her lips quivered. She turned her face away. "I didn't expect it to come quite this way."

C.J. cleared his throat and leaned forward. There were so many things he wanted to ask her…so many things he wanted to say. He didn't know where to start, so he murmured, "What way did you think it was gonna come?"

Her eyes crisscrossed him like searchlights, not silvery, now, but liquid and lost. Then, incongruously, she laughed, a soft ironic chuckle. "Well, for one thing, I never expected to be blind."

Chapter 4

Caitlyn listened to the silence and felt anger rising. Once, she had treasured silence, regarded it as a gift, and on those rare occasions when she found herself immersed in it, had taken pleasure in the experience as she might in a warm bath, with scented oils and wine and candlelight. Now silence was her enemy, unknown menace lurking in the darkness beyond the firelight. Silence made her feel alone, and afraid.

But it was not in her makeup to give in to fear, and at the moment her only weapon against it seemed to be anger.

"Say something, damn you." She shifted again, carefully. Despite the pain medication she'd been given, sky-rockets had a tendency to go shooting around in her skull whenever she moved.

She heard a sound—the clearing of a throat—and then the voice, Southern and soft as a summer evening. She'd liked his voice the first time she'd heard it, she recalled. She hadn't expected to hear it ever again.

"Sorry. Guess I don't know what to say."

Vaguely ashamed, she aimed a frown in the direction of the voice. "You knew, didn't you? About me being blind. They must have told you."

There was another cough and under it a faint sandy sound. Shoes. No, boots…sliding over a vinyl floor. He must be uncomfortable; he'd shifted position, perhaps leaned forward in the chair. How did she know he was sitting? Because his voice came from a level near her own. She was pleased with herself for being able to deduce so much.

"They told me you're damn lucky to be alive," he said, and there was a difference in the voice now. Something harder, denser. Emotion, certainly, but what kind? She made a mental grimace at the discovery that she wasn't nearly as good at deciphering emotional landscapes as she was physical. "They said a hair's breadth of difference and that bullet would have blown part of your head off."

The brutality of his words surprised her. With a bitter smile she answered in kind, "Yeah, but instead it only grazed me a little and hit Mary Kelly in the heart. So, she's dead, and I have some minor brain swelling that just happened to involve my optic nerve. What luck."

She heard the shifting sounds again. "They said the blindness might not be permanent. That your eyesight might come back as the injury heals, or if it doesn't, there's surgery they can maybe try later on."

"That's what they say." Caitlyn closed her eyes and carefully turned her head away from the man sitting beside her. *Might…maybe.* She felt so tired…and controlling her face and her voice took so much energy. If only he would go away. If only she could relax and let the tears come.

"Do you remember anything about, uh, the shooting?" His voice was raspy now, and again it vexed her that she couldn't read the emotions behind it.

She shook her head—bad move—and fought down the inevitable waves of nausea.

"You tried to shield her—Mary Kelly. Did you know that?" Oh, it was anger in his voice—definitely. It came through loud and clear, although he was obviously trying to hide it. It bewildered her, his anger, even as she felt a tiny flicker of triumph for having recognized it. "You threw yourself in front of her. That's why the bullet that struck her in the chest grazed you first."

"Who told you that?" The intense emotions were becoming too much for her. She felt desperately close to crying; there were strange sounds inside her head, and a panicky tightness in her chest. "The police? What...did they say...do they know—"

"*You* knew, didn't you? You *knew* Mary Kelly was the target, the second you heard the shots. You tried to tell me—"

The noises in her head had become a cacophony. Through them she heard footsteps, quick and purposeful, and C.J.'s voice, seeming to rise and float above her.

"It was Vasily, wasn't it? You told me he'd kill her. You told me, and I didn't—"

She felt a rush of air. Hands touched her, gentle and cool. "Look. I'm sorry...." She heard C.J.'s voice, moving away from her. "I'm sorry...."

Quiet came. And peace. With a grateful whimper she sank into the oblivion of sleep.

Summoning his courage, C.J. faced the people waiting at the nurses' station.

"I'm sorry," he said, squinting with the effort it took to meet their eyes. "I didn't mean to get her upset. I just wanted to say—" He lifted a hand and let it drop. Shook his head and said it again. "I'm sorry." Lately it seemed as if he'd been saying that a lot, both out loud and to himself.

Two of the four people there at the counter—a handsome, middle-aged couple—nodded their heads in mute un-

derstanding. It was to them he'd spoken—Caitlyn's parents.
Of the others, C.J.'s sister-in-law and lawyer, Charly,
clapped him on the shoulder and murmured supportive
monosyllables. Special Agent Jake Redfield of the FBI,
C.J.'s brother Jimmy Joe's in-law, leaned against the
counter and took in everything with quiet and watchful
eyes. He was a melancholy-looking man with stubbled
jaws, and the only one present wearing a suit.

A nurse came from the glass-partitioned cubicle where
Caitlyn lay, screened from view behind a curtain. "She'll
sleep for a while," she said in her high-pitched voice with
its thick upstate South Carolina accent. "If you want to,
you can go down to the cafeteria, get a cup of coffee, some-
thin' to eat."

Caitlyn's mother gripped her husband's arm as if drawing strength from that touch, and asked the nurse in her
quiet Midwestern voice, "Is it all right if I sit with her?"

The nurse nodded. "Sure. Go on in."

Watching Chris Brown walk away from him, C.J.
thought he could see where her daughter had come by her
looks. Not her grace, though, that quality of *lightness* that
made Caitlyn seem, in his memory, at least, fairy-like…not
quite real. Though tall and slender like her daughter, Chris
Brown moved with a coltish—he could think of no other
word for it—awkwardness that was in no way unattrac-
tive—and which made her seem much younger than he
knew she had to be. But her face was the same flawless
oval as Caitlyn's, her hair almost the same shade of sun-
streaked blond, but worn long and sleek and fastened at the
nape of her neck with a clip of some kind. She had the
same colored eyes, too—a clear and pale gray-blue—but
without that heart-stopping flash of silver C.J. couldn't
seem to forget.

Charly glanced at her watch. "Well. I think I'm gonna
go see about that cup of coffee. Any of you-all wanna
join me?"

Caitlyn's father smiled the kind of smile that probably came naturally to him no matter the circumstances, and shook his head. C.J. cleared his throat and said, "I think I'm gonna stick around here for a while."

Nobody asked Jake Redfield what his plans were; he'd already gone wandering over to join the uniformed police officer seated in a chair beside the door to Caitlyn's cubicle. Charly gave everyone a "See you later," and went off to the elevators, and C.J. found himself alone with the man whose only child he'd almost gotten killed.

Since he'd been raised by a mother who'd taught him to face up to the consequences of his actions no matter how painful they might be, he squared his shoulders and began with, "Uh, Mr. Brown—"

Before he could get another word out, Caitlyn's father took hold of him by his elbow and said in a low but friendly voice, "We might as well be comfortable, don't you think?" and steered him toward the waiting area.

They took chairs at right angles to each other, with a square table topped by a lamp and an assortment of magazines forming the corner. Perched on the edge of his chair, C.J. leaned forward, hands clasped and elbows on his knees, and tried again. "Um, Mr. Brown—"

Again he was interrupted. "I wish you'd call me Wood—most people do. I was given the name Edward Earl after my dad, but the only person who uses it is my sister, Lucy." His mouth tilted in a half smile. "Only my students call me Mr. Brown."

"You're a teacher?" said C.J., feeling dimwitted.

"Used to be. I'm a vice principal now."

C.J. tried a smile and he, too, only managed half of one. "Guess that explains why I feel like I'm sitting in the principal's office."

Wood Brown's smile was replaced by a look of dismay, then of compassion. He leaned forward, his pose almost a mirror image of C.J.'s. "Son—I know you feel responsible for what's happened to my daughter and that other woman, but you're not. Chris—Caitlyn's mother—and I sure don't blame you, and I don't think Caty does, either. She put you in an impossible position, and you did what you believed was the right thing under the circumstances. That's all any man can do.''

"If what I did was so right," C.J. said, looking at the floor and forcing words through clenched teeth, "then how come I feel so damn—excuse me—darn bad?''

Wood sat back with a sigh and ran a hand over his thick, iron-gray hair. His rugged features were somber. "It's not always a matter of a choice between a right and a wrong. Sometimes it's a matter of choosing the lesser of a whole bunch of wrongs. When that happens, you just do the best you can.''

He sat silent for a moment, looking at nothing, then shook his head. "I have—had—this great-aunt. She lived to be well over a hundred, but she's gone now, bless her soul. Aunt Gwen always believed if you wait long enough it usually turns out things happen the way they're supposed to. Providence, she called it.'' He smiled in a remembering way. "Take me, for example. I met my wife after I broke both my legs in a truck accident in Bosnia. At the time I thought it was the end of the world—the end of sports, my career, all the things I liked to do—but if it hadn't been for that accident I wouldn't have met my wife. And I wouldn't have been there when she needed me to save her life.''

C.J. gave a snort of surprise, and Wood smiled. "A long story and one for another time. I guess what I'm saying is, it's too soon to tell, yet, how this is all supposed to play out. Could be you were where you needed to be just so Caty could pick you to hijack.'' His smile slipped sideways, and he gave a one-shoulder shrug. "You never know…''

Since C.J. couldn't think of a thing to say that wasn't going to sound rude, he kept his mouth shut. Thinking about it, though, it occurred to him that whether he believed in all that Providence stuff or not, it was a remarkable attitude for a man whose only child was lying in a hospital bed with a bullet crease in her skull and blinded maybe for life. He felt humble and grateful and undeserving, which brought him back to what he'd wanted to say to Caitlyn's father in the first place.

This time he plunged right in, talking fast so he wouldn't get cut off again. "I appreciate your not blaming me for what happened to your daughter, but it doesn't change the fact that she wouldn't be where she is if I'd done what she asked me to. I'm not asking you to forgive me for that—" he held up a hand to stop Wood interrupting him "—but what I am asking is for you to let me have the chance to make it right."

He had to stop there and force his jaws to unclench, and into the pause Wood dropped a quiet "How do you intend to do that, son?"

"By getting the guy who did this to her." C.J.'s voice grated with rage.

"I think I know how much you want to do that," Wood said after a moment. "I think about it myself. But that's a job for the police and the FBI, isn't it? Realistically, do you think there's anything you can do?"

"Not by myself, no." C.J. was surprised at how calm and confident he felt. How certain. "But I'd have a whole lot of help. That man you met in there, he's FBI, true— Special Agent Jake Redfield—but he also happens to be married to my brother's wife's sister." He paused, and for the first time in a long while felt his dimples showing. "And I do know how awful Southern that sounds." The smile vanished as quickly as it had come. "The point is, we—and that means the FBI included—believe we can get the man responsible for all this. We have a plan, but it involves…" He sat back and sucked in a breath. "We need Caitlyn. We'll lay it all out for her, once she's up to it, and if she's willing—"

Wood let out air in a rush and once again ran a hand
back through his hair. He shook his head, and for the first
time C.J. saw the lines of tension and strain in his face…the
deep shadows around his eyes. For the first time he looked
like a man staring unthinkable loss in the face. "She'd say
yes, of course." His tone held more than a touch of irony.
"That's just Caty."

He leaned forward, his hands rubbing against each other
making a faint sandy sound, and gazed at the carpet as he
spoke in a soft, slurred voice. "It's been hell, these past
months. Especially for her mother. Right now all Chris
wants to do is get Caty home so she can take care of her.
She's been counting the hours…" He looked up at C.J.
"You have any kids?" C.J. shook his head and so did
Wood. "I don't know if you can understand, then. Your
child is always your child, even if she's grown-up. In fact,
that makes it worse because you don't have control over
what she does anymore. She makes her own decisions."

He slapped his knees and stood abruptly. He looked
down at C.J., forcing a smile. "Well. That's it, I guess. In
a nutshell. It's her decision to make, C.J., not ours. If Caty
wants to go along with your plan, we won't try to stop her.
We couldn't anyway, no matter how much we might want
to."

C.J. got to his feet and mumbled, "Thank you, sir." He
held out his hand.

The older man shook it briefly but firmly. Moving in the
jerky, uncoordinated manner of a man distraught, he turned
and began to walk rapidly away, but after a few steps he
whirled and jabbed a finger at C.J. "Promise me one
thing," he said, and his voice grated with emotion. "Just
get him, you hear me? You get that SOB."

Caitlyn drifted in a twilight zone that was not quite sleep
yet not full consciousness, either. Her mind wandered, as
it does in dreams, but with her permission; she knew she

was dreaming and took comfort in knowing she could wake up anytime she chose.

Images crowded into her mind, people and places and events—mostly people. One after another they clicked by, too quickly, like a slide show on fast-forward—her past in reverse order, beginning with the last image she remembered: the landscaped mall in front of the courthouse; a sea of reporters and video cameras; the sun glinting on their lenses and the windows of TV trucks; a brilliant blue September sky.

Back inside the courtroom a few minutes before that: the judge's face, fleshy Southern jowls, soft, smooth-shaven and unsmiling; Mary Kelly's face, gaunt and pasty, with blue smudges under her eyes and freckles standing out like blotches, trying hard to smile.

In the days and weeks before: Mom visiting her in the jail, her hair like sunshine in that drab and dismal room...frightened eyes looking out at her from the serene and lovely mask of her face; and Dad, calm and reassuring as always, but swiping at a tear as he turned to leave her.

Further back: a sultry April night; a big blue truck, powerful diesel engine idling away behind her; a man with a face like a Norman Rockwell painting, hair soft and thick, sun-streaked blond...eyes dark as chocolate and just as seductive...a sweet and dimpled smile; big hands gentle on her shoulders...lips moving, saying words hard and heavy as hammer blows. *I can't do it—I'm sorry.*

The same face in a rapid montage of swirling, overlapping images, like a kaleidoscope: eyes twinkling, smiling and flirtatious with her, nodding with good-ol'-Southern-boy courtesy to Mary Kelly; gentle and kind with a traumatized child; angry, hard as pewter in the bluish light of a yard lamp on an empty concrete apron; anguished, drawn and shadowed in the dimness of the truck cab as she'd seen them the last time. As he'd watched them walk away.

Mary Kelly again...then back through the faces of all

the fearful and damaged women she'd known, all the way back to the first and most beloved—her own mother's face…so young, so beautiful…so haunted.

There were children's faces, too, and even a few men among the victims—her cousin Eric and his precious baby, Emily, in their desperate dash for safety, bundled against the Iowa winter cold…could that only have been last Christmas?

She saw Eric in happier times, along with his sister Rose Ellen, saw them as the children she'd played with on Aunt Lucy and Uncle Mike's farm. There were Uncle Rhett's children, too, though she'd seen them less frequently. They were so much older than she: Lauren, who loved horses, older by eleven years; and shy Ethan, who'd grown up to be a doctor, older by seven. And they'd lived so far away.

She saw herself, a nervous teenager in a long slinky gown, dancing with Uncle Rhett, newly elected president of the United States, amid the dazzle and excitement of his first inaugural ball, and Dixie, the new first lady, radiant and laughing, dancing with a red-faced but determined Eric. She saw herself as a gawky child in overalls, riding on one fender of Aunt Lucy's green John Deere tractor, while Eric laughed at her from his perch on the other side.

And she saw an even smaller child, thrilled and scared witless, arms in a death grip around her daddy's waist for one exhilarating turn around the block on his Harley. Much later she'd learned to ride motorcycles by herself, and had even had her own Harley for a while, but it was that first terrifying trip she remembered most vividly.

Her parents' faces—her earliest memories. Their home in Sioux City. Her room. Pictures and more pictures…seasons and colors, places and faces…images upon images.

And now…nothing.

I'm blind now. What if I never see again? What if it's forever, and all I will ever have are these memories?

Chilled and sweating, she jerked herself awake. Her heart was pounding; nearby, a monitor was going off. A familiar hand was holding hers, stroking her arm. Touching her face. Her mother's voice crooned, as if to a very small child, "Hush, sweetie, it's okay…it's okay."

"Mom?" Caitlyn croaked. At least the pain was better; she didn't feel quite so nauseated.

"We're both here, honey," her dad said. His fingers felt warm on her wrist. She sighed, and the monitor went silent.

"Can I have some water?" A moment later she felt the top half of the bed rise beneath her, forcing her upright, and fought a momentary stab of panic. She fought the urge to put out her hand, to try to hold away the nothingness that hovered just above her like a solid ceiling. She felt the smooth, slightly crisp touch of the straw on her lips, tipped her head cautiously forward and drank. "Thanks," she said, and settled back, shifting to find a comfortable position.

"How are you doing? Can we get you anything?" Her mom's voice was unsteady, and that unnerved her. As a physical therapist, her mother was used to hospitals and hurt people; it took a lot to shake her.

She squeezed her mother's hand. "No, I'm okay."

Her dad, from closer by, said, "Honey, if you're up to it, there are some people here that would like to talk to you."

"I've already spoken to the police—"

"Not the police. It's…" He hesitated, which wasn't like her dad, either. "Honey, it's the truck driver you, uh… He has—"

Caitlyn's heartbeat stumbled, then quickened. She croaked irritably, "Is he still here?" She didn't feel up to soothing his guilty conscience.

"He is, and he has, uh, some people he wants—" the sigh of escaping breath interrupted the flow of words "—Caty, I think you should hear what he has to say."

Before she could answer, she was distracted by pain and pressure in her fingers; her mother was squeezing them so tightly they hurt. She resisted gently and murmured, "Mom…"

The pressure ceased instantly. She felt the cool press of her mother's cheek against hers, heard a quick, husky "I think I should go. I'll be outside."

There was a stirring, then an emptiness beside her. Caitlyn broke a brief and awkward silence. "Dad? What's wrong with Mom?"

"Bear with her," her father said softly. "This has been hard on her—" again, that whisper of breath "—on us all."

Silence came once more. This time the memories that filled it were gentle and comforting: the sturdy strength of a finger clutched in her chubby hand; the crunch of footsteps and huff of breath and a tall man running beside her wobbling bicycle on a hot summer day; a hug and a goodnight kiss that smelled of a brand of aftershave she'd never learned the name of.

"Daddy," she said as the easy and unbidden tears came, "I'm sorry. I'm so sorry…"

"Hey…" The empty space beside her was taken up by that familiar warmth…familiar smell.

"I didn't tell you…I couldn't—"

"Tell me what, punkin?"

"What I was doing. I couldn't—I still can't. It's so important—do you understand?" Her eyes stabbed futilely at the darkness; she'd have given anything to see his face. Anything. *Please let me see his face again. Please…*

She heard a gusty sigh. The hands that held hers tightened, then let go. "No, I can't say I do understand, Caty." There was a pause, and then her father added in a dry voice, "You're not helping, you know."

"I'm sorry." Weighted with a helpless sadness, she used her orphaned hands to wipe her face and heard a grunted "Here—" as a wad of tissues was tucked into her hand.

Drier-eyed and quieter inside, she said tightly, "I can't risk giving away the others. What we do is so important. The people we help have nowhere else to turn. It has to go on. Even if I can't…"

"So," her dad said, and she could hear him struggling to understand, "I guess it's like the old Underground Railroad, huh? During the Civil War. Only you help people escape…what? Domestic violence? Sexual abuse?"

"Abusers. Those the law can't—or won't—touch. Sometimes…the law and justice aren't the same thing." She sniffed and, feeling tremulous and exposed, fought to smile. "I guess it is a little like the Underground Railroad. With some witness protection thrown in. Sometimes it's not enough to just escape," she added somberly. "Sometimes people need to…disappear."

"Ah, Caty. I understand that. I do. But why you?" Her dad was silent again, but only for a moment. Then he gave a short, wondering laugh. "I guess I know the answer to that. But how in the world did you get into—"

"The Internet, of course." Her lips hadn't forgotten how to smile, after all, though it only lasted for a moment. "It was my first year away at college. I was lonely, homesick. And I'd get to thinking about how lucky I am…you and Mom…the way you two met…" The sentimentality embarrassed her; she shrugged it away with a sniff. "I wanted to find out more about it, that's all—domestic violence, abusers, stalkers, all that stuff. And, well, that's how it began. I'm sorry."

"Caty, honey. I'm the one who's sorry…" To her dismay, her father's voice was choked…thickened. Unable to think of words that would comfort him, she groped for his hand and patted it awkwardly.

From behind the glass partition nearby, C.J. watched the emotions play across Caitlyn's face, graphic and revealing as those lines of closed-captioning dialogue on the television screen. He watched her father bow his head to hide the anguish in his face from eyes that couldn't see it.

He'd been eavesdropping unabashedly, with arms folded and jaw tight...knots in his stomach he couldn't get rid of no matter how many times he told himself he wasn't responsible for those people being here, and this way. She'd made her choices, Caitlyn had, long before she'd ever met him, and she'd made him part of her crusade without ever asking him if he wanted to be. No sir, legally he wasn't to blame—probably not ethically, either.

He had a fairly clear understanding of all that. He also had a clear understanding, deep down amongst those knots in his belly, that there was another standard of measurement, one he didn't know the name of or where he'd learned it—the one that says when it comes to helping out another human being in dire need, a man doesn't stop to count the cost to himself. By that standard he'd fallen miserably short, and he was having a hard time living with that.

Furthermore, he knew he wasn't going to be able to live with himself until he'd figured out a way to make it right.

Right now, watching the two of them together, the father and his daughter, Wood and Caitlyn Brown, watching their faces—the grief in his, the fear in hers—what was giving him those knots in his belly was the realization that there maybe wasn't going to be a way to make this right. Ever.

Though C.J.'s eavesdropping hadn't given him much with which to console himself—and quite a lot that didn't make a lot of sense to him—he'd heard enough to be pretty sure the subject matter wasn't something either party to the conversation would want the FBI to know about. So when he saw his in-law-once-removed, Special Agent Jake Redfield, and his lawyer, Charly, approaching, he stepped around the partition and announced himself and them with a warning cough and a gruff "Hey."

"C.J.—" Looking relieved, Wood rose and motioned

him over. "I was just telling Caty—" ingrained honesty won out and he amended it to "—was *about* to, anyway. Here, why don't you…" He sidestepped hastily around the chair he'd been sitting in and offered it to C.J. instead. To his daughter he said unnecessarily, "Honey, C.J.'s here. I told you he has something he wants to talk to you about. Some people—ah." His eyes shifted to focus beyond C.J. as Jake Redfield and Charly filed into the room, filling it to its standing-room-only capacity. "Here they are. Well. Okay, C.J., I'll leave the introductions to you."

Though Wood backed out of the way of the gathering crowd around his daughter's bed, C.J. noticed he didn't leave the room. Finding himself a corner, he settled into it and stood erect with his arms folded on his chest in classic military style, like a sentinel. Like a bodyguard, C.J. thought, vigilant and ever ready. Determined to keep watch over his little girl but maintaining a low profile about it.

With so many pairs of observant eyes in the room, C.J. tried his best to avoid looking too long or too hard at the woman lying in the bed, lest he give away more of what he was feeling than he wanted to. But a glance gave him an image that lingered, of those delicate, fairylike features set in an expression both guarded and intent, and at the same time faintly annoyed. He focused on her hands, lying curled and slightly overlapping on the blanket that covered her to her waist, and a different kind of memory, sensual memories of their featherlight touch on his folded arms made his voice gruff as he introduced Charly, then Special Agent Redfield of the FBI.

The hands on the blanket jerked and clenched into fists. "I won't answer any more questions," Caitlyn said in a thin, remote voice. A voice beyond caring, C.J. thought; a voice that said to the world, "What more can you do to me?"

Unperturbed, Jake Redfield arched his eyebrows at Caitlyn as if she could see him. He'd taken the position at her

elbow across from C.J., with Charly back a little and toward
the foot of the bed. "That's okay," he said quietly, "I don't
plan on asking you any. Not right now. What I'd like you
to do, though, is listen to what I have to say. Can you do
that?"

Chapter 5

The silence in the room was intense. By contrast, the world outside seemed cluttered with sound: the rhythmic shushing of a ventilator in a nearby cubicle; the muted chirp of a telephone; a mutter of voices; the sandy slap of footsteps. C.J. found himself becoming aware of silences and sounds as if he were experiencing the world from the perspective of the woman lying in the hospital bed. A woman without sight.

The FBI man's long face and downward tilted eyes gave him a perpetually doleful expression that reminded C.J. of a hound dog he'd once known. He knew enough about Jake Redfield, though, to be pretty certain that behind those eyes lurked a keen intelligence—maybe even a sense of humor. Also a single-minded determination when in pursuit of bad guys that bordered on obsession. Which was not unlike a hound dog, come to think of it.

Now that keen and melancholy gaze was focused on the woman in the bed as intently as if she could actually meet it.

And almost as if she felt that gaze, Caitlyn's hands slowly uncurled, then brushed at the blanket in a self-conscious sort of way. Stabbing a sullen look in Redfield's direction, she uttered a quiet but firm, "All right."

When the FBI man seated himself on the edge of the bed and half turned so he was facing the woman lying in it, again as if she were capable of seeing him, as if she were someone he wanted to maintain eye contact with, a strange and unfamiliar disquiet stirred in C.J.'s belly. He hated to think it might be jealousy. He sure hoped it wasn't—he'd never been subject to such a thing before.

Nevertheless, he found himself squirming inside as Jake said in a soft, almost intimate voice, "Good for you...glad to hear it."

Then he paused, long enough for Caitlyn to stir restively and mutter, "So, *talk,* then."

When he continued, the FBI man's voice was brisk, all business. "Okay. Here's the deal. The man whose daughter you took—Ari Vasily—is a dangerous man."

Caitlyn interrupted with a faint snort. "Tell me something I *don't* know."

"We—the Bureau, that is—are very interested in Mr. Vasily," he went on, as if she hadn't spoken. "We have been for some time." Caitlyn had grown still and was listening intently, and though she couldn't see it, Jake nodded his approval. "We've been keeping a close eye on some of Mr. Vasily's business dealings since before the 9-11 terrorist attacks—we've always believed him to be a major player in the illegal drug and arms trade, possibly *the* kingpin in Miami and almost certainly a critical link between the Colombians and the Middle-Eastern dealers. Since the attacks, in following the terrorists' money trail, we've been turning up leads that suggest Vasily's links to the Middle East may involve a lot more than illegal drugs." He paused, creating a stillness nobody cared to break. "We believe that

Ari Vasily may be responsible for channeling hundreds of millions of dollars into terrorists' bank accounts.''

To C.J. the atmosphere in the room felt thick, as if there weren't enough oxygen to go around, and when Caitlyn finally spoke, her voice sounded starved for it. ''If you believed that, why haven't you stopped him?''

C.J. jerked his eyes from her hands to her face, then wished he hadn't. Her voice had been so thin, so frail—he wasn't prepared for the silvery flash of accusation in her eyes; the swollen, shiny look of her face, as if from the pressure of too much held-back pain, and the words unspoken: *Then none of this would have had to happen.* Seeing it, the disquiet in his belly became a building pressure that made him want to jump up and pace, punch something— *do* something, *anything* to make that look go away.

Again Redfield acknowledged her anger calmly, with a nod she couldn't see. He spoke with so much control his voice sounded gentle. ''We know the links are there, but so far we haven't been able to find the ones that lead back to Vasily. The man is clever and he's careful. And he has almost unlimited resources. He insulates himself inside so many layers of organization, it's been impossible up to now to follow a trail directly to him. We've been able to find and close off a lot of his—I guess you could call them fingers. Tributaries. Channels. What we haven't been able to do is connect any of them to the man at the top—we believe that's Vasily.'' C.J. wondered if he was the only one to see the FBI man's hand curl into a fist. For the first time Jake's voice betrayed tight-jawed, frustrated rage. ''We know it, but we can't *prove* it.''

Caitlyn spoke, not sullen or accusing, but quietly alert. ''What does this have to do with me?''

''I think you may be his first mistake.'' Jake's smile wasn't pleasant to see. ''We'd like to see that it's a fatal one.''

''A mistake?'' Caitlyn whispered. And then, referring to

the second part of the statement, a rather pugnacious, "How?"

Redfield shifted, in the manner of somebody getting down to the nitty-gritty. "This is the first hint we've had that Vasily might be human." He smiled wryly. "It's obvious that his daughter is important to him. So important that when faced with losing her, he's apparently willing to go to extreme lengths to get her back, even at unprecedented risk of personal exposure." He leaned forward and his voice hardened. "Spelling it out, I believe Vasily ordered the hit on his wife. I think that's obvious, even if there's no way in hell anybody'd ever make it stick in a court of law. Why would he do such a thing, effectively turning the spotlight of law enforcement on himself, when he's been so successful in avoiding it for so long?" He paused, then answered himself.

"Because he was driven to it by sheer frustration. All those months waiting for you to crack, not able to get to you, not able to do a damn thing to get his daughter back—it finally pushed him into doing something stupid. Now all we have to do is take advantage of that mistake."

"How can you?" Caitlyn whispered. "If you can't prove he did it—had Mary Kelly killed."

The FBI man leaned closer, and his voice grew softer still. "He had Mary Kelly killed for one reason, Caitlyn—to send a message to you. Look," he said, putting up a hand as if to block her gasp of rejection, "you were the one who had his daughter spirited away. He knows his wife didn't have the resources to do that. So, obviously, you're the one who knows where she is."

"But I don't—" He made a sound to cut off the denial.

"Vasily probably figured you'd be so shook up by the shooting you'd give in and spill what you know to the judge and he'd get the kid back and that would be that. He didn't count on you getting in the way of a bullet."

"How can you be so sure of that?" Caitlyn protested

faintly, voicing the same arguments C.J. and the others in the room had put forth when Jake had first laid out his theory for them. "There were bullets flying everywhere! Other people were hit—injured. Killed." Her eyes darted desperately around the room; she had that lost child look again. "Couldn't it have been...I don't know...*random?*"

"Anything's possible," Jake said solemnly, without an ounce of conviction. "But consider this—the first shots took out the guards, but only wounded them. Then one bullet got Mrs. Vasily square in the heart. The only reason it creased your skull first was because when you heard those first shots you got some crazy notion in your head that you'd protect her. Vasily must have just about had a heart attack when he saw that." His lips curved in his chilling smile. "It took a real pro and one helluva sharpshooter to do that, but I wouldn't give a bent nickel for the hit man's life right now. Vasily wants you, and he wants you *alive.*"

Vasily wants you.

This must be what drowning feels like, Caitlyn thought, as the wave of fear washed over her. To be engulfed in blackness...suffocating and cold.

And yet her mind was astonishingly clear. "I think I know where this is going," she heard her own calm voice saying. "You want to set a trap for Vasily, and you want me to be the bait."

There was a flurry of sounds and stirrings. Her mind's eye struggled to sort them out: a choked protest from Dad, hastily stifled; C.J.'s voice—an angry, growled "No. No way. You said that wasn't..." Background mutterings of protest from someone—that would be C.J.'s sister-in-law, the lawyer, probably; closer by, the FBI man's restless shifting and the barely audible hiss of a breath, exhaled through someone's nose.

The lawyer—Charly—said in a thick Southern drawl, "For Lord's sake, Jake, after you almost lost Evie—"

The FBI man cut her off, speaking directly to Caitlyn in a quiet but curiously vibrant voice. As if, she thought, he was trying to cover up some powerful emotion and not doing a very good job of it. "We do want to set a trap for Vasily, of course. Because if there's one thing in this world Ari Vasily would take care of in person rather than leaving to his loyal—not to mention untraceable—soldiers, it's picking up his little girl, once he finds out where she is. But the last thing we'd want to do is use you *or* the child as bait. Too many things can go wrong." He paused to clear his throat against a background of more shiftings and stirrings.

Undercurrents, thought Caitlyn, intrigued in spite of everything.

"What we want to do," the FBI man—Jake?—went on after a moment, raising his voice in a struggle to reclaim his self-control, "is get you under wraps and keep you there until we've got Vasily in custody. To do that—"

"You'll have to use me," Caitlyn said calmly. "You said yourself—he wants me alive."

"He wants his *daughter*," Jake corrected, his voice now hard and flat. "You're the means to an end, as far as he's concerned, nothing more. We'll set up the situation, and it'll be one that isn't going to put you or Emma Vasily in harm's way—leave that to us. Right now we're more concerned about getting you to a safe place without Vasily knowing about it."

A safe place… Her mind filled with achingly brilliant images of her room in her parents' house on its shaded street in Sioux City—soft-green walls and borders of pink tulips clashing intriguingly with the dark and brooding posters of Middle Earth from the Tolkien phase she'd dwelt in during most of her high school years.

I want to go home.

She couldn't go home, and knew it. So did everybody else in the room, judging from the silence and tension that had followed Jake's words. Caitlyn's sunny visions of home took on the grainy, shadowy shadings of an old film noir movie as she imagined Ari Vasily tracking her down…finding her there. She couldn't let him find out where her family lived. *Ever.*

She shivered, and felt isolated…alone.

A gruff and froggy sound reached for her in her cave of loneliness and yanked her back to the room filled with people. C.J., clearing his throat. C.J., sitting close to her, on the other side of the bed from the FBI man who'd demanded her focused attention so that she'd all but forgotten anyone else was there. C.J., the cute Southern trucker with the melting-chocolate eyes, sweet smile and wicked dimples, who she'd asked for help and who had let her down so badly and who she had expected never to see again, and yet—who was now so inexplicably and constantly *here.*

C.J. cleared his throat and said, "How 'bout this? How 'bout she comes home with me—to my folks' place in Georgia?"

Silence again—and Caitlyn thought she'd never known before how many different shades of silence there were. This one shimmered around the edges, balanced on the verge of sound, like that suspenseful moment of emptiness in a symphony just before the strings come in at triple *pianissimo.*

Then everyone spoke at once, a murmur and chatter of sound that blew past her ears like a capricious gust of wind.

In its wake, C.J. said, with what she thought was a touch of belligerence, "Look, it's the perfect place. Where we live it's way out in the country—"

"It is that," said Charly dryly. "C.J.'s right. Out there, the only neighbors are friends and family, and they all know one another. It'd be just about impossible for any stranger to get close enough to Caitlyn to do her harm, and anybody dumb enough to try would have to go through all the brothers and in-laws first—" she interjected a rich,

warm chuckle ''—not to mention Momma Betty. Personally, I'd bet on Betty Starr up against a hit man any day of
the week.''

Jake said, thoughtful and somber, ''Actually, it's got pos-
sibilities. There's no way to connect any of you with Caitlyn....'' She could tell by the clarity of his voice that he
was looking at her, waiting for her reaction.

''Honey?'' Her dad's voice, cautious and distant. ''What
do you think?''

What did she think? She couldn't think. The silence was
all around her...vibrant...waiting. Where was C.J.? Was he
watching her? Were they *all* looking at her, watching for
her response? Searching her face for revelations? Unable
to see them, she felt exposed...vulnerable...naked. In self-
defense, she fought to make her expression unreadable.

''In case she needs lookin' after, my sister Jess is a nurse,
lives right there with my mother,'' C.J. put in, rather like
a punctuation mark—as if that should settle it.

C.J., who'd let her down and turned her in to the police
and got Mary Kelly killed. Now he expected her to go
home with him? Let him and his Southern relatives take
care of her?

Caitlyn's head felt as if it might explode. Through the
hum of sound inside it, like the conversation of angry bees,
she heard a chorus of agreement:

''It's not a bad idea....''

''Actually, it's a *great* idea.''

''It'd be the ideal place....''

''She'd be protected....''

''It's the perfect solution.''

''We'd have to get her there without anybody knowing,''
Jake said slowly. ''And I mean *anybody*.'' Caitlyn felt his
weight shift as he turned from her to address the others.
She heard the rush of a sharply exhaled breath. ''Getting
her out of this place won't be easy. Camera crews and news
media everywhere you—''

"Do I hear somebody playing my tune?" That was a new voice, light and musical as birdsong.

Someone said, "Eve!" and it was echoed around the room in varying tones of surprise and delight, along with cries of "Hey, when did you get back?" and "I thought you were in Afghanistan!"

Jake's weight was gone from the bed. Caitlyn heard, "Hey, Waskowitz…" in a voice deep-throated and husky with intimacy, and after a moment, more softly, "You just get in?"

"Just," the newcomer murmured back. "I came as soon as I got your message."

"How was your flight? Get any sleep?"

"Okay…not much…never mind…"

Chafing with impatience, Caitlyn waited, listening to the exchange of mundane and essential information between partners and lovers—for that much was obvious from the first word spoken by the newcomer—reunited after a separation prolonged both in time and distance. She stared fiercely into the nothingness as if she could penetrate it with the sheer effort of her will, and was struggling against a childish sense of exclusion, the urge to cry out, "Hey! Over here! What about *me?*"

Then she felt her hand covered with one that was slender but strong…the skin roughened as if it had recently been too much exposed to hot dry winds and too little to soap and soothing lotions. The bright, musical voice said, "Hey, I'm Eve Waskowitz, Jake's wife. And you're Caitlyn, right?"

Before Caitlyn could utter a word, a new, lighter weight settled onto the bed beside her, and the voice became nearer and almost a whisper, like secrets whispered by best friends in the friendly dark. "They said you can't see at the moment—gee, I can't imagine how confusing it must be, surrounded by a bunch of strange people all talking at once. Are you doing okay?"

"Yeah…I'm fine." And for the first time in a long time, Caitlyn found herself thinking she might be. "Nice to meet you. Did…somebody say you were in Afghanistan?"

"Yeah…filming." There was a gust of breath. "Long story. In a nutshell, I make documentaries. Cable, mostly, although this one's for one of the major networks—*big* thrill. Not to mention more money than I'm used to having at my disposal." By way of changing the subject, she shifted her weight and turned to include the others in the room, although she kept her hand on Caitlyn's. "So, what's going on? What did I miss?"

"We're havin' a council of war," Charly said—and the last word sounded like *wo-ah*.

"Oh, goody," Eve chortled, while Caitlyn, talking over her, was saying flippantly, "We're planning to set a trap for the bad guy, and use me as bait."

Someone—C.J.—actually growled, and Jake sucked in air and said shortly, "We're not going to do that."

"Anyway, that's puttin' the cart in front of the horse," Charly said in her distinctive, dry way. "We need to get her well first. To do that, we've got to get her tucked away someplace safe where the bad guys can't get at her."

There were restless stirrings from C.J.'s side of her bed, and his voice said testily, "We have a place. What I'm gonna do is take her home to Georgia with me. The trick is getting her out of *here* without anybody catching on. The damn media—'scuse me, Eve—have got this whole place surrounded. Every TV station in the country's got a truck parked out there."

Eve made a sound like a self-satisfied cat. "Then nobody would be apt to notice one more, would they?"

There was a short, fat silence, and then Jake murmured, "Eve…" just as C.J. said, "Hah!" and Charly, chuckling, said, "It's perfect."

"Of course it is. Simple, too. We'll just smuggle her out as part of my crew." Eve's hand squeezed Caitlyn's and her weight was no longer beside her on the bed. "It'll take me a couple days to round 'em up—they're still trickling in from Afghanistan—I came ahead to get things set up for postproduction—but you're not going to be ready to go for a while anyway, right? She'll need to be on her feet, at least. And, hmm, let's see…those bandages might be—"

"Eve," her husband said in a low, warning tone, "nobody in your crew can know about this. I mean, *nobody.*"

"Well, of course. Not a word goes beyond the people in this room." Caitlyn felt the brush of a cool cheek and then Eve's voice, light with laughter, faded into distance. "Don't worry, my love—leave everything to me!"

To C.J., still tuned to the nuances of sound in a sightless world, the silence that followed her leaving had a vibrancy to it, like the aftermath of the ringing of a bell.

For long seconds nobody seemed to have anything to say. Then Charly, in her dry, sardonic way, said, "Well, I guess that takes care of that."

Jake cleared his throat, gazed distractedly after his departed wife and muttered, "I wouldn't quite say that…. Uh, there's a lot to take care of on my end. So…guess I better get on it. I'll be in touch." The last was for Caitlyn as he touched her hand in a brief farewell.

As if that was a signal of some kind, Wood Brown took a step forward and Charly glanced at her watch and said, "Well, I'm gonna head on back. What about you C.J.— you comin'?" He shook his head, and she gave the blanket-draped lump that was Caitlyn's foot a friendly squeeze. "Okay, y'all keep me informed, now, y'hear?" She and Jake went out together, as Wood moved to his daughter's side.

He took her hand and gently squeezed it. "Okay, honey, guess I'd better go see what your mother's up to. I'll tell her what we've decided." C.J. thought his quiet ways must be very reassuring under those circumstances. For a moment he felt a twinge of something akin to envy—he could barely remember his own father. And then Caitlyn's father leaned over and brushed her forehead with his lips and was gone.

It was the moment C.J. had both wanted and dreaded. Alone with the woman he knew deep down in his heart he'd wronged, he felt tongue-tied and useless. And yet, he didn't want to leave simply because, right then, at her bedside was the only place in the world he knew how to be. No matter how bad he felt being there, he knew he was going to feel worse somewhere else.

But in a way, it was even more fundamental than that, nothing whatever to do with thought, just a heaviness inside him that was bone deep, as if his body had somehow taken root in that hospital chair.

Seconds ticked by. Wood Brown's footsteps were swallowed up by the hospital sounds. C.J.'s breathing seemed loud enough to him to wake the dead.

"You're still here, aren't you?" Caitlyn said in a low voice, turning a shifting, unfocused gaze toward him. Searching for him in her private darkness.

"Yeah." He cleared his throat. With that sound her gaze found him and sharpened unnervingly, almost as though she could see. Uncomfortably he mumbled, "You need anything? Can I get—"

"I'm fine." But she flinched as she said it, as if she acknowledged the lie it was.

C.J. watched a frown pucker the middle of her forehead, the unmarred part just below the purple lump bisected by a dark line held together by neat, white butterfly bandages where she'd met the brick courthouse steps on her way down. From out of nowhere came a throat-tightening urge to touch his lips to the spot, and he swallowed rapidly and looked away, glad for once that the object of the impulse wasn't able to see him.

Oblivious, she gave a small, tired-sounding sigh. "I just wish I knew why you're here." He didn't know how to answer her, so he didn't try. After a moment she added in a soft, slightly thickened voice, as if she might be about to cry, "What is it you want from me?"

"I don't want anything." His quickening heartbeat seemed to fill his chest. Her vulnerability touched him with an unfamiliar fear that made him sound angry when he was anything but. "I'm just trying to help."

"I don't want your help." She threw it back at him, her voice as harsh and angry as his, and it never occurred to him she might be covering up something else, the same way he was.

"Look," he said, biting off words lest they give away too much, "you're gonna have to have help from somebody, might just as well be with me. They're gonna put you in some kind of safe house when you leave here, anyway, did you think about that? What, would you rather be with *strangers?*"

To his surprise she laughed—a single bright puff of air. "What do you think *we* are? We *are* strangers."

He clamped his teeth together and worked a muscle in his jaw while he thought about how to tell her what he knew in his heart, which was that she wasn't a stranger to him, not anymore. That during the past few months there'd been a bond formed that tied her to him in ways he didn't understand himself.

He leaned forward, shaking his head, then remembered she couldn't see that. "No, we're not," he said, in the flat, implacable way that had driven his brothers and sisters up the wall and won him a lot more arguments than he'd lost. "It's true we haven't known each other all that long, but we've sure enough had a profound effect on one another's lives."

She gave that little laugh again and was silent. Her lips held on to an ironic tilt, and her sightless eyes shifted past him while she thought about it.

He watched her for a moment, then said softly, "You're gonna like them, you know."

"Who?" Her eyes darted back to him and lit on his chin. He found himself smiling.

"My folks. They're good people. Hey, my mom was a teacher, too, you know. Like your dad."

She settled back onto the pillows with a sigh. "That explains it."

"Yeah? What?"

"The way you talk."

"The way I—"

"You use good grammar. Most of the time."

"Huh," said C.J., bemused that she'd noticed such a thing about him. It gave him an unexpected warming feeling inside.

As if she'd heard his thoughts, her lips curved again with that wry smile. "When your dad's a schoolteacher and you've had good grammar pounded into you all your life, you notice." She shifted a little, then murmured, "So, what about your dad? What does he do?"

"Died when I was little. Heart attack." He was still trying to get past that remark about his grammar.

"Oh—I'm sorry." She didn't say anything more for a while, and he got to thinking it was time for him to leave. He was getting ready to do that—shifting around and making rustling noises, trying to think what to say to end things—when she turned her face toward him and put out a hand. Searching.

His heart gave a bump, and he wondered if he dared take her hand and hold it, but before he could make up his mind she jerked it back and grasped it with her other one on the folded-over sheet across her middle.

"Please," she said in a soft but urgent voice. "Tell me about them—your family." She sounded nervous, he thought, as if she couldn't bear for him to leave. Like a little child asking for one more drink of water and a bedtime story because she didn't want to be left alone in the dark.

So he settled back in his chair with a silent exhalation, cleared his throat and began to tell her about the people most important to him in this world. He started with his mother, Betty Starr, five foot one on a good day, who'd taught school and raised seven children with a soft voice and an iron hand while her husband was off driving an eighteen-wheeler across the country. He told her about his brother, Jimmy Joe, who'd taken over the trucking when his dad died and built it into the company called Blue Starr Transport, and had given C.J. a job when he needed help to put himself through law school and nobody else besides his mother believed he could.

"How's that law degree coming along?" Caitlyn interrupted. She had that wry little smile on her lips, and C.J. knew she was remembering that April night they'd faced each other between the headlight beams of his truck and he'd told her he couldn't do what she was asking of him. And that she'd known the reason why without him having to tell her.

He told her it was coming along fine, that he'd gotten his degree in June and was just waiting to take the bar exam. He didn't tell her he'd most likely be postponing his scheduled date which was coming up week after next.

He went on to tell her about his brothers and sisters then, working his way down the list starting with his oldest sister, Tracy, the conventional one, a schoolteacher, too, married to Al who was a cop down in Augusta. Then Troy the ex-SEAL, now married to Charly, father of two and a private investigator. He'd made it as far as his sister Jess the nurse, mother of eighteen-year-old Sammi June, and was explaining how she'd been living with their momma since her husband, Tristan, had gotten shot down flying missions over Iraq, when he looked over and saw he no longer had an audience. Caitlyn had fallen asleep.

He cut himself off in the middle of the sentence and put a hand over his mouth, letting an exhalation sigh quietly from his nose while he studied her. Relaxed, the lines of stress and frustration erased by sleep, her face seemed to him flawless once more, fairy-tale lovely, the lump on her forehead, the swelling, the bruises beneath her eyes and the healing scrape on her chin of no consequence, invisible to his eyes.

Emotions tumbled through him like puppies, wreaking havoc on his piece of mind. Out of the chaos, he could find only one clear thought.

She sure doesn't look like a hijacker.

Chapter 6

On the day Caitlyn Brown was to be released, the hospital
held a press conference on the promenade outside its main
public entrance. The hospital's administrator and attorney
were featured, as was the doctor in charge of the patient's
care and treatment. So were Caitlyn's parents and the attorney they'd hired on their daughter's behalf. Various law
enforcement agencies were represented, including the FBI,
the district attorney's office and the local chief of police.

Throughout the conference, fit young men with somber
faces and flinty eyes kept watch from the steps in front of
the crowd, while somewhat scruffier individuals of both
genders bearing microphones and video cameras filled the
sidewalks and overflowed into the street, snarling traffic for
blocks around. The hospital parking lot was choked with
satellite trucks and vans bearing the logos of every major
news agency in the country and a fair number from over-
seas—it had been a relatively quiet news week and this was
the niece of the former leader of the free world, after all.

C.J. watched the news conference on a television set

mounted high on the wall of a waiting area on the hospital's quiet third floor. Except for one big-bellied, ruddy-faced man leafing through a tabloid newspaper in the row of chairs across from him, he was alone. Closed-captioning was off; the TV sound was on, turned down low.

Leaning tensely forward, clasped hands fidgeting, C.J. listened to the hospital personnel tell how Ms. Brown had received the best possible care and how pleased everyone was with her recovery thus far. Then he listened while the doctor explained about the swelling inside Caitlyn's brain, a result of the bullet that had grazed her skull, that was affecting the optic nerve. And no, there was no way of knowing at this point whether her blindness would be permanent; they would have to wait for the swelling to go down in order to determine whether or not there was significant damage to the optic nerve itself.

At that point the red-faced man, who was wearing overalls with a short-sleeved T-shirt, and a ball cap bearing a tractor manufacturer's logo over thick iron-gray hair, gave his newspaper a shake and grunted, ''Helluva thing, innit?''

Without taking his eyes from the screen, C.J. agreed that it was. He was watching the law enforcement contingent take over the microphones, shuffling around and muttering as they got themselves sorted into the previously agreed-upon speaking order. After some throat-clearing and fidgeting, the chief of police admitted there was no new progress to report in the search for the gunman who'd killed Mary Kelly Vasily and wounded Ms. Brown and two police officers. And that it was too early to determine whether the body of a male Caucasian in mid to late forties that had been discovered shot to death and dumped locally near an abandoned mill had any connection with the case.

The D.A. then stepped up to assert that the decision had been made not to return Caitlyn Brown to jail, and that the FBI would be placing her in protective custody at an undisclosed location.

The FBI representative's remarks consisted mostly of "I'm sorry, I can't comment on that," in response to questions fired at him from all sides by members of the press corps.

About the time the questioners were showing signs of impatience and the organizers of the press conference looked as though they might be getting ready to pack it in, a change came over the crowd. As if, C.J. thought, a stiff wind had sprung up out of somewhere. The young blond CNN reporter came into view, looking excited and holding a microphone in one hand. She had the other hand up to the side of her head, cupped over her ear.

"...word that Caitlyn Brown is coming out of the hospital at this very moment. *Tim, I'm going to try and get over there—"*

There followed a confusion of rapidly changing pictures, garbled sounds and jerky images, and then a partly obscured view of the hospital's ambulance entrance, where someone in a wheelchair had apparently just emerged through the automatic sliding door. The wheelchair was being propelled with some urgency across the pavement to where three dark sedans with tinted windows waited, engines idling. There were only glimpses of the chair and its occupant, surrounded as they were by hospital personnel in light-colored slacks and tunics and men in neckties and dark suits. Nevertheless, it was possible to determine that the figure in the chair was slender and slightly built and was wearing dark blue sweats and a black-and-yellow baseball cap that didn't quite cover the bandages swathing her head. Also a pair of dark-rimmed sunglasses.

"Why," the red-faced man said in an awed voice, "looka there, she ain't but a little bit of a thang."

C.J. nodded absently. His eyes were riveted on the TV screen and he was trying his best to follow the jerky, jostled images of a pale face all but obscured by huge dark lenses. Then there was only a closing car door, and dark-tinted windows reflecting back excited faces, open mouths and shoving microphones against a blue September sky.

The red-faced man said sadly, "It's just a shame, innit? A real shame…"

C.J. let out the breath he'd been holding and agreed that it was indeed a shame. Then, murmuring, "Would you excuse me?" he pushed himself up from the chair and lurched out of the waiting area. Halfway down an empty hallway across from an elevator marked Hospital Personnel Only, he pushed open a door, stepped into a room and closed the door behind him.

"Okay," he said, a little out of breath, "they're off. How's everybody doing in here? You ready to go?"

"I'm ready," Caitlyn said, breathless as he was. Her silvery eyes stared resolutely into middle distance as one hand lifted to adjust the scarf that framed her face, wound loosely and draped over her shoulders in the style of an Afghani woman. The other hand, relaxed in her lap, cradled a video camera.

Jake Redfield stood behind Caitlyn's wheelchair. His deep-set eyes, intent and somber, were on his wife. "Okay, then—I guess this is it." He took a breath, and it occurred to C.J. that the FBI man might not be as cool about things as he looked. "Eve, you know what—"

"Yes, love, I know what to do." Her tone was somber, too, but her eyes danced. "By now, I've made sure everyone in my crew knows about my new protégée from Afghanistan, here for a 'few days' to learn about documentary filmmaking. Her name is Jamille, by the way—which means beautiful, I think, in one of those languages over there. Perfect, isn't it?" Her smile burst forth, as if she couldn't keep it in check a moment longer.

She dropped into a crouch beside the wheelchair and placed both hands on Caitlyn's arm. Softly, as if for her only, she said, "Okay, just like we practiced. I'll be right beside you, you'll be able to feel me touching you all the time, but if you feel lost or woozy or anything, just stop where you are and keep looking through the camera. I'll get you, don't worry.''

''I'm not worried,'' Caitlyn said staunchly. ''You just have to keep telling me where to point this thing so I don't look like an idiot.''

Eve chuckled richly. ''We'll do the clock thing, okay? Twelve o'clock is straight ahead, ten's to the left, two's to the right, six is behind you. Then high or low—''

''So *that's* where it comes from,'' Caitlyn said in a wondering tone. '''Watch your six.' I've always wondered....''

''It means watch your back,'' Jake said. He kissed his wife and added a husky, ''That goes for all of you. I don't have to tell you—''

''No,'' Eve murmured, gently smiling, ''you don't. We'll be fine. Don't worry.''

''I think it's best we leave the chair here,'' Jake said, frowning at nobody in particular. ''On the off chance somebody sees you exit the elevator. You okay with that, Caitlyn?''

She nodded and said, ''Sure.'' She was already fumbling for the wheelchair's footrests with her toes.

C.J. dropped to one knee and folded the footrests out of her way. Then he took her feet, one at a time, and lowered them, like fragile artifacts, to the floor. She was wearing sandals, he noticed, and her ankles felt slender and strong in his hands. He rose, breathing hard and slightly light-headed, and put a hand under her elbow.

Murmuring a polite and barely audible, ''Thank you,'' she allowed him to steady her for a second, then unfolded herself in that graceful, lighter-than-air way she had. The robe settled with a whisper around her ankles. ''I'm okay— I'll be fine.'' Her voice was steady; the breathlessness was only excitement.

''Two o'clock high,'' Eve sang out, testing her, and C.J. barely ducked in time as Caitlyn swung the video camera toward him. He caught a glimpse of parted lips and silvery eyes as Eve said with laughter in her voice, "Well done!"

Jake was waiting with poorly disguised impatience beside the door. At his wife's nod he opened it a crack, gave the hallway a quick glance, then pulled the door wide. "All clear."

C.J. stepped across the hallway to the elevator and punched a button. Counted heartbeats until the doors clunked open.

"Off we go," Eve breathed from close behind him.

He turned and saw that she had linked her arm with Caitlyn's. He wanted to touch her, too—for reassurance, maybe, but for whose? Anyway, it didn't matter, because he didn't do it.

When the two women were on the elevator and had turned to face the open door, Eve blew her husband a kiss, then looked at C.J. and winked. He wanted to say to her, "You take care of her, now, you hear?" But again he didn't.

"We'll be right behind you," Jake said.

As the doors slowly closed, C.J. was conscious of a peculiar hollowness under his ribs. As he and Jake made their way to the stairs and down the four flights to the parking garage, moving with a tense and silent urgency, he felt as if he'd just put a newly hatched chick on a plank and shoved it out in the middle of a lake.

Something in the silence all around him made him steal a glance at the man next to him, and he saw that the FBI man's jaw looked as tense and bunched up as his was. He wondered if Jake was feeling the same way about Eve. Well, why wouldn't he? She was his wife, after all.

And Caitlyn was...

My responsibility. That's all. And he didn't know what he'd do if he let anything happen to her. Anything more than had happened already.

He and Jake found a vantage point near the garage entrance where they could watch the hive of activity around the media trucks from behind a planter filled with crepe myrtle. Over by the hospital's main entrance, some of the on-camera reporters were doing their wrap-up pieces against the backdrop of the building, while others were still finding people in the crowd to interview. Quite a number of people seemed to be doing nothing in particular, while others moved with the efficiency of a colony of ants, lifting, loading, packing up equipment and preparing to move on.

"There they are," C.J. said suddenly, his voice a fair imitation of a crow squawking from the top of a telephone pole. He'd picked up the glint of sunshine on Eve's blond head, and next to that the flutter of the pale blue scarf draped loosely around Caitlyn's. He saw Eve lean close and point, and Caitlyn swing her video camera upward toward a helicopter hovering overhead, just exactly as if she could see it there.

Jake didn't say anything, but C.J. knew he'd seen them, too. There was a certain *quickening,* a kind of electricity, an alertness that had nothing to do with the senses. Whatever it was, he recognized it in Jake because it was going on inside himself, too, and he felt a sense of kinship with the man that didn't have a thing to do with blood. Funny thing was, he didn't even know Jake Redfield all that well—they'd run into each other at the major family get-togethers, and that was about it. Now, though, he found himself thinking about the man, wondering what made an FBI agent tick, and how it must be to feel about a woman the way he obviously did for his wife, Eve.

And then out of the blue he was thinking about his brothers and their wives—Jimmy Joe and his feisty, redheaded Mirabella, Troy and Charly, with that dry sense of humor and chip-on-the-shoulder attitude of hers. For the first time ever in his life he thought about the people he knew who were head over heels in love with their mates, and knew how lucky they were. And for the first time ever in his life he knew that there was an emptiness inside himself and that it was called loneliness.

What he couldn't figure out was why he was having those thoughts and feelings while his eyes followed, as if stuck to her by a magnet, the slow and graceful progress of a woman who was, in all the ways that counted, a stranger to him. Yeah, a stranger; she was right about that, after all.

Strange? What else would you call a blind woman with silver eyes, a hijacker of trucks, a rescuer of battered women, and a kidnapper of children—an incredibly beautiful woman who at the moment was hiding herself and her bandaged head in the all-concealing robes of a woman from Afghanistan?

Strange…or crazy, maybe?

Jake, who'd been scanning the thinning crowd with eagle eyes, suddenly seemed to relax. He let out a breath and muttered, "She's something else, isn't she?"

C.J. replied fervently, "She sure is."

He was fairly certain they were talking about two different women, but that didn't matter. They were most likely both right.

They stayed where they were until the crowd began to thin out and they saw Eve give the wrap-it-up signal to her crew. They watched the two women make their way to the van followed by the other members of the crew, and then the seemingly endless process of getting all the equipment stowed, buttoned down and loaded up. Finally, Eve and Caitlyn climbed into the back of the van and disappeared from view. The rest of the crew sorted themselves out and found seats. Doors slammed. Nobody but the two men watching from behind the crepe myrtle paid any attention whatsoever as the van pulled slowly out of the hospital parking lot and bumped into the street.

Jake looked over at C.J. and let out a breath. "That's it, then. They're off. From here on I guess it's up to you."

C.J. glanced at him, then squinted off in the direction of the disappearing van. "Yes, sir," he said.

It was up to him, all right—tell him something he *didn't* know. Up to him not only to keep Caitlyn Brown safe, but to somehow put her life back on its rails. Seemed like a lot to expect of a man most people would have thought was still trying to figure out his own direction in life. C.J. was well aware there were some who'd have said it was *too* much.

They'd have been wrong. C.J. didn't know how he knew that, but he did.

He didn't know, either, how to describe the way he felt, watching that van drive off down the road with Caitlyn Brown inside. *Bigger,* somehow, than he'd felt only a few weeks ago. Definitely older, but also denser…stronger…more like steel than human flesh and bone. Maybe, he thought, thinking of fairy-tales again, it was something like the way one of those knights of old had felt when he strapped on his armor and took up his sword and shield and rode off to find him a dragon to slay.

Caitlyn woke from a light doze as the car's tires crunched over graveled ground. All motion stopped, and Eve's touch was a feathery tickle on her arm.

"Caty—honey, we're here."

She heard Eve's door open and felt the caress of a breeze that carried with it the smell of fall and the feel of evening…a coolness, a softness and the rich brown smell of leaves. Eager for more of it, she groped for the handle and opened her own door without waiting for help, and then she could hear the faint spatter of the leaves as they fell all around her, shaken loose by the breeze. In the distance she could hear doors opening and closing, footsteps and voices and the soft woofs of well-mannered dogs.

She swung her legs around, felt with her feet for the ground and stood up, and then had to clutch the door to keep from falling. Her head swam with dizziness—a little from car sickness, perhaps, but mostly just exhaustion. Though she'd managed to sleep a little after they'd exchanged the bumpy van for Eve's comfortable sedan in Atlanta, it had been hours since they'd left the quiet and safety of that hospital room. Too long for someone recovering from a head injury to be out of bed.

"Hold on, I'm coming…" Footsteps crunched and Eve's worried voice came closer. "How're you doing, hon'? You okay?"

"Just a little tired," Caitlyn muttered, hating her swimming head and hollow stomach. This weakness was new to her; she couldn't remember ever having had a sick day in her life before. Not like this. "I'll be okay…."

"It's been a pretty long day," Eve consoled, in her bright and cozy way, as she hooked an arm around Caitlyn's waist. "Don't try to be brave or sociable, nobody expects you to. You're probably going to want to go straight to bed. Plenty of time tomorrow to start getting acquainted…learning your way around. Hold on to me, now—"

"My head aches," Caitlyn said in a small voice. *Damn* the weakness. *Damn* the pain. Her ears rang; she drew a shivering breath, on the verge of confessing that she simply didn't have the strength to take another step. She thought how appallingly humiliating it was going to be to collapse in a heap in front of total strangers.

"Here—what the hell are you doing?" The voice was gruff as the welcoming woofs of the dogs, soft as the patter of breeze-carried leaves.

She shuddered and felt the breeze of movement and the warmth of a solid body, and an arm much bigger and stronger than Eve's wrapped itself around her waist. Another hooked behind her legs, and she gave a gasp as she felt herself swept up, then cradled against a heaving chest, a thumping heart. A warm, earthy scent filled her senses, strange but somehow familiar…a mixture of soap and Southern cooking and diesel fuel and man, and a hint of an aftershave she'd never learned the name of.

"I got you.…"

"Put me down," she said faintly. "I'm too heavy to carry."

"Shoot, you don't weigh as much as a feather," C.J. scoffed. But his breathing was quick and sharp, and she was certain he lied.

And yet she couldn't bring herself to struggle, or even argue, not another word. Which ought to have astonished her, alien as it was to her nature to surrender any kind of control without a fight. Except that this didn't *feel* like surrender at all. It felt…nice.

Was it shameful to enjoy this so much—the feel of muscular arms around her and the steadfast thumping of a man's heartbeat against her cheek? If it was, Caitlyn thought with a silent sigh, then so be it. *So be it.*

She only knew then that she was weak and he was strong, and it felt *good* to rest her head against his shoulder and let herself be rocked by the rhythm of his long, masculine stride. *Crunch, crunch, crunch, crunch* across the gravel…then the hollow thump of booted feet on wooden steps, scuffing and scraping across wood planks, the squeak of an old-fashioned screen door.

Soft voices, kind voices…

"Bring her right on in here this minute, son. Poor little thing…I expect she's about worn-out."

"Sammi June's room's all ready for her, C.J. It's the one closest to the bathroom, and she'll be next to me so I can look in if she needs anything. That's the second—"

"I know which one it is," C.J. said with an impatient-sounding grunt. "It was mine before it was Sammi June's."

"Are you hungry? I've got roast chicken and butter beans and mashed potatoes 'n' gravy and squash pie out in the kitchen.…"

They were all murmuring the way people do when they're trying not to wake up a sleeping baby. Caitlyn was neither one of those things, and it took just about that long for her pride to bestir itself from its unaccustomed dormancy. Her body arched and stiffened—a silent demand—and either C.J. understood or she'd caught him by surprise, because after the first instinctive tightening against her struggles, his arms relaxed and she found herself upright and on her own two feet.

Though none too steadily. As her world tilted on its axis, she clutched at one of those arms with one hand while she held out the other and said in as firm a voice as she could muster, "Hi, thanks so much for having me. I'm Caitlyn Brown."

The hands that sandwiched hers were small-boned but warm and strong. From a level considerably below hers, a no-nonsense voice crooned in the distinctive music of the South, "Well, we're glad you could be here. I'm Calvin's momma. Call me Betty."

Caitlyn blinked and adjusted her gaze downward. For no good reason that she could think of her eyes were stinging again. "Thank you," she whispered, then faltered. She could think of nothing else to say. She feared she was one good peppery sneeze away from bursting into tears.

"And I'm Jess—C.J.'s sister. One of 'em, anyway." The hand that claimed hers next was bigger, longer-boned, its touch cool and sure. The voice, with a more muted accent, came from higher up, maybe even a little above Caitlyn's five foot seven.

So, she thought, his mother is short and his sister is tall. "You're the nurse," she said, smiling. She felt a painful little bubble of fear. *I wonder what they look like. They're so kind…I wonder if I'll ever see their faces.* She imagined them both with C.J.'s chocolate eyes and dimples…golden hair for the sister, silver for the mother. She imagined them beautiful, to match their voices.

"Would y'all like to come on out to the kitchen and have some supper?" Betty asked. Her touch was warm on Caitlyn's elbow. "Eve, you'd better stay and have a bite."

"Thanks, but I need to be getting home." Eve's voice, from somewhere close behind Caitlyn, interrupted by a rustle and a breeze and the brush of a body…the soft murmurs and barely audible grunts people make when they hug "Before my kids forget they've even got a mother. I haven't seen much of them lately. Mmm, thank you so much, Betty…Jess."

Then it was Caitlyn's turn to be caught up in a brief but fierce embrace. Eve's hair, smelling faintly of lemons, tickled her cheek, and her voice said huskily next to her ear, "Caty, honey, you're going to be *fine*. You take care, now—I'll come see you soon…."

Caitlyn's mumbled thanks were swallowed up in the general babble of goodbyes and you-come-back-nows, and then Eve was gone, her leaving punctuated by the bang of the screen door.

Kind voices haggled good-naturedly over her, discussing her wants and needs as if she weren't there, the way people do with small children:

"Let's everybody come on in the kitchen, now, Caitlyn needs to sit down. You all can do with some supper—Calvin, I know you love my squash pie—"

"Momma, she's tired. She might just want to go to bed."

"Well, some soup, then. Build up her strength. Some soup, and—oh, I know, how about some hot cocoa? That's what Granny always used to fix us—"

"I think I would just like to go to bed," Caitlyn interrupted in a thin, unnatural voice. A child's voice. "If that's okay…"

A child was exactly what she felt like—a very small, bewildered child, lost in a vast darkness. She wanted nothing more than to crawl into a corner, curl herself into a terrified ball and howl until her parents came to find her.

Surrounded by well-meaning strangers, she wanted only to
hear a familiar voice, feel familiar arms around her, the
touch of gentle, loving hands.

"Of course it's okay. Momma, I'll just help her up—"

"Well, okay then, you go on. I'm going to make her a
cup of cocoa. I'll bring it in a bit."

"You think you can make it up those stairs, hon'?
Here—put your arm around my waist. C.J., if you take—"

"I've got her," C.J. growled.

There was an instant of silence, then the push of air,
warm and dense...and there were those arms again, seeming almost familiar now, one around her waist, the other
behind her legs. She was lifted, and there was the same
sharp, rapid breath blowing puffs at her temple and the
same steady heartbeat thumping under her cheek. She
caught a whiff of that half-forgotten aftershave, and the
other C.J. smells...and somehow those were already familiar to her, too.

The terror receded a little, but not the darkness. And not
the urge to cry.

Chapter 7

She couldn't give in to it. Not now. Not here.

She tightened her lips and muttered, "You don't have to do this." There was no answer. She could feel his chest and belly bunch and tighten, hear his breathing deepen as he took the stairs at a quick and steady pace. "You're going to kill yourself," she said grimly, breathing almost as hard as he was.

He let go a huff of laughter that sounded faintly wounded. "You don't have a whole lotta faith in me, do you?"

"I don't mean to insult you, but it's not like you're an athlete or something. You drive a *truck.*"

And yet, all along her side was the unmistakable resilience of firm masculine muscle, and somewhere in the neighborhood of her bottom she could feel the flat, rigid plane of a belly that carried not even a hint of a trucker's gut. An image rose in her memory…a long, lean form pacing across the barren concrete apron of an abandoned gas station. And the way he'd faced her, the angry-cat tension in him—a hissing, spitting fury one blink away from drawing blood.

Not *too* lean, though; his arms felt rock solid and steel strong. And—how could she have forgotten?—she remembered the way he'd overpowered her and so easily taken her gun away.

Plus, they'd reached the top of the stairs, and he hadn't dropped her or keeled over yet.

"I keep in shape," he muttered. She heard and felt the impact of his foot against a door. Her head reeled as he twisted his body and swung her around to carry her through it.

Before her head had stopped spinning, she heard a faint grunt and felt the bump of a mattress under her bottom...and before she was in any way ready for it, a fearsome emptiness all around her. Panic caught her up like a midsummer Iowa dust devil, taking her breath away. Strange that she should be so terrified at the thought of being left alone when only moments ago she'd thought that was what she wanted most in the world.

"Calvin—" she blurted out, and heard a startled grunt in response. She rushed on, desperate to keep him there if only for a moment longer. "I heard your mother call you that. Okay, so now I know what the *C* stands for. What about the *J?*"

"James." It was gruff and short, but at least he hadn't withdrawn from her any further. Listening hard, she heard the whisper of a reluctant exhalation. "After my dad. The Calvin comes from my grandaddy—on my momma's side."

"Calvin..." Caitlyn murmured it again, drawing it out slowly to divert his attention away from her momentary lapse of poise. The absurd attack of panic was ebbing. Now that she could be reasonably certain she wasn't going to be abandoned in the next second or two, she felt thoroughly ashamed of her neediness.

I'm only blind, after all, she scolded herself. I'm not a child. I'm a grown woman. I am not helpless. I just can't see.

C.J. was glad she hadn't been able to see him wince. His annoyance with her had evaporated. He wasn't sure where it had come from and was glad to let it go. Ashamed now of caring about which name she chose to call him, he stood looking down at her, thinking how small and hunched she looked—like a sick canary with those feathery tufts of blond hair sticking up out of the bandages around her head. Wishing he knew what to do for her. Wondering if he should go. Wanting to stay.

"I'd rather you didn't call me that," he said. "Momma's about the only one still calls me Calvin."

"Why? What's wrong with it?" Her eyes lifted, searching for him, but only made it as high as his chest. He could feel their touch there, a patch of prickly warmth as if he'd rubbed it with that salve his high school football coach used to use for sore muscles. "I loved that comic strip—what was it called?—the one with the little boy and his make-believe tiger?"

He thought about sitting down beside her on the bed, then decided he'd better not, not with sensory memories of the weight and shape and warmth of her body still burned into his muscles, nerves and sinews. He shifted his weight awkwardly instead. "Yeah, I did, too—used to doodle little cartoon pictures on everything, kind of like my signature, I guess."

"So?"

"So...I don't know. What was a pretty cool name when I was a little kid didn't seem so cool for a grown man."

She tilted her head to one side while she considered that. While he considered what it was about her and this conversation that was making him feel less like a grown man than he had in years. "So, why didn't you just shorten it to Cal?"

"I did, for a while in high school. I think I picked up the idea for the C.J. from my brother Jimmy Joe—he'd taken to calling his boy J.J., and well, you know…I thought it was—"

"Cool?"

He gave a little snort of laughter. "Yeah."

She smiled at him—or at his chest, rather—and he smiled back. And then it came to him that for the first time in his life he was in a situation with a woman where his smile and his dimples weren't going to be of any advantage to him.

Before he had time to mull that over in his mind, he noticed that Caitlyn was rubbing her hands back and forth over the bedspread she was sitting on, sort of stroking the delicate slipperiness of it, feeling it with her fingers in a way that made his mouth go dry. Her head was tilted to one side and there was an expression on her face he couldn't read.

"Did I hear you say this room used to be yours?"

Then he realized what the look on her face was. She was teasing him. Unexpected delight gathered in his chest like bubbles in a glass of soda pop.

"Yeah," he said, letting his grin leak into his voice, "but that was a while ago. The decor now is all Sammi June's—that's Jess's daughter—"

"You told me about her. You said she's away—in college?"

"That's right." C.J. snorted. "Here and I thought you were asleep when I was telling you that."

There was a pause while he watched a smile hover over her lips, the way he'd once watched, with breath suspended, a butterfly light on his finger. Then, hushed and husky, she asked, "Tell me the truth. Is it *pink?*"

In the same kind of voice, teetering on the edge of laughter, he intoned, "Oh, *yeah.*"

"Rosebuds?" It was a horrified whisper.

"Nope. Butterflies—little bitty yellow ones."

"I had tulips." She sighed, and her smile took on a wistful quality that made her seem even younger than she was. "Pink ones—two different shades, hot and baby—with green leaves."

He didn't know whether it was the smile or the silvery sheen that had come into her eyes, but all at once C.J. had a tightness in his throat and a tingling behind his eyes and nose. This, naturally, prompted the typically masculine urge to get the hell out of there before he did anything to disgrace himself. He was trying to think how to do that without coming across as a heel or a craven coward when Jess came in. He almost kissed her, he was so relieved.

"I brought up your things," Jess said as she set the small sports bag she'd brought with her on the foot of the bed.

"Can't be much." Caitlyn was groping for the bag with one hand. "The clothes I was wearing, um, before, I guess? They gave me the basic necessities when I was in jail, and Mom brought me some things in the hospital, but—" She stopped, and C.J. saw her throat move as she swallowed. Her eyes darted back and forth, and there was a desperate look in them now, as if, he thought, they were trying to find a way out of a trap.

"Well, I, uh, guess I'll leave you two to figure things out," he muttered, backing up until he bumped into the bedroom door, which he grabbed on to as if it was the only oar in a sinking rowboat. "I'm gonna, uh, I'll just…okay, well, I'll be down in the kitchen if you need me."

If you need me?

As he made his escape Jess was saying to Caitlyn, "Don't you worry about a thing, I'm sure we can find you anything you need. You're welcome to borrow Sammi June's clothes—she isn't gonna mind a bit. You look to be pretty near the same size."

His sister had the situation well in hand, it appeared. What he couldn't figure out was why he didn't feel happier about things turning out the way he'd planned. Maybe it was selfish, but he hadn't planned on and didn't much like feeling useless.

He went downstairs to the kitchen and found his mother standing by the stove stirring a big pot of butter beans. She looked around when she saw him, and her face lit up the way it always did when she set eyes on someone she cared about, even if it hadn't been but a few minutes since she'd seen them last. Unless she happened to be displeased with that particular person at that particular moment, of course. That was the great thing about Momma, C.J. thought—she never left you in any doubt as to what her feelings were.

"Sit down, son," she ordered as she put down the spoon and picked up a potholder, and C.J. did so with no arguments. His stomach had begun to growl with his first whiff of that roast chicken, and he watched hungrily as his mother took a plate out of the oven that was already piled high with chicken and mashed potatoes and what looked like fried okra. She added a spoonful of beans and then ladled some gravy over the mashed potatoes and set the plate in front of him.

Mumbling, "Thanks, Momma, looks good," he picked up his fork and dug in. The first bite tasted so good he caught himself making little humming, crooning noises. His mother chuckled. "Granny Calhoun used to say you know the food's good when you start singin' to it."

He grinned and took a big slug of milk, then said, "Guess I was hungrier than I thought I was." He was thinking about Caitlyn, up there in the dark, wondering if maybe she was hungrier than she'd thought she was, too. He thought he might take her up a plate, soon as he was finished....

While his mother was getting herself a glass out of the cupboard and pouring it full of buttermilk, he found himself looking around the kitchen, taking in the usual clutter of lists and notes stuck on the door of the fridge with magnets, the pencil and ink marks on the pantry door frame where everybody's height had been measured since long before C.J. was born, the sweet potato plant in a macramé sling left over from the seventies hanging over the sink and the row of late tomatoes ripening on the windowsill, the red teakettle on the back burner of the stove and the drainer that was never empty of dishes. He'd seen all those things so many times without thinking much about how they might look to a stranger, caring only about the warm fuzzy feelings they brought into his heart.

Now, though, everything looked and felt different to him. Instead of the familiar warmth there was a strange sweet sadness inside him because of one particular stranger upstairs who couldn't see any of it, and he wondered why he regretted that so much. He closed his eyes and tried to imagine himself being in that room and not able to see it. He thought how he'd describe it for somebody blind....

"You tired, son?" His mother's voice was gentle.

He shrugged away the sweet sad thoughts and didn't try to explain. He looked down at his plate, saw it was empty and pushed it away. Across the round oak table from him his mother sat quietly watching him and sipping at her glass of buttermilk. She'd take buttermilk, he remembered, when her stomach needed settling down—during stressful times, mostly. He cleared his throat and shifted awkwardly and wondered why it was so hard to tell somebody you love a whole lot how much you appreciated what they were doing for you.

"Momma," he finally said, "about Caitlyn—" Then he picked up his milk glass and set it back down and frowned at it. "I really do appreciate you doin' this. I mean—"

His mother waved a hand the way she might've batted at a fly and made a sound he couldn't have spelled if he'd tried, then added, "Lord knows it isn't the first time I've taken in something or someone you kids figured needed watching out for."

"Yeah," C.J. said, "but you never had to deal with somebody blind before."

"Phoo. Granny Calhoun was mostly blind, there at the end."

"Granny was old, didn't do much but sit in her rocker. Caitlyn is—"

He broke it off, and his mother prompted, "Caitlyn is…?"

But he didn't know what it was he wanted to say, so he snapped, "Well, she sure ain't *old*."

He waited for her to scold him for saying ain't, but she just looked at him and after a while she set down her buttermilk glass and said, "I know who she is, son. I've seen the news, read the papers. I know she's President Brown's niece. I know she's the one you told me about that hijacked you last spring."

C.J. scowled at the glass he was turning round and round on the placemat in front of him and cleared his throat a couple of times. "So," he finally said, "if you know all about her, how come you're still willing to take her in?"

His mother took a sip of buttermilk. "I said I know who she is. Didn't say I knew all about her. The question is, do you?"

He lifted his eyes and studied her face long and hard, but for once in his life he couldn't figure out what she was trying to say. After a minute or two she rose, picked up her glass and carried it to the sink. She took a plate out of the cupboard and picked up a pie server, and while she was cutting him a big slice of squash pie and topping it with a spoonful of whipped cream, she said with her back to him, "You know the fact she's kin to the president doesn't carry much weight with me. Any more than the fact that she hijacked you and your rig at the point of a gun." She whipped around to face him and pointed at him with the pie server, and her look was the one that could put the fear of God in a guilty man's heart. "Not that I approve of what she did, mind you. You told me she said she did it because she believed she didn't have any other choice, that she feared for that woman and her little girl's lives. Calvin James, tell me the truth, now. Do you believe her?''

''Yes, ma'am,'' he said, looking her straight in the eyes. ''I didn't then, but I do now. That's why—''

She shook her head, stopping him there. ''The newspeople can't seem to make up their minds whether she's a hero for refusing to tell the judge what she did with the child and going to jail to protect her, or a misguided do-gooder keeping a little girl from her daddy. I want to know what *you* believe.''

He leaned back in his chair and gazed at his mother with narrowed and burning eyes. He thought he knew, now, what she was angling for. The one thing that really counted in Betty Starr's estimation of a person's worthiness. ''Momma,'' he said with gravel in his voice, ''what you're wantin' to know is, what's in her heart. Is she a good person? Does she have a *good* heart…?''

''Well, *does* she?''

He nodded. ''Yes, ma'am, I believe she does.''

''Well, then.'' She plunked the pie down in front of him and turned back to the sink. ''That's good enough for me.''

C.J. let his breath out like a steam valve letting go. ''It's just real important nobody knows about her being here.''

His mother faced him again, leaning against the sink and smiling wryly. ''That's going to be a little bit difficult, isn't it? The way people come and go around here—your brothers and sisters, the grandkids—it's like Grand Central Station.'' Said his momma, who'd never been north of the state of Virginia in her life. ''We can't exactly keep a beautiful young woman hidden away in the attic, like one of those romantic suspense novels.''

C.J. grinned, thinking that his mother could surprise him now and then. ''It's not going to be for all that long, Momma. Just a few days…a couple of weeks…just while she gets her feet under her and some strength back.'' And her eyesight?

And, he thought, while the FBI guys are working out a plan to nail Vasily.

"Anyway, with Sammi June and J.J. just startin' a new semester of college, they're not going to be getting much time off until Thanksgiving break, probably, and Jimmy Joe and Mirabella off in Florida with the little kids for two weeks, that takes care of the closest ones. Jake and Eve are already in on it, and Charly and Troy—"

" 'In on it...' Just what *is* it we're all 'in on,' Calvin James? Who are we hiding her away from? They've been saying on the news they think it was somebody with a grudge against the local authorities up there in South Carolina that fired those shots, and it was just bad luck those poor women got in the way.'' His mother paused while her eyes took on a narrow, considering look. "But that's not true, is it? You and Jake—and that means the FBI—think it was that billionaire, the little girl's father. Isn't that right? You think he had his wife killed and that he's going to come after Caitlyn. That's why all the secrecy. Oh, my lands...'' She leaned against the sink, fanning herself.

Ashamed of himself for all the trouble he was dumping in her lap, C.J. rubbed his eyes and said unhappily, "Momma, I wish I could tell you more, but I promised Jake—"

She made that swatting motion again. "We'll handle things as they come, don't worry about that.'' She leveled The Look at him again, the one he was sure could see inside his brain. "What I want to know is, what's all this got to do with *you?*''

He shifted in his chair and squinted guiltily at her. "What do you mean?''

"I mean, you don't just offer up your family's home to shelter a notorious stranger without good reason.''

C.J. snorted. "I'd think it was pretty obvious why—''

"And by *good* reason I don't mean because there's somebody maybe trying to shoot her. The FBI is more than capable of stashing away people where nobody, not even billionaires, can find them, and I'm sure they'd've done just fine without your help." Her eyes narrowed even more. "But you didn't want that, did you? You wanted that girl where *you* could keep an eye on her—you personally." After a little pause to let him squirm some more, she asked softly, "So what is it about her, Calvin James? What does this girl mean to you?"

He knew from sad experience it wasn't going to do him any good to lie, but that didn't mean he wouldn't hem and haw and try and beat around the bush as long as possible. He stretched back in his chair and rubbed a hand over his face and finally settled on "It's complicated, Ma."

Typically she came to her own conclusion, and as usual, managed to hit the nail on the head without any help from him. "You feel responsible for her. For what happened to her."

He agreed defensively, "Well, yeah, I do. People keep telling me I shouldn't, but they're wrong." He gave his mother a hard, fierce look, but inside his head he was seeing himself standing in the yellow glare of a yard lamp with the racket of a springtime night all around him, and Caitlyn's silvery eyes pleading with him. "The simple fact is, she asked me to do something for her and I said no. Instead, I turned her in to the police. And I don't care how right-minded it seemed at the time, if I hadn't done that, none of what happened would have happened. A woman wouldn't be dead, *she* wouldn't be—"

"Son—" Gentle now, his mother pulled out the chair closest to him and sat in it. "You can't go back and undo it. No matter what you do, you can't unfire that gun." She reached to touch his hand, but he wasn't in a mood to be comforted.

"No, I can't." He snatched his hand away and felt

wretched and mean for doing it. "But I intend to do what I can to make it up to her. Set things *right*."

"How are you going to do that? You can't give her back her eyesight."

He was too angry with her to answer. Because, of course, he knew she was right.

She studied him for a while in a sad, faintly amused way that irritated him even more, then said softly, "I expect by making it up to her you mean you'd like to do something big enough and good enough to cancel out the wrong you think you've done her. What you want is to be her hero."

He snorted. "I'm no hero." No, his inner self said, but you want to be. You want to be a superhero and make the world turn the wrong way around, make time turn backward and give you another chance to save the woman you…

"Son, you're not a superhero," his mother said, in the uncanny way she sometimes had of seeing inside his mind. She rose up out of her chair and snatched his empty plate and milk glass out from under him, then stabbed at him with a spare finger. "You just remember that, when this— this *Vasily* fellow comes looking for that girl of yours, you hear me, Calvin James? Your body won't stop bullets."

Caitlyn woke to her perpetual darkness and, wide-eyed and listening, sought to understand what it was about this particular morning that was so different from other mornings in her recent past. It came to her at last. *It's so quiet.*

It came to her, too, that quiet was very different from silence. As she'd discovered during her time in the hospital, silence spoke with many languages; silences must be deciphered, interpreted, understood. Quiet, on the other hand, was…peace.

One thing hospitals and jails had in common was that they are never quiet. It occurred to her that this was the first time in many, many weeks that she'd had a chance to think…*really* think about everything that had happened and where she was now and what the future might hold, to think without shock and pain and fear, without the shadowy specter of Panic lurking like a stalker just beyond the edges of her mind's eye.

The first thing she thought about was what a wonderful relief it was to wake up this morning and not feel terrified. It was somewhat of a mystery to her why that should be so; she was still definitely blind, still almost certainly in danger, still very much alone among strangers, just as she'd been yesterday.

Unable to solve that puzzle, she put it aside and moved on to the second thing that was missing from her life this morning: pain. Okay, not *completely* missing; there was enough tenderness under the bandages that still encased quite a large part of her head to make her wince and gasp when she touched it with exploring fingers. But the pounding, nausea-inducing headache that had been her constant companion in the days following the shooting had faded to a hum in the background of her mind.

Having determined that much, her fingers moved on, lightly now, tracing the bandages…then her eyebrows…her nose…cheekbones…lips. Exploring the shape of her own face. How odd, she thought, that I've never done this before. *What must I look like?* She'd been swollen and bruised. Was she still? Were her eyes still bruised? *And my hair! Did they shave my head? Do I have any left?* Gingerly she felt the top of her head, breathed a long sigh when she felt the familiar short, slippery tufts. Badly in need of washing, she was sure, but *there.*

She'd never been vain, but now she would have given anything for the chance to look in a mirror and see her own reflection looking back at her. She'd never thought before how vulnerable it made a person, not to be able to check out her own appearance before presenting herself to the world. How awful not to be able to tell if she had a smudge

of dirt on her face, spinach in her teeth, food spilled down
her front, clothes that didn't match. A rooster tail in her
hair!

She threw back the covers. Tremblly, she sat on the edge
of the bed and explored her body as she had her face.
Arms…shoulders…collarbones…breasts. What was she
wearing? Oh, yes—cotton bikinis and a camisole top that
Jess had said belonged to her daughter, Sammi June. Jess
had told her they were pink—Sammi June had evidently
been very fond of pink—with a little edging of lace. Yes,
she could feel that and also three tiny buttons on the front
of the camisole near the top. She felt bones in unexpected
places; she'd lost weight. Small wonder…

She stood up carefully, feeling brave and very tall in her
personal darkness. She put out her hands and the left one
brushed something—a lampshade. Yes—on the nightstand!
And there were all the little plastic bottles with her medi-
cations Jess had put there for her the night before. A glass
of water.

Feeling her way, she moved clockwise around the room,
identifying the door to the hallway, then a tall dresser, and
another door, this one obviously a closet. Then a rocking
chair…oops, and a small desk. Then…a window. She explored it with her fingers and discovered that it was very
much like the one in her room in her parents' house in
Sioux City—an old-fashioned wooden sash, double-hung,
with a locking lever. She moved the lever and tried to open
the window. It slid up easily—evidently the former occupant of the room had liked fresh air, too. It rushed in, cool
and light across her face, and she gave a little sobbing gasp
of joy. Prickles filled her nose and eyes, then tears; she
hadn't expected she would ever feel *joy* again.

Sinking to her knees, she rested her arms on the windowsill, and then her chin. How do I tell, she wondered
wistfully, if it's morning or night?

But wait—it was the bright and busy twitter of birds she

heard, not the ratchety chorus of frogs and insects that filled
Southern nights. Daytime, then. As if in confirmation, she
heard the creak and bang of a screen door, and someone's—
Jess's—voice talking to the dogs. "Hey, Bubba... Hey, Blondie. Yes...good girl...down now. Okay...yes...aren't you a
good ol' boy...." And the eager woofs and grunts and whines
they made in reply.

How she longed to be out there, too! *Could* she? Why
not? *But...by myself? Do I dare?*

Yes, she told herself firmly. *I do. I must.*

Yes...because the one thing in the world she feared more
than being blind was being *dependent.* I won't, she thought,
as memories of last night's attack of panic rose like a nightmare specter to taunt her. *I can't.* She closed her eyes and
felt again the warm and solid strength of C.J.'s arms around
her...how good they'd felt...the chill of loneliness when
he'd left her. She shuddered. *Never. I'd rather be dead.*

Using the windowsill for leverage, she pulled herself up
and methodically continued her circumnavigation of the
room. Finding herself back at the foot of the bed, she discovered the pair of sweats she'd taken off last night and
put them on, being careful to get the backs and fronts right.
Tags to the back! She made the bed, taking quite a long
time at it and stumbling over her sandals in the process.
When she had it smoothed to her liking, she sat on the
slippery bedspread and put on her sandals, then rose, light-
headed and triumphant. *So far so good.*

What I need, she thought, is the bathroom and some
food. In that order. Jess had shown her last night where the
bathroom was. Her toothbrush awaited her there, at position
"two o'clock." She'd smiled when Jess said that. And
there was soap and a washcloth—nine o' clock—and warm
water and soft towels. How good it would feel to brush her
teeth, wash her face....

Her stomach growled. Lord, she was hungry!

*Yes! You're alive! Good morning, Caitlyn Brown...and
welcome to the first day of the rest of your life.*

Chapter 8

As she was going slowly and carefully down the stairs—and yes, she'd remembered to count them—Caitlyn heard voices and music. Following those sounds and the wafting smells of coffee, bacon and maple syrup, she felt her way to the kitchen. A U-turn to the left at the bottom of the stairs, Jess had told her, then down a long hallway with several doors opening off of it, all the way to the end.

On the way she marked the fact that there was a carpet runner on the floor and several creaky spots in the wood underneath and that the walls were papered. She could feel the seams with her fingertips as she trailed them along the surface.

The door to the kitchen was open, and she could feel warm, moist air on her face. As she stood sniffing the wonderful smells and basking in her own inner glow of triumph at having attained such a remarkable goal, she heard a voice say, "See, Momma, what'd I tell you?"

Then Jess sang out to Caitlyn, "Come right on in, hon', straight ahead about six steps and you'll hit the table." She paused, then added with a note of smugness, "Momma wanted me to go get you when we heard you up and around, but I told her you'd find your way down here just fine."

Behind those words, Caitlyn heard the sounds of a chair being scooted across linoleum and a wordless demurral that had a smile in it, and then someone short and soft put an arm around her waist and gave her a quick, warm squeeze.

"Oh, well," Betty's voice said near her shoulder, "I just thought, since it was your first day and all... Now, what can I get you, hon'? Coffee? You want some hotcakes and bacon? Or would you like some eggs? Jessie, turn that radio down."

"It's okay—" Caitlyn said quickly, but the country song had already faded to background noise. "Coffee would be great," she breathed as her fingers made contact with the back of a wooden chair. "Black, please," she added while she was easing herself into it. Safely seated, she let out a relieved breath.

Fingers brushed her left hand, and Jess said cheerfully, "You're doin' great, hon'. How're you feelin' this mornin'?"

Caitlyn gave a shaky little laugh. *"Hungry."*

Betty's voice came close again. "Here's your coffee, hon'. I put it in a mug and only filled it halfway so you don't need to worry about slopping it on yourself. Sure you don't want some cream in that?"

"No, thanks, this is fine." Fragrant steam drifted into her face. It smelled like heaven.

"Momma, quit tryin' to fatten her up," Jess said, and added in a murmur just for her, "Twelve o'clock, hon'...that's right."

Caitlyn's fingers touched, then closed on warm heavy crockery. She lifted the mug and inhaled, then carefully tipped the hot liquid to her lips. Warmth and pleasure flooded through her, and with it that strange, poignant joy she'd experienced when she'd first felt the morning breeze on her face. "Oh my," she breathed, "that's good."

"Well now." Betty's hand rested lightly on her shoulder. "What can I get you for breakfast? How about some—"

"Whatever you have is fine," Caitlyn said quickly, before she could go through the menu again. It had been mind-boggling the first time. Caitlyn's idea of a big breakfast was to put milk on her Cheerios instead of eating a handful dry on her way out the door. She couldn't recall the last time she'd eaten hotcakes. Or bacon, for that matter, except maybe in a tomato sandwich. "Please, don't go to any trouble."

Jess snorted. "Momma always fries bacon and makes hotcakes for C.J. when he's here." And there was that same wordless but good-natured denial from Betty as Jess continued, "We normally just have toast and eggs or cereal or something."

Caitlyn lifted her coffee mug, hoping the flush in her cheeks might be explained by the heat. "Is, um, is he here? I thought— I was under the impression he had his own place."

"He does. It's just up the road. Momma called him when we heard you were up. He said he was gonna jump in the shower and then run right over. Ought to be showin' up any minute. Right about *now,* in fact." She added that last part with a smile in her voice as somewhere outside a screen door banged—by the sound of it, the same screen door Caitlyn had heard earlier from her bedroom window.

She set her coffee mug carefully on the table but kept her hands curled around it, firmly anchoring them there so they couldn't betray her by reaching up to check on the state of what was left of her hair. She had that vulnerable, exposed, "Oh, God, what must I look like?" feeling again. *It's only because I can't see,* she told herself; *it must be.* She'd never worried about such things before.

Her heartbeat quickened inexplicably as she heard footsteps scrape and stomp across a plank floor. There came the sound of a door opening. Cool, fresh air flooded her cheeks and ruffled the short tufts of hair on top of her head.

"Calvin James," his mother exclaimed, "it's October! Where is your shirt?"

"Got it right here, Momma." C.J. wasn't about to tell her he'd taken it off because he didn't want to sweat in it. He didn't want for her—or Jess, either—to get the idea he was going to any extra effort on account of Caitlyn being there. He would never hear the end of it.

He glanced automatically at the digital clock on the stove and checked it against the stopwatch on his wrist. Still hadn't got his time down under five minutes, but he was gettin' there.

"Wash up, son, these hotcakes'll be ready in a minute."

He took the dish towel his mother threw at him and mopped his face and chest with it. After he'd done that, he let himself look over at the woman sitting there facing him across his mother's familiar old oak table.

He'd never seen anyone look so calm and cool...or so unbelievably beautiful. Seeing her in his mother's kitchen didn't seem real. Like finding a real-live fairy perched on the front porch rocker. To his eyes she seemed to shimmer around the edges; he had the feeling if he blinked she might disappear.

He cleared his throat and growled, "Good mornin'," as he pulled out a chair, the one next to Caitlyn and across from his sister. Caitlyn's eyes were hidden behind a curtain of eyelashes as she murmured, "'Morning," back to him. He hitched himself up to the table and parked his elbows on it while he tried to think of something else to say. It wasn't easy with Jess sitting there watching him, with her chin in her hand and a *way*-too-interested look on her face. He had to quell a shameful urge to kick her under the table the way he used to do when he was six and she was a brand-new and stuck-up teenager.

Reminding himself it wasn't good practice for a lawyer to be at a loss for words or thinking like a six-year-old, he frowned, concentrated and came up with, "How're you doin'?"

Caitlyn took a careful sip of her coffee and informed him she was doing okay. Which didn't give him much time to work on a rebuttal, but he had his next question ready for her, anyway.

"Sleep well?"

"Yes, very well. Thank you."

Then, thank the Lord, she looked as if she might be going to elaborate on that, and he held his breath, waiting for it. But before she got around to it, his mother turned from the stove with a plateful of hotcakes in her hand and said, "She found her way down here to the kitchen all by herself," sounding as proud as if one of her students had won the national spelling bee.

Caitlyn muttered, "It wasn't that difficult. Jess gave me good directions." And she was setting her coffee cup down, not realizing there was a plateful of food sitting in front of her.

Jess barked, "Plate!" C.J. reached for it to snatch it out of her way, but neither one of them was quick enough. Plate and mug made contact with a loud *clank,* Caitlyn jerked and coffee slopped out and splattered onto the hotcakes and her hands.

She gasped out, "Oh, God—I'm so sorry." But by that time C.J. had her hands safely wrapped in his.

That was the way he thought of it: *safe.* Lord, how fragile and fine they felt, her hands. And were they trembling or was that something way down deep inside of *him?*

"Didn't burn you, did it?" he calmly asked as he was rescuing the coffee cup and brushing cooling liquid from her skin. As an answer she gave her head a quick, hard shake. "Well, no harm done, then." He got the smile into his voice, but that was as far as it went; he'd never felt less like smiling. What he wanted to do more than anything was touch her face…brush away that stricken, frightened look with his fingers.

His mother was fussing over her, mopping up what was left of the spill with a dishcloth and scolding herself. "Hon', I just set that plate right down there without thinking. I don't know where my mind was. Don't you feel bad, now. That wasn't your fault, it was mine. Let me fix you some more hotcakes."

"Oh, no, please don't." Caitlyn's hands stirred in C.J.'s grasp, and when he reluctantly let them go she put one on each side of the plate and held on to it, guarding it like a big dog guards a bone. "These are fine. Really. I'll just, um…" Her eyes lifted from the plate and darted here and there in a way that made him think of panic-stricken birds.

He watched her swallow, and a patch of color appeared in each cheek. And it came to him—he didn't know where he got it, that faint flicker of insight, like lightning in the daytime. Maybe it was because he'd been thinking so much lately about what it must feel like to be blind, but all at once he knew, with absolute certainty, why she was looking so uncertain and scared. Hell, he thought, it's bad enough trying to eat when everybody's looking at you, when you can *see* what you're doing. *What must it be like to do it blind?*

He coughed and rubbed his nose and said gruffly, "Hey, you want some help with that?" Her eyes flicked his way, and he braced himself, but instead of the expected bright flash of silver, they held the dark and stormy, defiant look that made him abandon the idea of cutting up her food for her, right quick.

The same unbidden insight that had told him of her fear now warned him of her pride. He picked up the syrup pitcher and poured a puddle over her hotcakes with a deft little flourish.

"Bacon's at twelve o'clock," he said in a casual tone of

voice as he did the same for his own plateful. "Knife and fork on your right." He cut himself a wedge of syrupy hotcakes, put it in his mouth, chewed, and after he swallowed said thoughtfully, "What I'd do if I was you, I'd stick my fork in close to the edge of my stack and cut off what I'd got stabbed. That way, you'll know what you've got on your fork."

Jess gave a hoot of laughter. "Say *what?*"

Well, okay, he hadn't said it very well, but it was the best he could come up with on the spur of the moment.

But when he stole another glance at Caitlyn, he saw that her lips weren't clamped together anymore. In fact, it looked to him as if they might be working on a smile.

A pleasant warmth spread through him, and he ducked his head and attacked his own hotcake stack with extra concentration on the off chance his sister might be watching him and catch reflections of it in his eyes.

With his peripheral vision he could follow Caitlyn's progress as she picked up her knife and fork, gauged the size and location of the stack of hotcakes on her plate, cut off a chunk and lifted it to her mouth. Then he couldn't help himself, he had to sneak another peek at her. This time her eyes were closed and there wasn't any doubt about the smile. When the pink tip of her tongue emerged from between her lips to lick away a glaze of buttery syrup, his stomach growled and his mouth began to water in a way that didn't have anything whatsoever to do with the food he was eating.

He took a careful breath and cast a guilty look across the table at Jess, and yep, sure enough, she was watching him like a hawk watches a mouse. No, not like a hawk, come to think of it; the expression on the face of his oh-so-superior, usually teasing big sister was a lot kinder and softer than that. He didn't know what to make of it, but he wished to God she'd cut it out; she was making him squirm.

"So," he said after he'd washed down his last bite of

hotcakes with a big swig of coffee, "you're getting around by yourself okay, then? Feelin' okay?" When she'd nodded yes to both those questions, he said, "How's your, uh—" and was pointing to his own temple when he realized what he was doing and added on "head."

But just as if she *had* seen him, she'd already jumped in with "It's okay—aches a little, but I guess that's to be expected as long as there's still swelling. The doctors said I just have to take it easy…let it heal." Her fingers lightly touched the crown of bandages that encircled her head.

C.J. followed the gesture and felt a shock of surprise; it was as if he were seeing the bandages for the first time. They gave her a waifish, childlike look, he thought, like something out of a Dickens novel. Fascinated, he watched her fingers creep upward to pluck at the tufts of her hair. Like little golden rooster tails, he thought, or plumes of winter grass.

He was so taken up with watching those waving feathers that he forgot to worry about whether or not Jess and his mother were watching *him,* until Jess jumped in with, "That's right, hon'—you just need to give it some time."

Then he decided he didn't care who watched him watch Caitlyn, because a little bit of a frown had appeared in the middle of her forehead, like a ripple in silk, and he couldn't bring himself to take his eyes off it.

"What I was wondering—" she made a tiny throat-clearing sound "—what I'd really love to do is go outside. Do you think it would be—"

"I don't see why not," said Jess, getting briskly up from the table. "Long as you feel up to it. I've got to go to work, but C.J. or Momma can take you out after a bit."

"I'll take her," C.J. growled, and he shot his sister a look to make it clear he considered that was his responsibility and nobody else's. "I was planning on showing her around whenever she figured she was ready."

Then he said to Caitlyn, and it came out a lot gruffer

than he'd meant it to, "So, you want to go right now, or what?"

"Sure." She pushed back her chair and stood up, and so did he. Then, of all things, she gathered up her dishes and was about to carry them to the sink when he moved to intercept her.

"What do you think you're doing?" he said, taking hold of the plate in her hands.

"Clearing my dishes. What does it look like?" She was hanging on to the plate, and there was a stubborn edge to her voice that matched the steely gaze she aimed at his chin.

"You don't—" C.J. began, but his mother interrupted him.

"Plenty of time for that later, hon'. Nice of you to offer. Right now you run along and let Calvin show you around the place. It's just a perfect time to be outdoors—the weather's so fine. This is my favorite time of year, Calvin knows. Yellow-flower season is what I call it."

C.J. barely heard what she was saying. He was too busy trying to figure out the look on Caitlyn's face—several looks, really—different emotions that flitted one after the other across her face like images on a movie screen. A comical "So there!" look first, as if she was on the verge of sticking her tongue out at him. But then that vanished and he saw hope and wistfulness, sorrow and despair, but in such rapid succession he couldn't be certain he'd seen them at all. And finally, an almost angry sort of puzzlement as she realized that her hands, which had somehow gotten tangled up with him while he was trying to relieve her of her load of dishes, had come to be resting on his arms.

He realized it, too, about the same time she did. He looked down and saw them there, her fingers rubbing back and forth in a questing sort of way, burrowing down through the sunbleached hair to reach the tanned skin underneath, and he froze, rooted fast to the spot. Although "froze" wasn't anything like the right way to describe what he felt, the heat that was suddenly pouring through his body, the electricity skating around under his skin, the heavy thumping in the bottom of his belly. Terrible things to be happening to a man while his mother and sister were standing beside him; put it that way.

"You two go on, now, I'll do the washing up," his mother said, making shooing motions at them with the dish towel she was holding. "Calvin James, put on your shirt."

Caitlyn had snatched her hands away from him and was rubbing them as if she'd touched something she didn't like. "It's warm out, isn't it? I won't need a jacket...." She sounded as if she didn't have enough air to breathe.

"You aren't gonna need a jacket," C.J. muttered as he retrieved the T-shirt he'd left hanging over a vacant chair and pulled it over his head. He felt half-suffocated himself, his body blooming with heat and his heart pounding in a way it never did after the easy, one-mile run over from his place. He was good and angry with himself, and it came out in his voice when he snapped, "Are you ready? Well okay, then, let's go."

He felt sorry and ashamed for his sharpness when he saw the eager look on her face, and the searching, almost childlike way she reached for him with her hand. He took it and placed it in the crook of his elbow the way he might have returned a lost bird to its nest.

"Okay," he said with a more gentle gruffness, "this is the back porch. Watch your step, now...."

The screen door banged behind them. Caitlyn held her breath to contain shivers of delight...of anticipation and, yes, of sheer joy. At the bottom of the steps she paused, and C.J., obeying the tug on his arm, paused with her. She inhaled deeply, lifting her face to the sun's warmth. "Smells good," she said inadequately. "Like fall."

"Yeah," said C.J. Then, as she heard the eager wuffs and snuffles and felt the bump of warm bodies against her

legs, he said, "Guess I better introduce you to the dogs."
He paused, then went on talking as Caitlyn gave a gurgle
of laughter and dropped to her knees in a wriggling, licking,
wagging pile of friendly canines. "The big quiet one's
Bubba. He's a chocolate Lab and he's got yellow eyes—
looks like a lion without a mane. He's my brother Troy's
dog—you met his wife, Charly—but they live in Atlanta
and he's a whole lot happier out here. Can't say I blame
him. Anyway, he's getting up there—must be about ten,
now, so he's normally pretty well-behaved. Also the brains
of the outfit. The other one's Blondie. She's young and a
golden retriever, and as far as anything not having to do
with retrieving goes, dumb as a bag of rocks. Makes up for
it by being pretty and sweet natured, I guess. Just don't
count on her to bring you home if you get lost. She's as
apt to lead you into a pond."

The words startled her, though she doubted he'd meant
the remark the way it sounded, or had any idea of the notion—the hope—of independence that flashed through her
mind. *Could I? Could I walk out alone with the dogs to
guide me? Do I dare try?*

Before she could stop herself she jerked her face upward
as if to look at him—an automatic response from a different
life and futile now, of course—but it was to Blondie's advantage and utter delight. A huge tongue slapped joyously
across her face, and Caitlyn was caught between laughter,
the instinct to cry for help and mercy and the practical need
at that particular moment to keep her mouth shut.

She heard C.J. shout, "Hey, Blondie! Come here—
fetch!" then give a little grunt of effort. The tongue retreated with a happy "Wuff!" and a scrabble of claws on
gravelly ground.

Abandoned, Caitlyn teetered off balance and would have
collapsed in a breathless, laughing heap except for the solid,
furry body that moved in close to steady her at just the
right moment. Nudged up against her side, Bubba gave her

chin an encouraging lick as if to say, "You're okay, now. *I'm* here."

Murmuring, "Good dog…what a sweet ol' boy you are…." she wrapped her arms around the big Lab's neck and gave him a fur-ruffling rub. Then strong hands were under her elbows, and instead of the dusty, warm dog smell in her nostrils, there was that familiar, clean C.J. smell again. As he helped her up, just for a moment she felt the brush of his cheek—slightly beard-scratchy—against hers and the feathery tickle of hair. Something jolted under her ribs, and she caught at her next breath as if it were about to be taken from her.

"You okay?" he asked gruffly, and she felt the warm breeze of his breath, scented with coffee and maple syrup.

"Yeah, I'm fine." Back on her feet, she brushed at herself and pushed away from him, moving a few steps and covering her breathlessness with laughter.

"Ground's a little rough," he said as he caught her hand and brought it firmly back into the crook of his elbow.

Caitlyn didn't reply. Her feelings were a jumble—confusing, distressing—and as they walked on she kept her head turned so C.J. wouldn't see them written on her face. *Caty, make up your mind! What is it you want? One minute you're dreaming of walking out alone, the next minute you're terrified that he's not touching you. You were scared when you let go of him. Admit it. You felt safe when he took your hand again. Safe!*

But she knew safety that depended on someone else was an illusion. She'd learned from experience and example that no one could guarantee another person's safety, that the only real protection she had against the terrors and monsters of the world was inside herself. Her own inner strength— that was her armor. Without that she would be naked as a hatchling bird.

As she walked she chanted to herself, like a pledge, a credo, a prayer: *I must not lose my strength and my inde-*

pendence, no matter how good his arm feels here beneath my hand. No matter how nice it feels to walk like this beside his strong, warm body, I must not let myself like it too much.

"We're back a good bit from the road," C.J. said as they walked slowly along, feet swishing through leaf-covered grass, then crunching on gravel—no doubt the same gravel she'd heard the tires of Eve's car drive over last night. "The house is surrounded by trees—some poplars, hickories and a few maples...but mostly oaks, so the leaves haven't really started to pile up yet. There's an old tire swing hanging from one of 'em. I played on that when I was a kid."

The air did feel cooler now. They must be in the shade, she thought as she asked wistfully, "Have the leaves turned?" She'd always loved the colors of fall.

"A lot of 'em have. They're not at their peak, though. Farther north, up in the mountains, that's where they're pretty, right about now...." He paused for a moment, and when he went on there was an odd little break in his voice...another of those emotional nuances she hadn't yet learned to read? "There's lots of goldenrod along the roadsides and fences, with pink and purple morning glories mixed in. All sorts of grasses and other flowers, daisies, I guess, maybe sunflowers, mostly yellow—"

"Yellow-flower season," Caitlyn murmured, smiling. Her throat ached with longing.

"Yeah..." C.J. gave an uneven laugh. The fingers that covered her hand were stroking back and forth in a consoling sort of way. His voice became a soft sweet murmur, and she remembered that she'd liked the way it sounded a million years ago. "Anyway, where was I? Oh, yeah...there's fields over there on the other side of the lane—some farmer leases 'em out to plant crops on. Sometimes it's cotton, sometimes soybeans. This summer he had some kind of grain, but it's been harvested already, so there's just stubble out there now. Birds like it, though. You can see them flyin' in and out, looking for the leftover seed. And the turkeys, of course—they love it. Wild geese stop over sometimes to feed.''

"Canadian geese?" Her heart gave a leap, and in her memory's eye she saw the undulating arrows against a pale, cold Iowa sky. Homesickness washed over her, prickling her nose and eyes.

"Yeah. I don't see any out there now, though. Sorry." His voice was husky. "Maybe another time."

He paused, while his fingers went on stroking the back of her hand, and out of the blue she found herself wondering what he looked like. Not in general, of course—she remembered him the way he'd looked that night, remembered his warm brown eyes that crinkled at the corners when he smiled, and the sweetness of that smile—but at this particular moment. Right now she couldn't hear a trace of that smile in his voice. She didn't know what she did hear—warmth, compassion, kindness…other things she couldn't sort out or identify—and she couldn't picture the face that went with the voice at all. Her face felt stiff and achy with the effort of trying to penetrate the blankness. Frustration was a fine vibration that ran beneath the surface of her skin.

She felt his body turn toward her, become a close and humid warmth, and the vibration inside her became a jumpy current of electricity.

"Okay. Over here—" his voice was a spine-stirring growl near her ear, and she felt foolish as she turned, clumsy under his guidance, as if she'd missed a step in a dance "—on this side is mostly woods, but there's some cow pastures and hay fields with those big round bales still lying in 'em, and a pond down there, and a creek, too. And beyond that, more woods."

"No houses?" Her voice cracked.

C.J. gave a little laugh. "Told you we're out in the middle of nowhere. No, actually, Jimmy Joe—that's my brother—''

"The one you work for, who owns the trucking company."

"Right. His place is half a mile or so down the road from here. He used to run the business from there, until it got too big. Now he's got a regular terminal on the outskirts of Augusta. Then, just about a mile down the road in the other direction is my place. It's closer than that through the fields, but I like to come by the road so I can keep track of my time."

"So you did really 'run' over here this morning?"

There was a little pause, and this time when he spoke she could hear the grin. "Told you I keep in shape."

"Yes, but *running?*" It was unexpected; such a town-dwelling, yuppie thing to do, she thought. It didn't fit the image of C.J. Starr in her mind, sweet Southern good-ol'-boy truck driver who couldn't bear the thought of living in the city. But, she reminded herself, he's studying to become a lawyer, don't forget, and that didn't fit your image of him, either. Not even then.

You jumped to conclusions about this man once before and look where that got you.

"I got started running way back in high school," he was saying, as if he'd heard her thoughts. "The way it happened was, I was playing football and, like all good Georgia boys, dreaming of being a Georgia Bulldog one day. Since I was built on the lean side and had some fairly decent speed, I was a running back. Come the end of the football season, my coach wanted me to go out for track to keep in shape. Work on my time." He paused, and when he spoke again his voice had a distant sound, as if he'd gone into a private room and closed the door, leaving her outside. "I guess he thought I had some potential. Anyway, whether I did or not I never found out, but I got to like the running for its own sake, so I guess it wasn't a total loss."

She walked on beside him, unconsciously in step, listening to what he'd told her and what he hadn't. Listening to the faint elusive sadness in his voice that reminded her of the way wild geese sounded, far away in an autumn sky. After a moment she asked, "Why didn't you? Find out about your potential, I mean." And when he didn't answer she did for him, softly. "You never got to the University of Georgia?"

"No."

"Why not?"

He stopped walking, and so did she. She heard a dry, scuffing sound. He'd leaned against a tree trunk, letting her hand slide out of its nest in the crook of his arm. Distancing himself from her, she thought, and felt strangely bereft.

Needing to maintain some kind of contact with him but not wanting to admit to that need, she put out her hand and found the tree trunk instead. Splaying her fingers wide, she pressed her palm against the rough, crisp bark and tilted her head to listen as somewhere overhead a squirrel began to scold in outrage at the intrusion into his domain.

C.J. stared up into the bronzy-gold leaves of the hickory tree and located the squirrel, perched on the broken-off stub of a dead branch, tail held up behind him and fluffed out like a brush. He thought about describing it for her, but it suddenly seemed impossible, utterly beyond him. The truth was, no matter how hard he tried, he wasn't going to make her see.

The hurt that knowledge left inside him was a solid thing, like a fist in his guts. All in all, the vague ache of long-ago disappointments and failures seemed easier to deal with.

He drew a breath. "Preseason practice, start of my senior year. We were having a scrimmage and I got hit from the side—clipping, they call it—there's a good reason why it's illegal. Tore up the cartilage in my knee. They told me I'd be out the whole season, so there went my hopes for a scholarship to just about anyplace. I figured, the hell with it. I dropped out.''

''Out of *school?*'' He understood her horrified tone; she was a teacher's child, like he was. In families like theirs, such a thing was almost unthinkable. *''Why?''*

He laughed softly at the look on her face, intent and fascinated but frustrated, too, as if he were a puzzle she couldn't solve. Welcome to the club, he wanted to say. I've had some trouble figuring me out, too.

Then he thought about it and he realized that wasn't true; there were quite a few things about himself he'd got figured out, but he just hadn't ever wanted to share them with anybody before. Why he wanted to now—*that* was something he couldn't figure out.

''Why?'' He scrubbed a hand over his face. His grin flickered briefly before he remembered she couldn't see it. ''Oh, hell, what can I say? I was a kid. Spoiled. The baby of the family. Things had always come easy for me, and I guess I expected they always would. When I got hurt, from where I was standing it looked like my life was over. My dreams of football fame and glory, my easy-ride college career right down the tubes. I was mad, disappointed…it was easier to say the hell with it than to come up with a whole new set of dreams.''

Chapter 9

"'A new set of dreams…'" She whispered it, staring into nothingness. The bleakness in her face hit him like a body blow.

Turning so he couldn't see her face, she leaned her back against the same tree trunk that was propping him up and said in a not-quite-steady voice, "That's ridiculous. You could still have had your dream of going to the University of Georgia if you'd wanted to. If you'd worked at it. Even playing football—you might have gotten there by a different path—"

He shrugged, then sucked in air as their shoulders touched. It shocked him to realize how much he wanted to hold her. More than he wanted his next breath. His voice wasn't steady, either, as he retorted, "Yeah, well, maybe that was a dream that wasn't meant to happen. Maybe I wouldn't have been good enough to play college ball. How do I know? Like I said, things had always been easy for me. I'd never been tested, I guess you could say. And except for football, I didn't have the first idea what I wanted to do with my life. Without that, who knows, I might have squandered a whole college education and graduated still not knowing. Maybe dropping out of school at that point was the best thing I could have done.''

He heard a soft laugh and leaned over so he could see her face. A smile was tugging at the corners of her mouth. ''Providence,'' she murmured, angling her head toward him slightly.

'' 'Providence'?'' The word tugged at his memory and he frowned, trying to place it. But the top of Caitlyn's head was right there, just below his nose...those waving tufts of golden hair would tickle his lips if he leaned over just a little bit.

She tilted her face upward, and he caught and held his breath. Couldn't let it go—she'd know how close he was. Her lips quivered with her smile. ''Something my dad used to say.''

The memory snapped into focus, and he flattened himself back against the tree trunk and let out a shaken breath. ''Ah—your aunt, right?''

Surprised eyes reached upward toward his face as she turned fully toward him, her smile a hairsbreadth from where his lips had been. ''My dad's *great*-aunt, actually— she lived to be over a hundred. How did you know?''

His heart pounded; he fought to keep his voice even. ''Your dad told me—back there in the hospital. Said something about getting hurt and as a result of that, being where he needed to be to save your mother's life. And that your— *his*—aunt said it was Providence.''

''My dad told you that?'' The watermark frown had appeared in the center of her forehead, and her eyes flickered as if they were trying to search his face in the darkness.

''Yeah, he did. Is it true?''

''Oh, yes.'' She relaxed, sagging back against the tree. ''The way it happened... Dad was a marine. He was stationed in Bosnia, and he'd stayed on there even after he left the corps, helping out with one of those humanitarian groups, driving a truck—'' a startled look flashed across her face for an instant ''—um, bringing in food and medical supplies. He was injured when his convoy was shelled. Broke both his legs. So they sent him home for rehab. Mom was his physical therapist, and it just so happened that at the time she was being stalked by her ex-husband. He'd have killed her if Dad hadn't been there—or maybe she'd have killed him, I don't know. Either way, Dad saved her life, and he was in a wheelchair at the time.''

''Amazing story,'' C.J. murmured, and there was a swelling warmth inside his chest he recognized as envy. ''Your dad's a real hero.''

''Yes, he is.'' She pushed restlessly away from the tree, then halted…trapped, it occurred to him, on her own private island. ''Mom was one of the lucky ones.'' There was anger now in her voice, and he didn't know whether it was because of what they were talking about or her frustration at her own limitations. ''That's how I—''

He'd moved up beside her, to give her a point of reference, maybe, or walk with her if that was what she wanted. And she turned and reached out to him impulsively, the way she'd done that night in the abandoned gas station. That night her hands had landed on his folded-up arms with a touch light as leaves falling. Now since his arms weren't folded, it was his chest she touched. He looked down into her eyes, and for the first time in a long time saw that breathtaking flash of silver.

''C.J.,'' she said, earnest and intent, ''do you know what I *do?* I mean…have you guessed, or figured it out?''

''I think I've 'bout got it figured out, yeah. But why don't you explain it to me.'' His voice was harsher than he'd intended. Whether it was that or she'd felt the way his heart was knocking against her fingers, but she took her hands away from his chest. Regret swept through him, intense as a shiver.

"Well, that's what started it for me—my parents' story."
She was looking away from him now...far, far away.
"Mom and Dad were always open with me about what had
happened to her. She'd been abused by her father when she
was just a child, and finally the only way she could find to
escape him was to get married, when she was barely six-
teen. That was just as bad. Her husband was a violent,
controlling man, and when she left him he tracked her down
and, as I said, would have killed her if it hadn't been for
Dad. I used to think about that. What about the ones who
aren't lucky enough to have someone like my dad? Things
are a lot better now than they used to be. At least there's
more awareness of the problem of domestic violence...laws
are tougher. But there are still so many cases where—"
She paused, shaking her head, and the look she threw at
him was one of cold, bitter fury. Then, though he had nothing to say to her, she held up a hand as if to stop him—or
was it herself?—and went quietly on.

"I went into social work, first, thinking that was the way
to help. It didn't take me long to realize that Social Services
can only do so much. Social service agencies have to op-
erate within the confines of law. And the law—okay, the
law means well, but sometimes it seems like it protects the
wrong people. Then there are some people who don't know
about the law and others who don't care. And some—"
her voice and her eyes hardened "—who believe they are
a law unto themselves."

"Like Vasily..." He said it on an exhaled breath and it
sounded like a hiss. Even the name seems evil, he thought.

She gazed at him for a long moment without speaking,
and the healing bruises around her eyes seemed to shimmer.
Then she said softly, "I'm not going to tell you how I
found the group I work—" her mouth twisted "—*worked*
for. It's too important that the work they do be allowed to
go on." Her lips relaxed and quivered into a half smile.
"Dad says it's like the Underground Railroad—you know,

like during slavery?—but actually it's probably more like a witness protection program, only not sanctioned by any government agency. We get people who are in imminent danger to safety, then help them…disappear.''

"Is that what happened to Emma Vasily? She just…disappeared?'' His voice was gruff. He didn't mean to be judgmental, but he was thinking about the little girl with the big black refugee eyes, the way she'd leaned against him, wanting so badly to trust somebody. He wondered if she was happier now, living among strangers.

"C.J.…'' It sounded like a sigh of regret.

"I guess I can't blame you for not trusting me,'' he said. And he couldn't, but that didn't keep him from feeling hurt in some strange, illogical way.

She looked sideways at him. They'd begun walking again, swishing their feet through the leaves on his mother's lawn. "It's not that I don't trust you,'' she said, still wearing that little half smile. "The funny thing is, you know, I do. I trust you to behave exactly as you have been, with honor and integrity.…'' C.J. snorted. Why didn't he feel complimented? "The problem is, you and I are on opposite sides of the fence, C.J.''

"I don't think that's true—'' The denial was automatic and held no conviction at all.

She shook her head. "You still plan on being a lawyer?''

"Yes, I sure do.''

"Well, then? As a lawyer, you are bound as an officer of the court to uphold the law. And there's no getting around the fact that I—'' her smile wavered ''—for the best of all possible reasons, am often, shall we say, *forced* to circumvent it.'' She shrugged as if to say, That's the way it is—what can you do?

What *could* he do? What could he say? The answer to that was: not a damn thing.

"I think I'd like to go in now,'' Caitlyn said softly, and

she gave a shiver that was only perceptible because his arm happened to be touching hers.

"Getting cold?" he asked, and she shrugged.

It did seem cooler there in the shaded yard, or maybe it was just the chill he felt deep down in his insides…of loneliness, maybe? Of regret?

All he knew was that a few moments ago he'd felt so close to her it had seemed to him one good puff of wind could have brought her into his arms. Now she was a million miles away. On opposite sides of the fence, she'd said, and he couldn't think of any way to tell her she was wrong. And if she wasn't, he wondered how in the world he was supposed to help her, whether that meant make things right for her, be a hero to her, save her life or just *be* there if she needed comforting. How was he supposed to do any of those things with that fence between them?

"Hey, hon', how're you doin' out here?" The screen door creaked, then banged shut. Jess's footsteps scuffed on the planks of the front porch floor.

It was late afternoon, coming to the end of Caitlyn's third day in the Starr household. She was becoming more comfortable there and less fearful, gaining confidence as she learned her way around. Her days were already developing a routine: in the mornings, breakfast; then, while Jess went off to her shift at the hospital in town and Betty to her shopping or volunteer work for the church day-care center, long, leisurely walks with C.J. and the dogs. During those walks, C.J. tried, rather touchingly, she thought, to describe everything for her in great detail, while she tried very hard to keep from him the fact that she was counting footsteps and memorizing the locations of trees and fences.

Later, after C.J. had gone home to study for his bar exams, she would help Betty with the housework or in the garden. She was learning how to water by hand with the garden hose during the autumn dry spell, and to tell the difference between crabgrass and vegetable plants by feel.

The hardest times were the quiet times, like now—what could she do if she was too restless to nap? Reading and watching TV were definitely out. She wasn't accustomed to being idle, but so far, sitting on the front porch listening to the cassette tapes Betty had found for her was the only activity she'd been able to come up with to combat the loneliness of those empty hours.

"You got a minute?"

Caitlyn had nothing *but* minutes, but thought it would be self-pitying to say so. She stilled the rocking chair, felt for the Off button on the portable tape player in her lap and pulled off the headphones, then turned toward the voice with a welcoming smile. "I was just listening to these 'Lake Woebegon' tapes your mom gave me."

"Garrison Keillor? Oh, I remember those." The rocker next to hers gave a groan and Jess's voice came from a new level. "It's been a while since I've heard them, though."

"My parents always put them on in the car during long trips." She leaned over to put the tape player on the floor, and her foot nudged a large furry body that twitched and emitted a patient sigh. "Sorry, Bubba," she murmured.

"He sure has adopted you," Jess said.

"Yeah, I know." Caitlyn settled back in the rocker with a short laugh. "It's funny…it's almost as if he *knows*."

"Dogs have a sense about 'em. The intelligent ones do." There was a pause and then a laugh—a dry, soft stirring, like the rustling of leaves. "The day I found out my husband had been shot down, ol' Bubba, there, wouldn't leave my side. Came right in the house and would not be put out…and Bubba is *not* a house dog. That night and for a long time after that he slept on the rug beside my bed."

"Shot down?" Caitlyn sat forward, frowning. She had a vague memory of C.J. telling her something about that, but

she rather thought she'd dreamed it. It had occurred to her
to wonder why Jess and her daughter were living with
Jess's mother, and what had become of the husband and
father, but she would never in a million years have been
so rude as to ask. "You mean…"

"Yeah…as in killed." It was a gentle exhalation.
"Didn't C.J. tell you? Tristan's officially listed as KIA,
although they never did find his remains—and how they
could *know* anything, considering he went down in
Iraq.…"

"I'm so sorry." Such a loss seemed beyond imagining.

Jess let out another of those careful breaths. "That's
okay. It was a long time ago—God, eight years. Sometimes
I can't even believe it. But I have accepted it."

"But you haven't remarried, or…"

"Or…?" The rocking chair's creak seemed to accent the
question mark. "No, but it's not because I didn't—that I
wouldn't have, if—" The chair creaked again, more like a
protest this time.

"I'm sorry," Caitlyn said quickly. "It's none of my—"

"No, no, it's okay—it's just that I haven't thought about
it in a while, is all. It's not that I wouldn't have, if I'd
found anybody I wanted." She hesitated, then, "Problem
is, Tris is a pretty darn hard act to follow."

As she nodded her understanding, in her mind's eye Caitlyn pictured a smile, poignant and sad. Jess's, she wondered, or her own? She could imagine…had grown up in
the shelter of such a love…could readily understand why
someone who had known that kind of love would never
settle for anything less. She couldn't imagine, for instance,
either of her parents remarrying, should anything—God
forbid!—happen to the other. She could understand…but
would she ever *know?* Looking ahead at her own prospects
for finding love like that, she saw only a vast and hopeless
emptiness.

"But," Jess said briskly, to the accompaniment of a loud

creak from her rocking chair, "that's not what I came out here to talk to you about. I've been looking on the Internet at work—" there was a papery rustle "—and I found all sorts of stuff I think might be really helpful for you. You know—programs, services, gadgets. Technology is amazing, isn't it? Like, they have this little thingy you put in your coffee cup, so when you pour, it beeps to tell you you're close to the top. Cool, huh?"

Cool. Caitlyn's smile had frozen on her face. If she moved, if she uttered a word, it would shatter into a million pieces. *She* would.

"You wouldn't believe the stuff they have to help blind people be more independent—gadgets, but more important, they teach you how to do for yourself. There are schools, counseling programs—you know, to help you cope.... They even have people who come and help you get set up, organize your clothes, teach you how to use everyday things like the stove, money, how to use a cane. There are Seeing Eye dog— Hon', where y'goin'? You okay?"

She wasn't okay, and she didn't know where she was going. Nowhere. *Nowhere.* She was standing up, driven to her feet by the desperate need to flee, to escape from the kind voice and well-meaning words, from the intolerable, unthinkable pictures they painted of the future...*her* future.

I'm not blind. I can't be blind. Not forever. My vision's going to come back. It has to come back. It has to.

Fear gripped her; fear such as she'd never known in her life. She felt cold to the center of her soul. She was shaking.

"Caitlyn, honey, what's wrong? Did you want to go inside?"

"What? Oh. No—I just..." She shook her head and put out a groping hand. Where could she go? *Nowhere.* She was trapped—trapped in a box of nothingness.

"I'm sorry, hon', I didn't mean to upset you." Jess's hand was on her arm, guiding her back to the rocking chair, and Bubba's nose nudged a question against her knee. Absently she gave his ears a reassuring fondle.

"You didn't upset me," she said, and her voice was calm and even. "It was kind of you to go to so much trouble, but… It's just that…well, I can't very well do any of those things as long as I'm in…" *In what? In hiding…in limbo?*

"In FBI custody?" Jess finished it for her in a wry tone, and Caitlyn gave a shaky laugh.

"Yeah, something like that. Nobody's supposed to know where I am. So I can't very well go to classes or see a counselor…."

"No, guess not." There was a small sigh, lost in creaks and rustlings. "Well, okay, I'm gonna hang on to these— might come in handy later on. I just thought, you know…it might make you feel better to know there's help out there. That you're not alone." A hand squeezed Caitlyn's shoulder, and Jess added in a soft-gruff voice that sounded a lot like her brother's, "You gonna be okay out here? You sure you don't want to go in?"

Caitlyn wanted to scream at her. *No, I'm not okay! I'm blind, you idiot! I can't see! I'm blind and I'm trapped and I'm terrified, can't you see that?* She wanted to scream and swear and punch and kick something. She wanted to crawl into someone's lap and cry.

"No, that's okay, I'm fine," she said softly. "I think I'll just sit out here a little while longer." Her hand moved in the warm silkiness of Bubba's fur.

"Sun's going down—you want me to bring you out a sweater?"

"No—I'm fine."

"Okay, hon', if you're sure you're okay." After a moment's hesitation the screen door creaked, then banged shut.

The sun's going down. I wonder where? I can't feel it

here. I must be facing the wrong way. Or maybe it's the trees. I wonder if it's a beautiful sunset....

Caitlyn sat and listened to the rhythmic creak of the rocking chair and the rustlings and scufflings of squirrels in the leaves on the lawn. As she rocked, her hand stroked gently over Bubba's head. And she shivered...and shivered...and shivered.

C.J. could see her as he came up the lane, sitting in a rocking chair on the front porch with Bubba alert and on guard beside her. Funny—he remembered he'd thought her being in his mother's house was like finding a fairy perched on a front porch rocker, and here she was. But right then what she looked like more than anything was a statue, lovely and graceful, yes, but lifeless and stone cold.

He slowed to a walk as he turned onto the grass, but didn't look at his watch to check his time. He knew it had to be one of his best, but the truth was he'd forgotten to set the stopwatch when he'd taken off out of the house after Jess's phone call. If his sister was worried enough to tell him to "get your butt over here," well...

He knew Caitlyn had to have heard him coming, but she didn't call out to him or give any sign she knew he was there. So he called out, "Hey, how'y'doin'? Ready to go for a walk?" Careful not to let any sign of his concern show in his voice.

Not that he fooled her for a minute.

"I suppose Jess called you," she snapped at him as he came up the steps, chin jutting. Her eyes, thundercloud gray, sparked a warning, and her hand moved restlessly in Bubba's neck fur.

"Yeah, she did." He smiled gamely at her, panting a little. "But I was comin' over, anyway."

"Well, you don't need to worry about me, I'm a grown woman, not a child. I don't need a baby-sitter. And I'm not a dog, either. I don't need to be walked twice a day."

Her grumpiness amused him. Maybe because Jess had warned him, or he was getting used to her, but where her frosty tone might have intimidated him a few days ago, now he only thought how cute she looked with her hair lying on her forehead and cheekbones like petals of a pale yellow flower. She'd gotten the last of her bandages off this morning, after a consultation set up by Jake between Jess and the doctor, and his mother had trimmed her hair and shampooed it for her. It covered up most of what was left of her bruises and scalp wound so that she looked not so much like a convalescent, now, as a little child woken up from a nap too soon.

"I like your hair," he said. "Looks good."

Her hand flew up to touch it, a jerky, involuntary motion that reminded him of a drunken butterfly landing on a flower. Warring emotions flitted across her face: a uniquely feminine pleasure at odds with the darkness of her thoughts. Finally she made a throat-clearing sound and grudgingly muttered, "Thanks."

He took her hand and drew her up and out of the rocking chair, but let go of it when she tugged, and let her find the railing and feel her own way down the steps. After a moment Bubba hauled himself up and lumbered after her, and C.J. followed, fighting the useless feeling that came over him so often when he was with her.

He moved up beside her as they walked across the leaf-littered grass. He could smell strawberries. He wondered if it was the shampoo his mother had used on her hair. "So, where do you want to go? Wanna go down to the creek? Probably just got time enough before it gets too dark."

She gave a sharp, bitter laugh at that, and for a moment or two didn't answer. Then she lifted her head and paused, as if listening to a distant sound. "I want to *run*," she said, and her voice was breathless and suspenseful, as if she were already in the starting blocks.

What the hell, he thought. Why not? "Okay," he said, and was rewarded by her look of surprise.

He took her down to the hayfield, which the farmer had finally cleared of bales the day before. It hadn't rained in a while and the ground was hard and dry, the grass gone dormant until spring. It was quiet and empty out there, away from the stirrings of trees and the rustle of falling leaves. A little breeze lifted the feathers of her hair as he stood behind her in the lavender dusk, carrying the sweet strawberry scent of it to his nostrils. With his hands gentle on her arms he turned her to face the open field.

"Okay," he murmured, "nothing in front of you but grass. Go for it. I'll be right beside—"

She was off before he'd finished, jogging tentatively at first while he stayed where he was and watched her, his soul lifting with purest pleasure at the sight. Then Bubba whined; he looked down and saw the big dog gazing up at him with reproach.

"Wha…at?" he said, grinning. "What's she gonna run into? She's got the whole—" Bubba gave a sharp yip and took off. C.J. looked up, and what he saw was Caitlyn running as if the hounds of hell were after her.

"Holy sm—" He took off after her, swearing under his breath.

She was faster than he'd expected, a whole lot faster than anybody who'd almost been shot to death a short time ago had any business being. Plus, the field had a downward slope—not too steep—but way down at the bottom of it, what he'd mistakenly considered to be a safe distance away, far beyond her reach, was the pond. And the direction she'd picked, she was headed right for it, with Bubba loping along at her heels.

C.J. yelled at her to stop, but that only made her run faster, damn her, and ol' Bubba wasn't doing anything to stop her, either. Come to think of it, why would he? Bubba was a water dog—a dip in the pond probably seemed like a great idea to him.

C.J. hadn't ever been much of a sprinter, but adrenaline gave him the push he needed, and he caught up with her a yard or two from the edge of the pond. She was gasping, her breath coming in sobs, while Bubba sat on his haunches and watched her with his tongue hanging out. C.J. had hold of her arm—he was well ticked off at her and prepared to bawl her out good for scaring him like that—but she whirled and struck out at him, catching him in the chest with her fist.

Even with twilight coming on he could see she was crying.

"Leave…me…alone," she yelled, and her voice was a terrible, raspy sound, like cloth tearing. "Can't you just *leave me alone?* I said I wanted to *run,* damn you. You said— Why can't you—"

"Dammit, I'm trying."

"*Don't* try! Don't *help* me. I just want you to let me *go!*"

Well, damn. He couldn't let her go, because if he did she was going to wind up in the pond for sure. And he couldn't get her to listen to him even long enough to tell her that; he had his hands full just trying to keep her flailing arms and hammering fists from doing either one of them damage.

Truth was, she was starting to scare him. Having grown up with sisters, he was no stranger to feminine tears and histrionics, but this was clearly beyond his experience. If she kept on like this, he thought, she was liable to hurt herself.

"Come on, calm down, dammit!" he yelled at her. "Can't you see I'm tryin' to help—"

"Don't…help." She bit off the words like a snapping turtle, spitting fury.

And tears! He'd never seen tears like that in his life. It

was eerie, seeing all those tears pouring out of sightless eyes, seeing the emotions—silvery flare of passion and darkness of pain—knowing the windows of her soul were only one-way glass. It was almost too much for him. Dammit, it *was* too much. He could feel his eyes burning, his own emotions heavy in his chest.

"Don't help me. You can't *help* me," she choked out, "don't you *get it?* You can't fix *this*—" she jabbed a finger toward her streaming eyes "—can you? You can't make me *see!* What are you going to do, lead me around like a puppy on a leash for the rest of my life? You want to *help* me? Well, I'll tell you something—it's too late. It's too *late.* I asked you for help and you wouldn't give it to me. And now Mary Kelly's dead and I'm blind and you…can't…fix it." The thumping of her fists against his chest grew weaker. She sagged against him. *"You can't fix it! Damn you…"*

He didn't blame her for saying that. How could he, when he'd said the same thing to himself so many times over?

When he went to put his arms around her, he was meaning only to give her comfort. That was his honest intention. He had no idea what happened next. He sure as hell never saw it coming. Just, one minute he was reaching out for her, his heart warm and aching with sympathy—and all of a sudden he felt a completely different kind of pain in his midsection, and where his next breath should have been there was…*nothing*.

He was looking desperately for it, doubled over and clutching his belly, when the next thing he knew he was flying through the air, and the cold, murky waters of the farm pond were rising up and hitting him in the face.

Chapter 10

Caitlyn heard the splash and then some hoarse, honking sounds, followed immediately by a smaller splash and a canine yip, though that didn't fully register in her consciousness until a little later. The rage that had enveloped her cracked like an egg's shell. The anger drained out of her, leaving her hollow…cold…shocked to her core.

"C.J.!" she screamed. She *thought* she'd screamed; all she heard was a raspy whimper. She tried it again, then again, and she was staggering, stumbling toward the gasping, whooping sounds, hands thrust out before her like Frankenstein's monster.

The ground squelched under her feet. Razor-leaved grasses slashed at her clothes. She heard smaller splashes inside the larger ones, which seemed to be of the magnitude of those produced by frolicking whales. Cold water seeped into her shoes; it rose with each step she took until it had engulfed her to the knees. The terror that engulfed her heart was far colder.

"C.J.!" she shrieked. "Oh, God, C.J., I'm coming. Where are you? Answer me, damn you! C.J.—"

The whoops changed to swearing—some really remarkable swearing, she considered, to be coming from someone raised by a Southern Baptist schoolteacher. Then, "Stay there! Don't—"

A wave caught Caitlyn in midstep. Knocked off balance and with her feet rooted firmly in mud, she sank gracefully into the frigid water like an empress lowering herself onto a throne. Water that smelled of mud and moss and wet dog and other things she didn't want to think about rushed into her mouth. She spat it out with a bellow of disgust, coughing and clawing wildly at the unknown things she imagined must be crawling over her face. Hitting out as well at the hands that were reaching to help her.

"Cut it out!" C.J. yelled. "You're all right, dammit, I've got you. *I've got you.*"

She gave a squeak of sheer relief and launched herself toward him. Sobbing, "Oh, God, C.J. Oh, God." She hauled herself along the lifelines of his arms until she'd reached the safe harbor of his chest.

Safe? She'd thought so, believed so, until she heard him grunt, felt him sway backward, pulling her with him. She gasped, then held her breath and clutched at the arms that were wrapped around her, and for a few suspenseful seconds they teetered together, swaying back and forth like dancers in the midst of some complicated step—a tango, maybe.

"Hold...still," C.J. ground out savagely, and he was so close she could feel his lips move against her temple.

Her heart jumped like a frightened rabbit. Afraid to utter a sound, she felt his arms tighten around her and the muscles beneath her hands bunch and harden. It flashed through her mind—just one incredibly crazy thought—that he was about to kiss her, but of course he was only turning her around, shifting her position so he could maneuver them both to shallower water.

Moments later, streaming water and pond weeds and hanging on to each other, they were struggling uphill over slippery, squelchy mud with Bubba bumping unhelpfully against their legs, and shortly after that Caitlyn knew that she was standing once again on dry, solid ground.

Shock—the mind-numbing kind that protects people and enables them to function during times of disaster—was ebbing, but for Caitlyn, shock of another kind had taken its place. Shaking so hard she could barely speak, she clung to C.J.'s arm and felt with her other hand for his chest, patting at the soppy sweatshirt material as if to reassure herself that a heart still beat beneath it. "Oh, C.J.—I can't believe I did that. I'm so—"

"Yeah, well, believe me, I can't, either," he muttered bitterly. "Come on—you're freezing. Let's get you—"

"No, I mean it. I can't believe I could do such a thing. C.J., I am so sorry—"

"Forget it. Let's just get you home before you catch pneu—"

Impulsively she slipped her hand upward and covered his mouth with fingertips that trembled. "No—please. I'm really, *really* sorry. I don't *do* things like that. I *don't*. I don't know what came over me. I *hate* violence. I mean, my whole life is one big fight *against* violence. To think that I could—that I—" Her next word was muffled, swallowed up by a hard, cold mouth.

He'd had no idea in the world he was going to kiss her. One minute he was standing there shivering and shaking and grinding his teeth, wishing to God she'd shut up, and so cold and ego battered he could barely think straight. Then the next second her lips were slippery and cool under his, and the shape and feel of them was well on the way to becoming a permanent imprint on his senses, and his brain was filled with light and music like a Biblical revelation.

That shocked him so much he stopped what he was doing, letting go of a short sharp breath as he lifted his head.

She did the same, and followed it with a squeaky and airless, ''What'd you do that for?''

His thoughts were murky as that pond they'd just climbed out of. Gazing down at her in the near darkness, all he could think was that she looked like a half-drowned puppy.

''I was tryin' to shut you up,'' he heard himself say in a voice he didn't recognize.

''Oh.''

Then for a long, tense moment neither of them said anything. The only sounds came from Bubba, patiently panting somewhere nearby, and the sharp chirp of bats hunting in the twilight.

C.J. realized he was shaking all over but not from the cold. Somewhere along the line *that* had ceased to be a problem, because now there seemed to be molten lava flowing through his veins. He decided the shakes must be from the strain of keeping himself from kissing her again—for real, this time, with her mouth hot and open and her body growing eager and trembly pressed up against him. It occurred to him that that effort would be a whole lot easier if he could just bring himself to let go of her. Her body was still enfolded in his arms, shaking nearly as badly as he was, and her hand, trapped between them, was making little stroking motions on the upper part of his chest.

He cleared his throat. She whispered, ''What?''

And he said, ''Nothing. I didn't say anything.''

''Then what did you want me to shut up for?''

Damned if he could remember. He scowled up at the flitting bats and after a moment began to laugh silently.

''What?'' It was quick and suspicious now.

''Nothing. Not a damn thing.'' A distinct clicking noise

distracted him and he growled angrily, "Listen to you—your teeth are rattling. I've got to get you home before you catch your death of cold. And just so you know, it's *dark*, dammit. That may not matter much to you, but it would be nice if *one* of us could see where we're going."

She pushed abruptly away from him, and he had to shift his arm to her waist and get a grip on her belt to keep her from slipping out of his grasp.

"No problem," she said, and her voice was artificially light and frosty and carefully restrained. "Bubba can lead us home—can't you, Bubba? Where are you, boy?" She paused, and then a dark shape separated itself from the grasses and thumped wetly against her legs. "Oh, there you are. Yes, you're a good dog. Let's go home, Bubba. That's a good boy...."

The dog took off walking and so did she. C.J. didn't have much choice but to do the same, so he did. "I was kidding," he muttered after he'd wrapped his arm around her shoulders and gotten her tucked up securely again against his side. "Dammit, I can see well enough to get us home."

In that same annoyingly prissy—and obviously ticked-off—voice she said, "Then you were probably kidding when you said that about catching cold, as well. You do know you don't get colds from being wet? You get colds from germs."

"Huh. Is that right, Dr. Brown?"

"Yes, it is—and don't be sarcastic."

"Well," he said after a moment, "I'm not about to argue with a woman who just threw me into a pond."

He was caught by surprise when she jerked and then tried to turn within the circle of his arm. "Oh, God. C.J., I'm so sorry about that. Really. I don't know—"

"Don't start that again," he growled, reeling her back against him. And after a moment, he said, "I just want to know one thing. How did you do it? I mean, where did somebody who looks like—'' He squelched the fairy-tale images in his mind and began again. ''Where did you learn a move like that, anyway?''

''Oh…it's no big deal.'' He felt her shrug. ''I've had some self-defense training—quite a bit, actually. In my line of work it's pretty much a necessity. And then, after I got involved with the organization…well, we deal with some very violent people, after all. And since I don't like guns—''

Yeah, right. After the calm and efficient way she'd pointed a loaded one at him? He snorted and muttered, ''You sure coulda fooled me.''

He felt her flinch again. ''Oh, C.J., believe me—''

''You pointed a damn gun straight at me! Hijacked me!'' The anger bubbled up like an unexpected burp and was out of him before he could stop it. ''A loaded gun. Aimed right at me. Do you have any idea what that feels like? Lady, I coulda gone my whole life without having something like that happen to me!''

She paced beside him in silence while he thought over what he'd said to see if he regretted any of it. He'd about decided he didn't when she heaved a sigh and said unsteadily, ''You have every right to be mad at me.''

Mad at her? It astonished him to realize that he was and probably had been mad at her all along, deep down, telling himself he wasn't because he didn't think he ought to be angry with someone who was in such trouble, and wounded and blind and vulnerable. It astonished him, too, to realize that as soon as she said that, all the anger seemed to leak right out of him.

''I'd never have shot you, you know.'' She paused, then went on in a grave, shivery voice, ''I only decided to carry a weapon that one time because of Vasily—because I knew how dangerous he was. Now I'm sorry and I wish I hadn't, but…all I can say is, it seemed like the best thing to do at the time.''

The best thing to do at the time. Images flashed through his mind: Mary Kelly's eyes and her sad little smile when she said, "You just don't know what it is you're doin'." Two women and a little girl walking away from him across a deserted parking lot toward the lights of a police station....

He took a breath. "Yeah, I guess I know how *that* is." She tilted her head toward him in an inquiring way, and he gave a huff of laughter that hurt him inside. "That's what I keep tellin' myself about turnin' you guys in. It seemed like the right thing at the time. Looks like we were both wrong."

She didn't reply, and they walked on together, just the two of them now. With the house lights visible through the trees, Bubba had evidently figured his job was done. Chills still racked her from time to time, and him, too, but it seemed to him there was something sort of companionable about it now—shared shivers in a friendly darkness.

Maybe it was that cloak of darkness, making her a faceless, warm and vibrant presence, but he didn't think about how otherworldly beautiful she was, or how bruised and battered, but only how real…how human.

Somewhere along the line her arm had crept around him, and her fingers were hooked into the waistband of his jeans. He thought how nicely she fit there against his side, and how much more comfortable she seemed to be with him now. And how comfortable he was not. That was when it hit him. That was when he knew that he wanted her. It felt to him now that he had done so for quite a long time.

When had it happened? It couldn't have been from the first moment he saw her. He'd thought her barely a girl then, in punky spiked hair and hooded sweatshirt, with a cell phone stuck in her ear. A girl with silver eyes, it was true, but since when had he lusted after a woman because of the color of her eyes? Shortly after that she'd pulled a gun on him and hijacked his truck, not exactly actions designed to excite a man's libido. And yet…and yet. He *had* found her exciting. He had. In some strange way she'd fascinated him…troubled him. And he definitely recalled the way her body had felt, pinned under him while he'd wrested the gun away from her, every slender, well-muscled writhing inch of it. But then, he was only human…wasn't he?

He'd thought of her for weeks after that, second-guessing his decision to turn her in to the law, anguishing over mental images of her in a jail cell, and while he distinctly remembered her voice and her eyes and the reproachful looks she'd given him, he hadn't once pictured her naked in his arms…had he?

Then had come the shooting, and the terrible images on the television screen, and the hospital. He didn't like to think about the hospital, especially those first hours—the way she'd looked, lying there, bruised, bandaged and blind. The way he'd felt. The pain, the awfulness of it, was too recent and far too vivid still; his mind shied away from it with a shudder.

So, when had it happened? Was it when he'd carried her up the stairs to his old bedroom, showing off a little bit because she'd taunted him, and her body thinner and lighter than he remembered, and a strange and unfamiliar tenderness filling up his insides? Or later, those embarrassing moments when she'd gotten tangled up with him in his mother's kitchen, and he'd lost his breath and his composure because she'd touched his naked chest? Oh, yeah. But by then the lust that had lit up his insides had already seemed familiar to him.

So, in the long run, he supposed, *when* it had happened didn't really matter. The fact was that it had. He wanted Caitlyn. He wanted her in his bed. He wanted her in his arms. He wanted her body warm and naked and trembling, tangled and intertwined with his in all the ways two bodies could be. The fibers of his being had known these things for a long, long time, and now his mind did, too. The only thing he didn't know was what he was going to do about it.

That night, for the first time since the shooting, Caitlyn dreamed of Ari Vasily. Or rather, she dreamed of being chased by cloaked, faceless men, and the sound of gunshots zipping past her, and all the people she loved in the world falling down around her, one by one, in pools of thick crimson blood.

She awoke drenched in sweat with her head pounding so fiercely she feared for a moment C.J. was right, and that she had after all contracted some awful flu bug as a penance for dumping them both in the pond. Her weakness frightened her. She was so recently out of the hospital and her customary confidence in her own good health so badly shaken that she wavered on the brink of rousing Jess.

But as she lay rigid, trying to work up the courage to get out of bed, her galloping pulse slowly receded and so did the throbbing in her head. She drew long, measured breaths and concentrated on relaxing every part of her body, but she knew it was no use trying to sleep again. Every time she closed her eyes she saw those puddles of blood...viscous and unimaginably *red*.

She got out of bed, taking the bedspread comforter with her, and felt her way to the rocking chair. She pulled it close to the open window and sat curled up in it with her feet under her, wrapped in little yellow butterflies dancing on a field of pink, until she heard the birds begin to chirp in the dawn.

She didn't want to tell C.J. about the dream. She wouldn't tell him. Damned if she would. It was a dream, and she wasn't a child; she didn't need anyone to soothe her nightmares away.

She didn't need *him*.

But the feel of his arms around her, warming her wet, shivering body like a warm fire on a wintery Iowa evening…of his mouth, cold and hard on hers. The memory of those things was like a haunting and annoying phrase of music that had stuck in her brain and kept recurring when she least expected it, no matter how hard she tried to push it away.…

It was Sunday. They were returning from their walk, strolling slowly along the grass and gravel lane, side by side but not touching, each occupying one of the low, graveled tracks where the tires ran, separated by the grassy hummock between. It had been scary for her the first time they'd done that, and she'd reached for him across the median, needing the touch of his hand to give her courage. Gradually, though, she'd stopped feeling as though she were about to fall off the edge of the world, and learned to judge her way by the feel of the gravel under her feet and the rise of the ground on either side of the path. She was learning to walk with her head up and the sun on her face and the morning breeze in her hair.

Normally, those things would have made her smile, drink deeply of the winey autumn air and quiver inside with that recurring and always unexpected happiness. This morning, she smiled, but the muscles of her face felt pinched and achy, and the restless emotion that vibrated through her wasn't joy.

No, she ruthlessly told herself, I won't tell him about the dream. I don't need him to comfort me. I don't need him to hold me. I don't need— Oh, God…I can't.

They were approaching the yard. She knew that because there was shade from the oaks and hickories that sheltered the house, and because the dogs had left them and gone off to their favorite nap spots in the flower beds. She veered onto the grass that grew along the sides of the lane, kept neatly mowed by Jess to the place where the ground rose to the pasture fences. There she knew, because C.J. had told her, began the riot of yellow sunflowers and black-eyed daisies and goldenrod and tall grasses headed out with waving plumes, the thickets of scarlet sumac and tangles of pink and purple and white morning glories, all laid out in a glorious harmony no human floral designer could ever hope to match.

"I want to pick some flowers to take back to the house," she announced, breathless for no reason, holding her hands out in front of her and finding nothing. She'd taken several reckless, unsteady steps toward the fence when she felt C.J.'s body brush against her back. Her breath caught and her heart gave a scary lurch. *I can't let him touch me...I can't let him hold me again. I can't.*

"Whoa, hold up," he murmured, his voice a vibration near her ear. She felt his arms extend along the outsides of hers. "Okay, now...turn to your left, about...ten o'clock. Couple more steps...now you've got it...feel that?"

She nodded and gave an uneven cackle of laughter as she felt leaves prickle her hands and then the sturdy stalks of goldenrod...the spindlier stems of some sort of flower. A grass plume tickled her face and drifted into her mouth. She spat it out and waved it impatiently aside, focusing with all her concentration on what her hands were feeling. *Seeing with my hands...is that what I'm doing?* A strange, fierce excitement rushed through her, sanding her skin with goose bumps.

C.J. made a gruff sound, the beginnings of words, and she silenced him with a shake of her head and a sharp "No, don't tell me. Let me do it...." as her fingers climbed a stalk of goldenrod and found the feathery yellow plumes. She let them trail through her fingers. They felt silky soft, delicate as lace. She measured an elbow's length down and broke one off, then two more. Her insides quivered, emotions as finely balanced as drops of dew on the edge of a leaf.

"I can hold those for you," C.J. offered, but again she shook her head, forcing his nearness from her mind.

Her fingers were busy, following a slender, slightly furry stem to its terminal. *Yes!* There it was—a daisylike flower. She broke it off with her right hand and added it to the collection in her left. With a little burr of tension humming in her chest she picked daisies—sunflowers?—until she couldn't find any more, then seined the air with her hands until they snagged the tickly plumes of grass that had teased her face at first.

Oh, but the grass leaves were sharp and left her hands and forearms stinging with tiny cuts, and the stems were tough and resisted her efforts to break them. She straightened, brushing tickling leaves—or bugs? Flies? Bees?—away from her face and gave a small grunt of frustration.

"Let me get that for you." C.J.'s warm shape brushed her back...her shoulder...her arm. His clean, familiar scent mingled with the dusty smell of weeds and grass in her nostrils. It took all her willpower to hold herself still. Trembling, she listened to the squeaky, popping sounds the grass stems made as he broke them, knowing that if she turned her face toward him, his would be right...*there.* In her mind a vision rose, indistinct and soft with lavender shadows—crinkly brown eyes, a lock of sandy hair falling over one, a sweetly smiling mouth. *Dimples—yes, I remember now...he has dimples.*

"Looks nice." His voice was much too near as he added the stems of grass to her bouquet. "Think you've 'bout got enough?"

For some reason she couldn't answer him. Gathering the sheaf of flowers and foliage close to her chest, bugs, prickles and all, she felt her lips part, then close again.

"Ready to go back to the house?" A hand was firm and warm on her elbow.

She nodded but didn't move. A shudder rocked her. "I dreamed about Vasily last night."

Her eyes burned and the shivers were sweeping through her in waves, deep inside where they wouldn't show. And now she knew why the nightmare had upset her so and why she hadn't wanted to tell him about it. Why she dreaded needing him so. They were shivers of shame.

She heard a breath taken and released, and C.J.'s arm came across her shoulders. She slipped away from that gentle promise of comfort and stepped carefully from the grass to the gravel...then across the center ridge of grass...more gravel, and then the leaf-strewn grass that began the broad sweep into the yard and under the trees. She felt him moving beside her, but he didn't speak and didn't touch her again. She tried to fool him with a soft, breathy laugh.

"It's the first time, can you believe that? The first time since the shooting."

"Can't see how that's a bad thing," C.J. said. His hand on her arm as he guided her around a tree trunk had a diffident, tentative feel. "He wouldn't be pleasant to dream about."

She felt a solid, but giving, bump against her hip. Her searching hand caught at the rope attached to the old tire as if it were a life preserver rather than a child's swing. She fingered the rope and leaned into it casually, swaying a little to disguise her relief at finding something to hold on to. Something to give her her bearings. From here it was exactly twenty-two steps to the front porch.

C.J. watched her sway slowly in the dappled light, one arm hooked around the rope of the swing, the other cradling sprays of grasses and sunflowers and goldenrod. But though pollen from the goldenrod spangled her hair and cheeks and the shoulders of her sweatshirt like pixie dust, it wasn't fairies and fantasies he thought about when he looked at her now. And though the bottom edge of the sweatshirt played peekaboo with her slender and supple flesh when she lifted her arm, he didn't think about how firm and soft it would feel...not then. There was something weighing her down—a misery, a sadness he could almost see, as if a heavy net had been thrown over her. He wondered, he hoped she'd tell him what it was, if he was patient enough not to rush her.

"I haven't…" She hesitated, and he held his breath; her voice seemed to come from a great distance, from across a chasm he didn't know how to cross. "I haven't even thought about him, about…the shooting. Even when we've talked about it, I haven't really *thought* about it. Felt it—" she let go of the rope and touched her chest "—in here."

"That's understandable." He found himself moving toward her—toward that chasm—and made himself stop. "I guess you've had one or two other things on your mind."

She tilted her head toward him and gave a brittle laugh. "Yeah? What's the second one?" He stared at her, not understanding, and she made a disgusted sound and began walking away from him. Pacing, rather; he could hear her counting under her breath as he quickened his own pace to catch up with her.

"I've been thinking about *me*—that's all. *Myself.* Being blind. Worrying about whether I'm going to see again. Oh, *damn.*" She halted and threw up her arms with a cry that was half a sob. "Where *are* they?"

Ignoring the question, which made even less sense than the rest of what she'd said, C.J. said in bewilderment, "Jeez, Caitlyn, why shouldn't you? That's a hell of a lot for anyone—"

"Yeah?" A look—silver daggers—slashed past his shoulder. "So I'm blind—big deal. At least I'm *alive*. What about Mary Kelly? Where is she? She's *dead*." Her eyes darkened, and without their silvery flash her face became a mask. She turned away from him, thickly muttering, "Where are the damn steps? I counted—they should've been here. Dammit, where—"

"Your vector's a little off," C.J. said with dazed relief. This, at least, was something he could deal with. "You missed by about ten feet. If you come around to...oh, say two o'clock—''

She came around, all right, but not toward the house. She kept right on coming until the sheaf of wildflowers whacked him in the chest, and her face, uplifted to his, was a mask of grief. ''Mary Kelly's dead,'' she whispered through lips that barely moved. ''I had her blood all over me. I didn't—I never—''

Her face crumpled. With an anguished cry she turned and stumbled away from him, fleeing blindly across the lawn, leaving wildflowers scattered like jackstraws at his feet.

Chapter 11

He was sitting in the front porch rocker when his mother came out with her Sunday dress on to tell him she was heading off to church.

"Well, aren't those pretty," she said when she saw the flowers in his lap.

He nodded glumly. "Caitlyn picked 'em."

"By herself?"

"Yep."

"Bless her heart." His mother moved to the top of the steps. "Where is she?" she asked, surveying the empty yard. "I didn't hear her come in the house."

The chair creaked as C.J. tipped it forward. He stared down at the flowers dangling between his knees and muttered, "I don't know, she's out there somewhere."

"By herself?"

"Yep." The chair creaked again as he leaned back in it and defiantly met his mother's mildly disapproving look.

"You think that's a good idea?"

He shrugged and scowled down at the wildflowers, no-

ticing as he did that they were looking somewhat the worse
for wear. He picked at a floppy daisy and his heart grew
heavier. "Probably not. However, she definitely does not
want me with her. She's grieving," he said, and took a
long breath that didn't do much to ease the tightness in his
chest. "For Mary Kelly."

"That's the woman that was killed?" C.J. nodded.
"Well," his mother said after a moment, "she needed to."
She settled herself against the porch railing and hooked her
pocketbook over her arm as if she meant to stay awhile. "I
expect she'd like some comfort, though, no matter what
she told you."

"It wasn't what she said," C.J. said bleakly. "It was the
way she looked." He was surprised when his mother
laughed and made a "shame on you" sound with her
tongue.

"Son, I'm afraid you don't know very much about
women."

He didn't like hearing that, even if it was true. "Well,
shoot, Momma," he said, bristling, "I know enough to
know when I'm not wanted—or needed."

"You do, do you?"

He was getting tired of being the source of his mother's
amusement but knew better than to say so. Instead, he
whacked the flowers across his knee without much regard
for their condition and muttered bitterly, "That is the
strongest, most independent, stubborn and bullheaded—"

"Whoa, now. That's a lot for one woman to be, and not
necessarily all bad."

"Well, it ain't all that good, either," C.J. growled.

"So," said his mother, ignoring his grammatical lapse,
"I guess that means you'd like a woman to be weak, clingy
and wishy-washy?"

He snorted, though he could feel a lightening of his spirits and a grin trying hard to break through. "After growin'
up in this family? Momma, I've never even *met* a woman

who fit that description.'' He paused to think about it, and the heaviness settled back around his heart. "*No,* I don't want that. Of course I don't. I just want—'' *What any man wants.* He stopped, frustrated, because he didn't know how to say it. Or didn't want to say it, not out loud. *To be needed...wanted. To be, for one person, at least, big shot...superhero...knight in shining armor...the alpha and omega. The light in one particular woman's eyes.*

"You want to be her hero," his mother finished for him, but her voice was gentle and for once her eyes weren't smiling.

He let his breath out in a gust of exasperation. "Momma, you're always sayin' that, but that's not what I mean. It's not what I mean at all." He aimed a scowl at her and hoped he was going to be able to tell her what he did mean without making a damn fool of himself. No man wants to look like a fool, even to his momma. "I'd be happy just being her friend, if she'd let me. All I want to do is help her get through this. Sure, I'd like to be able to fix everything for her, put everything back the way it was. And, okay, I know I'm not gonna be able to do that, but at least I'd like to—" he swallowed hard, lifted a hand and finished lamely "—*be* there for her. You know?"

"Calvin." His mother straightened up and walked over to him. Her hand rested briefly on the back of his neck, then moved to his shoulder and gave it a little squeeze. "What on earth do you think being a hero *is?*"

He looked up at her and frowned. And what did she do? Just smiled back at him, then turned and started down the steps. He was about to yell at her in protest for leaving him with an exit line like that one, but after the first step she stopped abruptly and hesitated a moment before turning halfway back to him. The protest he'd planned died on his lips; the look on her face was one he'd never seen before.

"Son, your daddy was a hero to me every day of his life. Did I need him to take care of me? I most certainly did not. I was a strong and independent woman when I met him—I had a college degree and a good job teaching school. Did I *need* him? No more than I needed sunshine, and air to breathe. He worked hard, your daddy did—he was away a lot, driving trucks, and Lord knows it's a good thing I'm as strong and independent as I am or I don't know how I'd ever have been able to raise seven children with him gone so much of the time. But he loved me and he loved his kids, and let me tell you, he never thought he was too much of a man to fix a meal or change a diaper or put a load of laundry in the washing machine, either! Lord knows he had his faults. He wasn't perfect, but that didn't matter.'' She paused, a fierce light shining in her brown eyes and spots of color showing through the face powder on her cheeks, and when she spoke again her voice was husky and uneven. ''I'll forgive a man a lot, for his eyes lighting up every time he sees me.''

She stomped on down the steps and around the corner of the house to where the cars were parked and didn't look back or wave goodbye.

C.J. sat where he was with his forearms on his knees and a bunch of wilted wildflowers drooping in his hands and watched her car back out onto the lane, then head off toward the highway. After a while he took a big breath and brushed at something that was crawling down his cheeks—some kind of bug, he told himself.

Yeah, that's what it was. Had to be.

Scaredy-cat, Caitlyn scolded herself. The voice in her head kept time with the scuffing sounds her feet made as they felt their way along the gravel track, like a schoolyard taunt: *Scaredy-cat, scaredy-cat, 'fraid of the dark.*

She wasn't afraid of the dark. Or she never had been before, even as a child. She remembered playing with her cousins, Eric and Rose Ellen, on Aunt Lucy's farm, where, far away from city lights, on moonless nights the Milky

Way made a shimmering path across an inky black sky. She remembered playing games of hide-and-seek in the big old barn on nights when clouds hid even the starlight, and the darkness was like a blanket across her face, and they'd taken delicious shivery delight in scaring each other silly.

This is no different, she told herself. *It shouldn't be. Why should it be, just because it's the middle of the day and I can feel the sun on my face and the autumn breeze in my hair? It shouldn't be, but it is.*

For one thing, the scary things lurking in this darkness weren't giggling children poised to jump out at her and yell, "Boo!" They were evil men with guns and no compunction about using them to snuff out the life of an innocent young woman…a little girl's mother. *Or mine.*

And in this darkness there were no farmhouse windows ablaze with light, beacons to guide her home. In this darkness she was all alone.

You don't have to be.

The whisper inside her head was enticing…insidious. She squelched it ruthlessly. She couldn't allow herself to think like that, even for a minute. She didn't dare.

She wondered now if she'd dreamed of Vasily last night for a reason. Because C.J. had kissed her, because it had felt so good to be held and to walk with his arm around her. Because it was so tempting to give in, abdicate responsibility, let someone take care of her, let someone *else* take care of Vasily. Only, she couldn't do that. This was her trouble, her battle, her war, and she couldn't risk the possibility of anyone else getting hurt fighting it for her.

She could learn to live with being blind, if she had to, but she could *not* live with that.

The dream remained vivid in her mind's eye as she shuffled along the lane that ran between fields of hay and stubble, and although the autumn sun was a toasty burn across her shoulders, she shivered. Once again she could hear the bullets making angry zapping sounds as they whizzed past,

missing *her*.... Once again she saw the bleached faces of
people she loved lying in pools of thick red blood, dead
eyes staring up at the sky—Mom and Dad were there and
Aunt Lucy and Uncle Mike, Eric and Ellie. It shocked her
now to realize that one of the faces was C.J.'s.

What had she been thinking, to run away from him like
that?

You wanted him to come after you, answered the trai-
torous voice inside her head. *You hoped he would.*

As before, she slapped the voice away, but not before
she heard it jeeringly ask, *Well, why didn't he?*

I shouldn't be doing this, she thought, quickly redirecting
her thoughts. *It was selfish. I shouldn't be out here alone.*

She felt as exposed as a duck in a shooting gallery. What
if Vasily's men were out there now? What if they'd been
watching her? Just been waiting for their chance to grab
her?

If they get me, she thought, then Jake will have nobody
to use as bait to catch Vasily. He'll get away with it—with
killing Mary Kelly. He'll get away with everything!

I shouldn't be here. I have to go back.

But where was "back"? She'd long ago lost count of
her steps. And now she realized that she wasn't walking
on the gravel lane and that the ground under her feet was
spongy with thick layers of fallen leaves. Oh, Lord—she
was in the woods, she had to be. She'd never tried to orient
herself or count footsteps in the woods—it was too big, too
cluttered, too confusing. All the tree trunks felt alike. Now
sapling trees slapped at her and their huge dying leaves
rustled like dry bones as she brushed them. An exposed
root rose up beneath her foot; she gasped and, stumbling,
threw out a hand and scraped her knuckles on bark.

It came upon her so suddenly, as if she'd triggered a
trap, one of those nets that fall out of nowhere and instantly
immobilize: *fear.* Fear that had nothing to do with stalkers
and snipers and nightmare visions of blood. This was fear

as old as humankind, instinctive fear of the darkness and the unknown. Icy sweat sprang from her pores and her skin shivered. Fine hairs rose along her arms and shoulders and the back of her neck. Her heartbeat thundered in her ears, so it was a moment before she realized the whimpering sounds she kept hearing came from *her*.

Something rustled through the branches above her head and fell with a *thump* nearby. Adrenaline shot through her and in her panic she pushed away from the relative safety of the tree and fled, stumbling through thick drifts of leaves on legs that felt like melting rubber, arms thrown up to protect her face, her breath like sobs. A thorny vine caught at her, tore her clothing and slashed her skin, and she fought it as desperately as if it had been a wild animal attacking her with intelligent intent. Trying to elude it, she turned this way and that, becoming only more hopelessly confused, more terrified, more lost. This was worse than being lost in darkness—she was lost in *nothingness,* populated by terrors of her own imagining.

How long she thrashed and stumbled through the woods she didn't know—probably no more than minutes…seconds, even. It seemed like hours. Like forever.

It ended abruptly when her foot sank into a hole left by a long-decayed stump. Pain shot through her; she pitched clumsily forward, half falling, half stumbling as she instinctively fought to forestall the inevitable. Then, suddenly there was an embankment, studded with moss-covered rocks and rotting logs—and down she went. She rolled…and slid…and bumped to a stop.

For a few minutes she lay as she'd landed, on her back, feet downhill on a steep incline. She felt oddly peaceful now; the terror, the nightmare panic, seemed to have vanished as quickly as it had come upon her. Covering her face with her forearms, she began to laugh silently—partly from relief, but mostly with chagrin and shame. She'd panicked—utterly and completely panicked. Never in her life had she done such a thing. She felt unbelievably foolish. Unforgivably stupid.

As she listened to the quietness fold itself around her she realized that it wasn't *silence*—she could hear the musical tinkle of running water. She put out an exploring hand and felt cold liquid slide through her fingers. And now…yes, she could feel wetness soaking into her jeans on one side. *The creek.* She was lying on the edge of the creek, partly in the stream, which was barely a trickle this time of year.

At least, she thought, I know where I am now. She'd been to the creek with C.J. enough times; surely she could find her way back to the lane from here.

But when she tried to stand, the pain she'd forgotten about exploded through her leg. She gasped. Her head reeled and she sat down much more abruptly than she'd intended. Breathing hard and swearing fiercely, she rocked herself back and forth while she took stock of her situation. Oh, yes, she remembered stepping in that hole, now. *Stupid…stupid.* But she didn't think her ankle was seriously injured—probably only sprained—and if she could manage to crawl out of the creek bed, she might be able to hobble— *No.* She mentally slapped a hand over her mouth. *Caitlyn, haven't you done enough stupid things today?*

She sank back against the creek bank, closed her eyes and once more lifted both hands to cover her face. Oh, how she hated feeling helpless! But there was no getting around the fact that she *was,* at this moment, anyway. Like it or not—there was no way out of it—she was going to have to sit here, a classic maiden in distress, and wait for someone to come to her rescue.

''Okay, Bubba, ol' boy,'' C.J. said, giving the lab a neck-ruffling hug, ''let's go find her, shall we? Where's Caitlyn, huh? Let's go, big fella—go on, find Caitlyn.''

He was surprised to hear how calm and ordinary his voice sounded. Inside, deep in his guts, he was beginning to get worried. More than worried—scared to death. Okay, so Jake had assured him they were in the clear, that according to the FBI's surveillance sources Vasily had no idea where Caitlyn was. Nobody had noticed any strangers lurking in the neighborhood, either, but that didn't make C.J.'s mind rest easy. He had an idea he wasn't ever going to rest easy again until Ari Vasily was either dead or behind bars.

Bubba gave his wrist a swipe with his tongue, threw him a panting, grinning, "Why didn't you say so?" look and went trotting off across the hay field toward the woods. C.J. sighed. He knew Labs weren't trackers, and ol' Bubba was as likely to be after wild turkeys as anything, but what the hell.... He took off after him. After a few steps he broke into a run.

He'd lost sight of the dog by the time he got to the woods, but he could hear him rustling around amongst the leaves not far away. "Hey, Bubba, where you off to, boy?" Then, with accelerating heartbeat, and feeling funny and self-conscious about it, he called out, "Caitlyn? You there?"

She didn't answer, but in the tense and suspenseful silence, he could hear Bubba making happy yipping-whining noises down by the creek. He huffed out a breath and headed that way, forcing himself to walk easy, telling himself his thumping heartbeat was because he'd been running hard. Although he hadn't.

She was still some little distance away when he caught sight of her, mostly because Bubba's tail whipping back and forth marked her location as effectively as a flare. Without that, downhill from him and up against the near creek bank as she was, one leg tucked under her and the other in the water, he wasn't sure he'd have seen her at all. In Sammi June's old faded jeans and an even older Georgia Bulldogs sweatshirt that had most likely belonged to him once upon a time, her pale gold hair the color of birch leaves, she seemed to blend right in with the autumn scenery.

It had been a long time since he'd thought of her in conjunction with fairy tales. He did now, but not the Disney-type, enchanted-princess, Sleeping-Beauty-type of fairy tale. She called to mind things he hadn't even realized he knew about—things like nymphs and elves and sprites, spirits of nature, of woods and trees, water and earth…creatures of superstition and ancient legend…beings, so those legends said, that had once populated the earth, long before mankind.

"Hi," she said, and the vision vanished like an elf into shadows. Her voice was breathless. Her face, turned toward the sound of his approaching footsteps, was dusty and tear streaked and crisscrossed with scratches.

When C.J. saw those, the anger he felt toward her for her foolishness, which had begun welling up in him like an incipient sneeze, dissipated like pollen in the wind. Unable to say anything, he let out a half grunting, half snorting sound of sheer relief and sat down on the edge of the bank just above where she was. He was surprised to discover that his legs had become unreliable.

Bubba gave Caitlyn's nose and mouth one last swipe with his tongue and went splashing off to see if he could find anything interesting in the creek. Her hand followed the dog in an involuntary groping motion, and a look of uncertainty flashed across her face. "C.J.?" There was fear in her voice. "That is you, isn't it?"

"Yeah," he said sourly, figuring it was okay to go ahead and let her think he was mad, now they both knew she was okay. "It's me. Lucky for you." He eased himself over the edge of the creek bank. "How in God's green earth did you get down here?"

Her mouth tilted sideways. "I sort of…fell."

"You…fell."

She nodded and gave a gallant little gulp of chagrin.

"Yep—spectacularly. I must have been a sight—too bad you missed it."

Not thinking about what he was going to do, he hunkered down beside her in the rocks and ferns and dipped his fingers in the trickle of creek water. His hand felt unsteady as he brought it to her cheek. She flinched just a little when he touched her, and her eyes held a wary look. He slid the ball of his thumb across a scratch, spreading cool water over it like a salve. "You hurt yourself." His voice felt and sounded like sand.

"Oh—" she touched a hand to her cheek, nudging his away "—yeah, actually, I did." Her voice was quick, breathy. "I think I turned my ankle, too. Stepped in a hole—that's why I fell. I don't think it's too bad, but I can't put weight on it yet. I was going to try to crawl up the bank. I thought I could make it home, if I could just—"

"Cait," he said as he let his hand drop away from her and drape across his knee, "what am I gonna do with you?" When what he really meant was, *What am I going to do with these feelings inside me?*

She made that funny, half-embarrassed gulping sound again. "Well, I was hoping you were going to take me home."

He didn't feel like laughing. "Don't tell me you're gonna let me help you."

Her smile disappeared and she turned her face away from him. "I don't think I have much choice, do I?"

With a sigh of exasperation that was more like a growl, he shifted his weight, pivoting on the ball of his foot so he could reach the leg that was stretched out in front of her, making a bridge across the tiny stream. "This it?" he muttered, and she nodded. He'd barely touched it when she stiffened and jerked her other foot out from under her, then used both it and her hands to brace herself for what was coming.

She didn't utter a sound as he lifted her leg into his lap and, as gently as he knew how, drew back the stiff wet fabric of her jeans. He eased off her shoe, then peeled away the sock. His heart hammered beneath his breastbone as he cradled her foot in his hands. Funny—he'd never noticed before how vulnerable and sweet a woman's bare feet were. Come to think of it, he didn't remember ever noticing a woman's feet, *period.* To hold one—*her* foot—like this, the skin so cool and silky soft like a baby's, the bones so fragile and yet so strong…it was vulnerable, yes, and even sweet, but incredibly *intimate,* too. It must be the intimacy, he thought, that made it so erotic.

"Yep, sprained," he said in a strangled voice, as he eased the foot off of his lap and set it gingerly on a moss-covered rock. "Not too bad—that cold creek water'll probably keep the swelling down some."

He retrieved her sock and stuffed it inside her shoe. When he trusted himself to look at her again, he saw that her eyes, focused on the place where a moment ago his face had been, were shimmering like sunlight on gray water.

"Tell me something," he began. She jerked toward him in surprise as, instead of preparing to haul her up out of the creek, he settled himself beside her in the nest of crushed ferns. With his back propped against the creek bank, he asked in a conversational tone, "Why do you hate it so much? Askin' for help, I mean. Hell, not even asking—just accepting it when it's offered."

She was sitting forward, her body tensed and wary, her face turned away from him. He saw her shoulders lift. "I don't know," she said in a muffled voice. "I guess it's just the way I am."

Exasperation rumbled in his throat. He scrubbed a hand over his face and fought it down, and after a moment was able to quietly say, "That's no kind of answer. What I was asking is for you to *tell* me the way you are."

He stared at her silent back, a bulwark against him, and felt defeated. Then…as his gaze traveled upward to her neck, rising pale as a newly sprouted shoot from the neckline of her sweatshirt, the bumps of her spine downy and delicate as something newly born, and as vulnerable, revelation came to him, not in a blinding flash, but as a slow and gentle warming…. She's afraid of this, he thought. *Even more so than I am.*

He put his hand on her back, between the draped mounds of her shoulder blades, and began to move it with a relaxed rhythm…a kneading pressure. She said nothing, but after a moment her head sank forward. Closing his eyes in thanksgiving for that small acceptance, he let his hand work its way along the valley of her spine to the top of the sweatshirt…and then beyond. Her skin was satiny and cool where it stretched across her shoulders, warm and damp farther up on her nape beneath the slightly curling ends of her hair. He thought how small and slender her neck felt in his hand. He marveled at the vibrant strength in it even as desire mushroomed inside him, wallowing like a bathing hippo in his belly. Slightly seasick, he mumbled, ''How's that?''

Her reply was faint. ''Heaven.''

A tiny thrill of triumph shivered through him. He lifted his other hand to her shoulder and raised himself so he was sitting upright, the way she was, moving slowly and carefully as he might if he were trying to tame a wild animal. Leaning toward her, he slid his hands lightly down the sides of her neck and curved his palms over the places where the rounded ridges of muscle were the thickest, kneading gently while his fingers brushed the velvety hollows above and below her collarbones and his thumbs probed the wells of muscle along her spine. He smelled sweet strawberries and closed his eyes and concentrated hard on not burying his face in her hair.

She said something he couldn't quite hear, and he leaned closer to her ear to dazedly mumble, "What?"

"I said, that feels incredible," she said in a thickened murmur. "I never realized—" She took a breath; her chin tilted sideways. "I don't think anybody's ever done that to me before."

He felt a smile coming on and didn't try to stop it. "Is that a fact?" He slowed the motion of his hands, making a new rhythm at once gentler and deeper…more like a caress. In a voice to match that motion he said, "Well, I'm glad I'm your first."

She answered with a high, short laugh.

Then there was silence, while he allowed his mind to wander down impossible paths….

I wish, Caitlyn thought, as an ache came from out of nowhere, swelled through her throat and face and threatened to blossom into tears. *I wish you could have been my first.*

Her "first" had not been a wise choice—or for that matter, her choice at all. It had come about in the wee hours following her senior prom, in the back of her date's parents' station wagon. He'd had too much to drink, and she…well, maybe she hadn't had nearly enough. She remembered being frightened and overwhelmed and all too aware that he was twice her size and that she had no hope of preventing him from doing what he was so determined to do. She remembered pleading with him, though that may have been only inside her head. In any case, he'd neither heard nor heeded. She remembered the pain, and what was worse, the helplessness. She remembered the humiliation, too.

She'd never told her parents—it would have hurt them too much. Though they'd wondered why she hadn't wanted to go out with Tyler again. He'd kept asking her—pestered her, in fact, right up until the day she left for college. But she'd never been able to look at him again after that night without revulsion, and had taken care never to allow herself to be caught alone with him. She hadn't liked him all that much to begin with, she realized too late, and had accepted his invitation to the prom for all the wrong reasons: because he was handsome and popular and a star athlete, and she, a rather gawky, skinny late bloomer, had been flattered by his attention.

Later choices hadn't been much wiser, perhaps, but at least she'd made sure they were *her* choices, and the partner, the circumstances and her emotions always under her strict control. She'd been content with that, and had never wasted time on regrets, or wished things might be otherwise…until now.

I wish… She put her hands over C.J.'s, stopping their seductive caressing motion. Her skin felt tight…stretched…on the verge of tearing. She didn't lift her head; her neck felt too frail to hold it. "I think," she said, and her voice was frightened and airless, "that's the reason I hate needing help."

"What is?" Warm puffs of breath stirred the hair above her ear. Goose bumps sprang up all over her body. She shivered, and her nipples tightened until they hurt.

"I don't want to need *anyone*. I won't—I can't—I'm afraid—"

"What are you afraid of?" His hands, ignoring the restraint of hers, moved back and forth across her shoulders, gently stroking over the rounded part, moving the fabric of her shirt in a way that made it part of the caress.

Her breath caught in her throat. She cleared it and tried to speak calmly…rationally. "I suppose a therapist would say that I'm afraid of losing control. Of being weak."

He was silent for a moment, considering…then softly touched the shell of her ear with his hoarse whisper. "Needing somebody doesn't make you weak, it just makes you human. In fact, I'd say just about everybody needs somebody—"

Desperate laughter rippled through her. She sang the

words of an old song in a fruity, somewhat inebriated—
and shaken—tone, "'Everybody needs somebody some-
time...'"

His hand swept upward, changing the contours of her
throat and nudging her chin up and back, and the last note
of the song died a burbling death as his mouth closed over
hers. The breath she hadn't had time to exhale swelled in
her chest, her breasts tightened and her belly quivered.

His fingertips stroked up and down along the taut curve
of her throat. His lips didn't quite withdraw but brushed
hers lightly, back and forth, and even though she could
have taken that breath now, she didn't. So enthralled was
she with the smooth, silky firmness of him that she forgot
she needed air, forgot she couldn't see. Light enveloped
her, lovely and golden.

"I suppose," she whispered, searching for him in the
light, "you did that to shut me up...."

He didn't answer, not with words. His mouth came
closer. She felt its warmth, and her own softened in a smile.
Her breath bathed his lips. They parted. So did hers, just
as they touched.

"But I'm not..."

"Hush up." His mouth bore down on hers, increasing
its pressure with exquisite slowness while his hand cradled
the sensitive underside of her chin and tenderly and almost
unnoticed, lifted and turned it toward him. His tongue coming inside her mouth seemed only a natural progression of
that growing pressure...a completion, not an intrusion.

Her body grew hot...her skin stung with a thousand tiny
points of heat. Melting inside, trembling, she felt her neck
muscles dissolve and her head slowly sink into the nest that
seemed specially made for it in the hollow of his shoulder.
Weak as a newborn, she almost sobbed when she felt the
warm strength of his body...his arms...fold around her,
trapping her arms against her sides. *Helpless.*

She'd never felt so weak...so helpless. And she never
wanted it to end.

Chapter 12

When he felt her begin to lose control, his instincts responded to the surrender with a surge of primitive masculine triumph. But then…she trembled. And it hit him. What he wanted from her wasn't surrender. And he didn't want her to *lose* anything, either.

Bleakly he realized he'd been feeding himself a lie all along, telling himself he only wanted to help her, to *give* her something, those things that had been taken away from her—her life, her eyesight, her sense of safety. And he did; sure he did. Only, with this terrifying revelation, he understood finally that what he really wanted to give her, in his deepest darkest secret soul, was *himself*.

And even that wasn't ever going to be enough for him, because what he wanted just as much was for her to give him something back. Give him, in fact, the very things she didn't want—and was bound and determined *not*—to give. And do it willingly, joyfully, unreservedly.

He wanted her to want him. In spite of what his mother had told him, he wanted her to, yes, *need* him—at least now and then. He wanted her to give him her burdens and let him help with the load. He didn't just want to give her back her life, he wanted her to share it with *him*.

What he wanted was for her to love him.

For long, fierce moments he fought to deny it; the primitive male part of him, confident he had a victory on his hands, battling with the reasoning human being that knew damn well if he took advantage of the woman lying soft and trembling in his arms, it wouldn't be any kind of victory at all. Acceptance of that fact came as a slow chilling in his blood, passion's heat congealing into shame as he pulled away from her and looked down into her upturned face. As always the sheer loveliness of it took his breath away. This time it left a chunk of pain behind.

What were you thinking? he bitterly asked himself as he watched her eyelids flutter open and saw the silvery light in them fade like a dying ember. *It wasn't impossible enough you expect her to forgive you, now you want her to love you besides? After what you did to her? What were you thinking?*

The sheer audacity of that leavened his spirits with irony, and on its yeasty bubble—temporary, he knew—it was possible for him to ease her upright and shift himself away from her. Not far, just enough to free him—temporarily—from the Siren spell of her sweet woman's scent and warm, pulsating body. Enough to allow him to say, with some degree of masculine stoicism and authority, "You're hurt. I'd best get you home."

Caitlyn calmly nodded. She was in shock, she supposed. Shivering and cold inside, her mind a blank, barricaded against thoughts too devastating and emotions too confusing to cope with. She felt something thrust into her hands— her shoe, with the sock stuffed inside. She clutched it to her chest as C.J.'s hands came under her elbows.

"Easy now," he murmured as he lifted her. "Just keep

your weight off that foot.... Now, put your hands on my shoulders. I'm gonna lift you up onto the bank.''

And her heart thundered and she felt her cheeks flame as he came around in front of her. *Oh, God, what must I look like? Can he see it in my face, what he's done to me?* Her hands stung where they touched his shoulders. Her stomach flip-flopped when she felt his hands on her waist. His muscles surged beneath her fingers, and her lungs gave up an involuntary gasp as he lifted her. Then she was sitting on the top of the embankment with her feet dangling over the side. Her stomach righted itself, her lungs pulled in air and her mind cleared. And she knew that she was angry.

Angry. And battered, bruised and thoroughly humiliated. She felt, in fact, very much the way she had when Tyler Webb took her virginity in the back of his father's station wagon. Not in body; what C.J. Starr had taken was something she didn't have a name for and hadn't even known she possessed. *Emotional virginity. Is there such a thing?* What was more infuriating—and confusing—was the fact that she didn't know how he'd managed to do it. She only knew he had.

She held herself rigid, seething inside, as he lifted her once more to her feet. Clutching her shoe and hopping a little to balance herself, she said coldly, ''I can walk, if you'll just give me something—''

He muttered, ''Don't be stupid,'' and swept her up and into his arms, not gently. She heard him exhale sharply through his nose as he began to carry her through the woods, striding heavily, feet crackling in the litter of leaves and twigs.

''It'd help,'' he said after a while, in a voice that seemed to come from between clenched teeth, ''if you'd quit bein' so stiff. Relax a little—maybe even put your arms around my neck?''

''Oh...certainly.'' With an exaggerated flourish, she lifted her arm, the one not holding her shoe, and draped it across his shoulders. "Is this better?" she inquired politely, trying so hard not to let him hear the breathlessness. Though she didn't want it to, her hand had already strayed to the smooth, warm column of his neck, damp with sweat and taut with strain.

He grunted and hefted her, settling her closer against him. And she could feel two hearts hammering against her ribs, one from outside, one from within. She couldn't tell which was beating harder…faster. What's my excuse? she thought. He's the one doing all the work.

"It's a long way home," she said tartly. "You're going to give yourself a heart attack."

"Wish you'd quit worryin' about my health," he snapped back, not breathing hard at all. "There's easier ways to carry you, you know. Would you rather I throw you over my shoulder, like the firemen do?"

The image that called to mind compelled Caitlyn to mutter, "Not especially, no."

But her anger had begun to erode, leaving exposed the hurt she'd tried to bury beneath it. Yes, she was *hurt*. Bewildered. Why would he do such a thing—kiss her like that—and then behave as though he'd done something shameful or, worse, as if he'd done nothing at all?

The why of it tormented her like an itchy place she couldn't reach to scratch, until even the humiliation of asking didn't seem as bad as wondering. Heart pounding, nerves vibrating, she pushed the words out of herself as she'd once forced herself to jump off the high diving board, with the exercise of sheer willpower. "Tell me—" and her voice was brittle, a little too loud and artificially light "—do you always make a habit of kissing women, just out of the blue? Whenever it suits you? On a whim?"

"Just the pretty ones," C.J. said without missing a beat.

Which was a conversation stopper if ever she'd heard one.

As she gulped back the scathing retort she'd planned,

she felt shaky still, but now with a strange new excitement. And secret, shameful pleasure. *He thinks I'm pretty?*

It occurred to her that it must be a beautiful day—one of those utterly gorgeous autumn days when the sky is a brilliant, aching blue, and the breeze smells of just-cut hay, and the sun feels good on your skin. Where it touched the back of C.J.'s neck his skin felt hot and velvety, with deep solid muscle running underneath. She discovered that, without her ordering it, her fingers had begun to stroke it like the sunbaked hide of a healthy animal.

Her own skin felt hot, too, wherever he touched it: his arms across her back and under her thighs, his belly against her hip, his chest pressed to her side. She felt his muscles flexing, nerves vibrating, blood pumping through his veins. Wrestling with a powerful urge to smile, she drew in a breath and let it out in careful bits, like a miser doling out pennies, and lifted her face to the warmth.

Light stabbed her; it was as if she'd come from total darkness to look straight into the sun. She gave a cry, jerked reflexively and hid her face against C.J.'s chest.

Her cry of pain struck deep into C.J.'s heart, broke through into virgin strata where nothing had ever touched him before. Tenderness, and other emotions he couldn't name from wellsprings he hadn't known he possessed, came bubbling up through all the layers of ego and protective bravado and shook the very foundations of his masculine soul. His voice quivered with it when he mumbled, "Almost there. Hang in there, darlin'...." And he found that his lips were pressed against her hair.

Furious with himself—and, irrationally, with her—he thought, How could I have been so stupid? How could I not have known I'd fall in love with her? It seemed so obvious to him now, he wondered if everyone had seen it but him, and he felt foolish, like one of those embarrassing moments where everybody jumps out from behind the furniture and yells, "Surprise!"

Bubba and Blondie came bounding out to meet him when he turned into the yard, Bubba panting and grinning as if to say, "What took you guys so long?" and Blondie jumping up and down in giddy delight and trying her best to slobber all over Caitlyn's face, evidently thinking this was some cool new game, or maybe that Caitlyn was a pet he'd brought home for her to play with.

"*Down,* dummy," he snarled, secretly glad to have something on which to vent his chagrin. Caitlyn was quaking in his arms, her face damp against his chest. And he could feel his arms beginning to quiver; his whole body seemed to be going weak with the need to hold her…comfort her. Growling and swearing, he danced his way through the canine welcoming committee, and on will alone, surged up the steps and across the front porch.

There was a suspenseful moment while he balanced Caitlyn on his knee, wrestled open the screen and then pirouetted himself and her through both doors. There in the cool, quiet dimness of the front hallway, he paused to catch his breath.

"You can put me down now," she said. Her voice, muffled in his sweat-damp shirt, sounded quavery and indistinct.

"Uh-uh." Grim-jawed, he eyed the staircase. She was right; he was going to give himself a heart attack. "Almost there," he muttered, gathering himself for the final assault.

How, he didn't quite know, but somehow he made it to the top of the stairs and was quick-stepping down the hallway. The door to the room that had once been his was open. He swept triumphantly through it. His heart filled his throat, his legs shook and his arms felt like lead, but he managed to cross the room and deposit his burden, with a grunt of effort, on the pink bedspread decorated with little yellow butterflies.

And it was only then that he discovered she was laughing.

For a while he couldn't say anything, which was probably just as well; his thoughts and emotions weren't up to forming coherent phrases. Surprise, chagrin, bewilderment, relief, enchantment—those were only the ones he could put a name to.

He was glad she wasn't crying, glad she didn't seem to be in pain. He didn't know what could be the cause of her mirth, but watching her, he decided he didn't care what was causing it, because he'd never laid eyes on anything that gave him more joy. He realized he'd never seen her laugh, hadn't had any reason to think he would for a long, long time to come, not like this.

She lay on her back with one arm covering her eyes and the other clutching her stomach as she writhed in paroxysms of mirth that did rather resemble pain. Ah, but her laughter... It was a contagious cackle; it was howls and peals of pure delight, uninhibited as a child's.

It came to him from out of all his confusion that what he wanted more than anything in the world was to share it with her. To collapse beside her on that frothy pink bed and roll and howl and snuffle with her until, with arms around each other and bellies aching and tears flowing, the laughter began to die and become gradually...with little hiccuping, settling sighs...the beginning of something else...a discovering...a different kind of intimacy...a different kind of sharing.

Why didn't he? He didn't believe he had the right. Maybe someday he would, but not now...not yet. There were things he had to do first. Things he had to put right.

"I'm glad you think it's funny," he said mildly, when he had his breath back.

Oh, Caitlyn thought, if only I could tell you! *Oh, C.J., I'm going to see again!*

There was so much joy inside her—too much to be contained, so much that she'd had to let it out somehow or explode. But more than anything in the world, she wanted to share the joy with someone— *No,* with *him!* Just him.

But she couldn't—not yet. There was something she had to do. Now that her vision was coming back she knew the time had come...time to set the trap for Vasily. In spite of Jake's reservations, Caitlyn knew she was the only one who could lure that evil man into the open. She was also sure that C.J., with his overdeveloped sense of responsibility, would try to keep her from doing it.

No, she couldn't let him know her eyesight was return-ing, but that didn't mean she wanted him to go right this minute. Her happiness was like effervescence inside her— she felt buoyant, infused with sparkling bubbles of energy, like champagne. She wanted to share her laughter and her joy with him, even if she couldn't tell him the reason for it. She wanted him to lie down with her and hold her in his arms and laugh with her and little by little merge his laughter with hers until it stopped being laughter and be-came...something else entirely. A different kind of sharing. The deepest, most perfect kind of sharing.

She wanted him to make love to her.

"I'm sorry." Her laughter, already dying, came fitfully now. From behind the shield of the arm covering her eyes—she must not let him see their response to the light— she murmured, "I'm not laughing at you—really I'm not. It must be just...some kind of reaction." *That* much, at least, was true. "You have to admit, the whole thing was pretty ridiculous, me going off in a-an emotional huff, turn-ing my ankle and falling into a creek—"

"Ridiculous isn't what I'd call it," C.J. said in a distant and disgruntled tone. "*Stupid* is more like it. No tellin' what coulda happened to you out there. What did you think you were doing, anyway?"

What *had* she been thinking? It was hard, now, to re-member the depths of her grief just a few short hours ago. It had been such a roller-coaster day.

She heaved a sigh and sat up. This wasn't going the way she wanted it to. She wiped her face with her hands, then left them to cover her eyes while she tried to think what to say next, wondered what she could say or do to make him know how much she wanted him to come closer. It wouldn't have been easy for her under the best of circumstances; she'd spent most of her life discouraging men's attentions and she didn't know how to seduce.

If I could just look at him. If only I could see his face. She'd never realized before what a vital tool eyes were in the art of seduction. Without them she was hopelessly handicapped. How could she speak to him with her eyes or read the response in his? How was it possible to flirt without fluttering lashes and come-hither looks? What about all those references to eyes in language and literature, poetry and song? Like: "Drink to me only with thine eyes and I will pledge with mine."

Overfilled with emotions she couldn't express, she smiled and shook her head in wordless apology. "What happened to my wildflowers?" she asked through her spread fingers.

He made a breathy sound she couldn't interpret, the kind that went with a gesture she couldn't see. "I think they're on the porch. They were looking pretty sad. Wildflowers don't hold up all that well after you pick 'em, you know."

"Well," she said, lowering her hands to her drawn-up knee and tilting her face away from him, "I guess I'll have to pick some more." She closed her eyes and remembered the feel of his body behind her...of his arms stretched alongside hers...the sun's heat and the dusty smell of pollen. The smell of *him.* The room around her seemed to fill with his clean, masculine essence.

"Yeah, I guess you will." His voice was low and growly. She felt the mattress sag with his weight, and her heart soared. "How's your ankle?"

She braced her hands behind her and clutched at the

bedspread for support as he lifted her ankle into his lap. "Stiff." She couldn't feel her lips move. Her heart hammered; she trembled inside. *I wonder,* she thought, *if he can feel it, all the way down* there.

She hadn't known how much she wanted him to touch her. Touch her other places. Everywhere. Her skin broke out in shivery prickles in anticipation of his touch. And her mind called up all the touch memories of him stored in its meager archives to compensate her for the touch she knew in her heart was not going to happen. At least...not today. Would it ever?

The surprising wiry strength of his body pressing down on hers as she lay across the center console of his truck. The unexpected silkiness of the hair on his forearms, folded in implacable barrier against her pleas.

Those same strong arms across her back and under her thighs, carrying her, and his chest and hard, masculine belly against her side. The steady thump of his heartbeat just out of step with hers.

The brush of his silky-soft hair and beard-prickly cheek against hers as he picked her up after the dogs had knocked her on her fanny. Her hand nested in the crook of his elbow.

The cold, hard press of his lips stunning hers to silence. His arm holding her tightly against him as they walked together, bodies chilled and wet on the outside, furnace-hot underneath.

The unexpected gentleness of his hands as they cradled her injured foot, and then...and then. The terrible tenderness...the devastating sensuality, the deliberate eroticism of that kiss.

She couldn't help it; she shuddered.

"Still hurtin' you, I guess," C.J. said in a strangled voice as he shifted her foot off of his lap. Caitlyn held her breath, and the bed creaked a small protest as he left it. "I'm gonna go get some ice to put on that."

She heard his footsteps cross the room and the door whisper open...then softly close.

Alone, she turned toward the window, took a deep breath...and fearfully opened her eyes. The breath left her body in a long, shivering sigh. Yes—it was still there. The miracle. A window-shaped rectangle of light in her darkness.

C.J. was standing in front of the open refrigerator door when his mother came back from church. He had a plastic zipper bag of ice cubes in his hand and was regarding it sourly, trying to decide which part of his anatomy was in need of it most.

"You trying to cool off the whole house?" his mother asked, as she had no doubt asked each of her children, countless times before.

He closed the door and turned to her, hefting the ice bag in his hand. "This is for Caitlyn. She turned her ankle."

His mother's brows rose. "Oh? How did that happen?"

"Stepped in a hole. Out in Parker's woods."

"Out in the—" She set her pocketbook down on the table with a thump. "You didn't let her go there alone, did you? Calvin—"

"Momma, it's not like it was my—"

"Calvin James, don't you make excuses to me. You were sitting on the front porch nursing your pride, is what you were doing. You *know* you had no business letting her run off, not with those evil men still out there looking for her."

"I know," C.J. said with a gusty sigh. He juggled the ice bag from one hand to the other as he added dryly, "For what it's worth, I think she's learned her lesson. I don't believe she's going to be doing that again anytime soon."

"Well, I should hope not," said his mother. And with a nod toward the ice bag in his hand, "You planning to take that up to her before it melts?"

"I was sort of hoping you'd do it, since you're here,"

he muttered, and added in a darkening tone, "I think she's had 'bout enough of me for a while."

"What, have you two been quarreling?"

C.J. shot a fired-up look at his mother before he realized she was teasing him. He swallowed his retort with a gulp and said, "Naw, it's nothing like that, I just think I'm gettin' on her nerves, is all. She's doing so well by herself, you know, it's not like she needs me baby-sittin' her all the time."

"Well now, that's true."

"That's why I was thinking…" He set the ice bag down on the countertop and looked at it for a moment, then turned around and leaned his spine on the edge of the counter and folded his arms over the pulse that was tapping away in his belly. Trying to look casual about what seemed to him the momentous announcement he was about to make. "I was thinking, if you and Jess are gonna be around the next few days, I might call up Jimmy Joe and see if he's got a load for me."

"Well," said his mother, picking up her pocketbook and the bag of ice, "I think you should."

"I can't sit around and do nothing forever," he argued, trailing after her into the hallway. "I've got bills to pay."

"Son, you are absolutely right," his mother said cheerfully as she started up the stairs. "After all, as you said, Caitlyn's a grown woman, she doesn't need a baby-sitter, and you're a grown man with responsibilities, you *should* get back to work. Go right on—and don't you worry about Miss Caty. Jessie and I'll look after her. She'll be just fine."

"Well…okay, then," C.J. breathed to his mother's back as she reached the top of the stairs and disappeared from sight.

He hesitated, then shook his head and turned around and walked back into the kitchen where he spent another minute or two frowning at the place on the countertop where the ice bag had been. He had the disoriented, slightly foolish feeling he remembered getting when he'd swung with everything he had at a pitch and missed it by a mile. He knew he must have missed *something* by a mile; he just didn't have any idea what it was.

Since the answer didn't appear to be jumping up at him from out of the Formica, he muttered, "Okay then," under his breath and wandered on outside.

It's the best thing, he told himself, shifting his shoulders and trying to make himself believe he was happy with the decision he'd made. After today's revelations it was going to be pure hell being around Caitlyn and constantly having to remind himself he wasn't the kind of man to take advantage of a woman in her state of vulnerability. At least, he hoped he wasn't. When he thought about kissing her back there in the woods, and realizing how long he'd been wanting to do that, and that he wanted to keep on doing it for a long time to come, and everything else that just naturally came after it, he broke out in chills and his stomach turned upside down. He hadn't brought her here for that...had he?

No, dammit.

Angrily he checked his wristwatch and broke into a run. But he discovered that his legs were weak and his heart rate was already way up there, and after a couple hundred yards he stopped and walked home instead.

"Caty, honey, Jake wants to know if you're sure you're ready to do this. Are you sure it's not too soon?" Eve's voice on the telephone was full of concern.

In the alcove between the kitchen and dining room where Betty Starr kept her household business clutter—and the household's only telephone—Caitlyn hitched the chair closer to the desk and said with determined brightness, "I'm okay, really. The headaches are much better. I'm feeling really strong."

She wasn't; she'd never felt more fragile. She, who'd always been so confident, so self-assured, now couldn't trust her own feelings...her own judgment. Ground she'd thought solid under her feet had shifted. She'd never experienced an earthquake, but she thought she now understood why they made people panic and animals stampede.

"The swelling's almost gone. I look fairly normal—so they tell me. I can't see any kind of detail yet, just light and dark shapes...silhouettes, sort of. It just started today, after all. But the doctors told me once it started to come back it might happen pretty quickly. That's why I thought—"

"Caitlyn, that's such incredible news," Eve breathed. "You must be six feet off the floor. I'm so happy for you—Jake is, too. And I'll bet C.J.'s about the happiest man in Georgia."

Caitlyn planted an elbow amidst the litter of grocery lists and junk mail, receipts, bills and correspondence that covered the desktop and rested her forehead in her hand. The house was empty—Jess working late and Betty gone to a Sunday evening potluck supper at her church—and its quietness seemed a growing pressure in her ears. Like the way it feels to dive into the deep end of the pool, she thought. *And that's what I'm doing—going off the deep end.*

But it was too late to turn back now; she'd made her decision for better or worse. Tomorrow Eve would put the first part of the FBI's plan in motion. In two or three days it should all be over. For better or worse.

"He doesn't know," she mumbled, carefully massaging the tender places around healing scar tissue. "I haven't told him." Eyes closed, she waited out the shocked silence on the other end of the line.

Finally, in the careful tone of voice usually employed with the mentally deranged, Eve inquired, "Why in the world not? You know he's taken what happened to you awfully personally—"

She let out an exasperated breath. "Eve, that's why I can't tell him. He has this idea that he's responsible for everything that's happened—for Mary Kelly getting killed, for me being blind—even though I've told him and told him he's not. And I know—I *know*—that if he knew what I'm planning to do, he'd do everything in his power to keep me…" She stopped, her voice choked with helpless fury and other emotions less easy to name.

"Maybe he's right," Eve said softly. "I know Jake's not all that comfortable with it, either. There are other ways—"

"No. There aren't. I know Vasily—you don't. He's not stupid, he's not going to be lured into the open by a decoy. It has to be me. And look—the plan has all sorts of safeguards, they're not going to let anything happen to me. *Don't worry.*"

"I'm not worried," Eve said with an unconvincing huff of breath. "Okay, then. So, I'll pick you up tomorrow for the interview. What time?"

"Late morning should be fine. Jess'll be at work and Betty drives on Monday for seniors' meals, so there won't be anybody around to make a fuss."

"And C.J.? How are you going to keep him in the dark?"

"It's okay, I don't think that'll be a problem." With an effort Caitlyn kept her voice neutral, her emotions ruthlessly suppressed. "He probably won't even be here. I heard him tell his mom he's going back to work. He should be off on a long haul with his truck by then, but if he's not…"

"If he's not," said Eve, "you'll let me know and we'll go to plan B. All right, then—if I don't hear from you otherwise, I guess I'll see you tomorrow morning."

"Right," said Caitlyn.

She said her goodbyes and cradled the phone, then sat for a moment while tremors rippled through her stomach. Butterflies, she thought. Nervous anticipation.

She nudged back the chair, rose and pushed through the swinging door to the kitchen. There she halted while the door whapped back and forth behind her in time with her thumping heart.

The kitchen was awash with light. She was certain she hadn't turned any on—why would she? She was blind.

Silhouetted against the light, someone was sitting at the kitchen table, holding something—a newspaper. She could hear it rustling. The Sunday paper, of course.

She stood frozen to the spot. *Oh, God—C.J.!*

There was barely time for her to register that thought before it came to her—the hospital smell, faint, unmistakable. Relief made her knees buckle. She put out a hand to steady herself. "Jess? Is that you?"

"Yeah." The newspaper rustled; the silhouette turned to face her.

She felt out of breath, as if she'd been running. "I didn't hear you come in. How…how long have you been here?"

"Long enough," Jess said.

Chapter 13

Caitlyn moved toward the table on feet she couldn't feel. Her groping hands found the back of a chair, but she didn't sit down. Magically, her butterflies were gone. She felt instead a strange icy calm. "How much did you hear?"

"Enough to know your eyesight's come back," Jess said quietly. "That's great. I'm as happy as I can be for you."

"Thanks—"

"And that you're about to do something that'd be dangerous for a professional law enforcement person with perfect vision."

"It's…something I have to do," Caitlyn muttered, staring fixedly at the pale-gray shapes that were her hands.

"Yeah," Jess said in a voice that cracked, "that's what my husband said when he went off to Iraq. Tell me something—were you going to tell any of us? Momma and me? Or were you just going to sneak off with Eve tomorrow and leave us sitting here in the dark? So to speak."

Caitlyn gripped the back of the chair and leaned her weight on her hands. Her face felt hot…swollen, and she

had to swallow twice before she could answer. "I don't
know. Please don't think— It's not because of you. I
just…I can't let C.J. find out. He'd have a fit. He hovers
over me like a…like a mother hen with one chick, as my
Aunt Lucy would say. He acts as if I'm completely helpless…as if he's afraid I'll break. He's never—"

"Well, of course he does," Jess interrupted in exasperation. "He's in love with you!"

"—going to let me… What?" The last word came out
in a wheeze, much as if someone had punched her in the
stomach.

Slowly, patiently, Jess repeated it. "C.J.'s in *love* with
you. Don't tell me you didn't know!"

Caitlyn gave her head one quick, dazed shake. She was
feeling earthquakes again. As the ground shifted beneath
her feet, she pulled the chair out and lowered herself into
it.

"You *have* been blind, haven't you?" Jess said in a
kindly way. "The rest of us knew from day one." Her tone
betrayed a smile. "Right from when he insisted on carryin'
you up those stairs in true Rhett Butler style."

"Rhett…Butler?" Caitlyn whispered, still disbelieving.
"I thought he just felt guilty. Like…I'm this huge responsibility, because he blames himself for what happened."

"He may very well," Jess said, nodding, "but believe
me, I know my baby brother, and if he feels he's responsible for you, it's not because of guilt. It's because as far
as he's concerned, you are *his,* honey chil', and he is not
about to let any harm come to you, not if he can help it."

Caitlyn put both hands over her eyes, but it couldn't stop
what was happening. To her dismay, she had begun to cry.
She wept in total silence while images played across the
blank screen of her mind: Ari Vasily's cold black eyes
watching her from his seat in the courtroom the way a
snake watches a mouse, sensuous lips curved in a cruel
smile; Mary Kelly's sweet face and sad, gentle look; the

scars and bruises on her body; Emma's frightened eyes; the blue September sky over the courthouse steps; dreams of people she loved lying dead in pools of blood.

Other things, too…not images, but sensory impressions even more profound: C.J.'s warmth and arms closing around her; his smell, that unique amalgam of soap and clean clothes, diesel fuel and a familiar aftershave she didn't know the name of; his deep-throated voice, growly in her ear; *I've got you…*

She drew a quivering sniff and wiped her cheeks with her hands. "Oh, dear," she said, and this time her voice was soft and purposeful. She cleared her throat and pushed back from the table. "Jess—what time is it?" Wired with a terrible sense of urgency, she didn't wait for a reply. "Would he be home…do you think? Right now?"

"He was when I drove by. His pickup was in the driveway and the lights were on." Jess had risen as well. "Why? You want me to call him for you?"

"No—" vaguely Caitlyn shook her head "—not on the phone. I…I have to tell him something. Have to see him. Before—" *Before I go. If something goes wrong, if Vasily kills me, I'll never get to tell him. He'll never know. I'll never know.…*

She didn't say any of that, but strangely, Jess seemed to understand. She touched Caitlyn's arm and said gently, "You want me to take you over there?"

"Oh—" relief trembled through her, almost like a sob "—would you? Please."

"Sure. Just let me get my keys." Counting heartbeats, Caitlyn listened to the scuffling, jingling noises Jess made, rummaging through her purse. "Okay. You ready?" she asked, and Caitlyn nodded, too choked with fear to speak.

"Are you sure you don't need a jacket?" Jess asked her as they were going down the steps. Caitlyn shook her head; it wasn't cold that made her shiver.

The one-mile trip to C.J.'s house seemed to take for-

ever—and was much too short. Bewildered, Caitlyn hud-
dled like a sick sparrow on the front seat with her hands
tucked between her knees to stop the shaking and thought
about all the reasons she shouldn't be doing what she was
doing. *What if he's not there? What if I'm too late? What
if Jess is wrong? What if I'm making a terrible, colossal
fool of myself?*

She didn't understand it. She'd never felt so uncertain in
all her life, or so scared. *She,* who'd faced wife beaters and
child abusers twice her size, violent men, often armed, with
everything from guns to broken beer bottles and most of
the time drunk besides. How was it that she should be more
afraid of a man with only goodness in his soul, kindness
in his heart and gentleness in his hands?

Could be, a voice inside her replied, *there's never been
so much at stake before. Could be that you're afraid to
hope....*

"Look's like he's home," Jess said. "His pickup's
here." Tires crunched as she turned onto a graveled driveway. "Want me to come in with you? Need any help finding the door?"

Caitlyn shook her head; she could make out the light-
colored door and the steps against the darker building. "As
long as the lights don't go out before I get there, I should
be okay," she said with a wan attempt at humor, taking
determined hold of the door handle. "Any obstacles on that
grass I'm not seeing?"

"Not a thing. You're clear all the way. I'll wait till
you're inside, though, just to be sure."

Caitlyn nodded and slipped out of the car. Her heart
knocked against her rib cage as she started across the gentle
grass-covered slope, Jess's car engine idling softly behind
her. And maybe it was the crisp autumn feel of the air, or
something about the way it smelled—of hay and drying
cornstalks, of burning leaves and pumpkins ripening on the
vine—that   took   her   suddenly   back   to   another

time…another place…another Caitlyn. A Caitlyn just as apprehensive and uncertain as this one. A very small Caitlyn, picking her way across a leaf-strewn lawn while her daddy's car idled at the curb, holding the flapping pieces of her Halloween costume together and gathering up the courage to knock on an unfamiliar neighbor's door.

The memory and the cool October breeze lifted her spirits. Dizzy with nervous excitement, she mounted concrete steps and felt her way across a small front porch. Unable to find a doorbell, she raised her hand and knocked. The sound seemed frail and timid against the heavy wooden door. Would he even hear it? She waited, rocking gently with her own heartbeat, like a boat tied up at a quay.

Her throat closed when she heard the doorknob rattle. A rectangle of light appeared, and in it a shape that seemed already familiar to her—though how could that be? She heard a shocked, "Caitlyn. Oh, my God…"

"I've lost track of what week it is," she said in a droll but unsteady voice as somewhere behind her Jess's car whined in reverse down the driveway and purred away into the night. "Am I too early for 'trick-or-treat'?"

He was losing his mind. It couldn't be Caitlyn standing in his doorway, like the answer to some adolescent dream.

At first he could only stare at her, tongue-tied as an adolescent would have been, beholding the object of his fevered imaginings. Then he saw her eyes, misty and lost above the stretched mask of her smile, and he forgot everything in the fervency of his desire to fold her into his arms. Not knowing what it was that had brought her to his doorstep, he restrained the impulse and, heart flapping furiously against his rib cage, waved his pancake turner at her instead.

"I was just— Here…come in, for Pete's sake. How'd you get here? Was that Jess? Why didn't she…" He took her arm and cast a quick look over her shoulder at his empty front yard as he drew her into the entryway.

He didn't know what to do with her. What to say to her. He'd never, except perhaps in his dreams, imagined her *here.* "Uh, look, I was just...I'm making myself grilled cheese. You want one?" Her eyes had been aimed past him toward the living room, separated from the entryway by a half wall partition. "I make a pretty fair grilled cheese," he added, attempting a smile as her gaze, vague and bewildered, swiveled slowly toward him.

"Thank you. That would be nice." She sounded like a well-brought-up child.

C.J.'s heart was about to choke him. Juggling the pancake turner, he did an awkward little do-si-do to switch sides with her so he could usher her down the hallway to the kitchen, and everywhere her body brushed his felt like he'd been lit on fire.

"You have a nice house," Caitlyn said, tilting her head as though she was listening to voices.

He glanced down at her, curious. "How can you tell?"

She lifted the hand she'd been trailing along the wall. "You have wallpaper," she explained, smiling crookedly. "And hardwood floors." There was a patch of color in each cheek.

"Huh," said C.J. "I guess it is...nice, I mean. Not mine, though. I'm just renting the place—people that own it are getting up there, so they bought a place in town. He used to be a friend of my daddy's, actually, and his wife's Momma's cousin, second or third once removed—something like that—so I get a pretty good deal. No sense in buying a house, not until I pass my bar exams and figure out where I want to hang out my shingle, right?" He realized he was babbling and made an effort to stop.

"Where *do* you want to hang out your shingle?" she asked in a breathless voice, half polite and half distracted. "Atlanta?"

He gave a dry huff of laughter. "Not if I can help it." He guided her to the small maple table shoved under the window that overlooked the backyard and pulled out a chair. She lowered herself into it and he turned back to the stove. "No," he said, squinting as he relit the burner he'd shut off to go and answer the knock on the door, "the way I see it, people who live in small towns need lawyers, too."

"So, that's what you want? To live in a small town?"

"Live, practice law, raise a family…I don't expect I'll get rich, that's for sure," he said, aiming an ironic smile at the slice of butter he'd just dropped, sizzling, into the frying pan. "I guess," he said after a moment, "what I'm lookin' to be is the lawyer equivalent of a small-town family doctor. Know what I mean?" He said it casually, but having laid out his future as a kind of offering to her, the way he felt was *exposed*. As if he was standing on the edge of a cliff with a cold wind blowing against his back.

He waited an interminable time for her to answer, and when she didn't, briskly clapped his hands, rubbed them together and announced, with thumping heart, "There…that's comin' along good. Now, how 'bout some soup with that? What kind of soup goes good with grilled cheese?" He opened a cupboard door. "Let's see…we got—"

"Tomato," Caitlyn said. "Tomato soup goes with grilled cheese."

"Tomato it is." He plucked a can from the shelf, closed the door, opened a drawer and took out a can opener. Closed the drawer. Opened the can. Opened another cupboard and took out a pot. Closed the cupboard door.

And on and on, doing the normally routine things required to heat up a can of soup, something he'd done a few thousand times, probably, in his lifetime. Only, tonight he had to think about each step, recite them to himself as he checked them off, one by one. Why? Because it was impossible to concentrate, hard to even hear himself *think* above the voice inside his head screaming, *For God's sake, Caitlyn, why are you here?*

More than once it was on the tip of his tongue to ask her. Each time, he bit the words back, thinking they'd sound too blunt...even rude. Or maybe he didn't want to ask because he wasn't in any hurry to hear the answer to that question. Because he was so certain it wouldn't be the one he wanted.

What *did* he want? Not so very much, really, no more than any man wants. To have the woman he's chanced to fall in love with by some miracle love him back. To lay out his dream for the future in front of her and find that by some miracle it's her dream, too. Nothing special. Nothing out of the ordinary.

So why did it feel like he was hoping for the moon? His whole body prickled when he thought of the implications of her coming to his house, alone, in the evening like this. Prickled...why? With fear? Excitement? *Uncertainty?* Being a man, he feared feeling uncertain more than anything.

"My mother used to fix me this when I was a little girl," Caitlyn said. She was hunched over her bowl, spooning soup, and her voice sounded husky. "When I'd walk home from school on cold winter days...and my nose would be so cold I couldn't feel it...and she'd make grilled cheese sandwiches and Campbell's tomato soup. I had this special plate with a big matching cup, with the Campbell's Kids on them. I remember that little burn you get in the back of your throat. Tomato soup. It always does this—makes my eyes water and my nose drip."

She touched the back of her hand to her nose, then abruptly remembered the napkin she'd spread across her lap and snatched that up instead. She wiped her nose, then her eyes, then laid the napkin on the table and gazed at it helplessly. Her eyes were still streaming.

"Caitlyn?" C.J. said in a wondering tone.

"I'm sorry," she whispered, gulping softly. "I'm so sorry. I know you have to be wondering why I've barged in on you like this. You're just...too darn well brought up to *ask*—'' A hiccup interrupted her, and she put her fingertips to her lips and muttered, *''Damn.''*

''Caitlyn—'' He scraped back his chair and reached for her, but she had risen to her feet at the first sound and eluded him, pushing at him with a groping hand.

''No—don't. I wanted to tell you…something. You asked me a question and I…didn't answer. I don't know why I didn't—I wanted to tell you. I want you to know…I think you *should* know—''

''For God's sake, Cait…'' Quaking inside, he interrupted her hurried and gulping babble. ''Tell me *what?* Whatever it is—''

''You asked me why I can't stand needing help, and I…I think I said it was because I'm afraid of being weak…something like that? The truth is—'' she took a breath and let it out, while her cheeks turned rosy pink ''—I probably have some control issues.''

Control issues. He was thinking the phrase, like so many others commonly referred to as psychobabble, had become nothing but a clichéd excuse…meaningless crap. And then she went on.

''Because of something that happened to me…a long time ago. I've never told anybody. I was raped by my prom date the night of my senior prom. I felt so helpless. He was much bigger than I was…so much stronger. He wouldn't listen. There wasn't anything I could do to stop it. But I made up my mind I wasn't ever going to be that weak and powerless again. And I haven't been. Until now. And that's why…it's hard.''

C.J. stood absolutely still while the last of her words went rumbling and echoing off into the distant reaches of his mind, like rocks falling into a canyon. He couldn't seem to feel anything, not even his own body. And he didn't notice the lengthening silence until he heard a tight and airless whisper.

''Say something, damn you.''

He couldn't, not yet, but the thought of what the silence must feel like to her after such revelations tore at his heart. He took a step and folded her into his arms. The air and the tension seemed to flow out of her as she melted against him, and he cradled the back of her head in his hand and tucked it tenderly under his chin. Eyes closing, throat aching, he nestled his face in the sweet-smelling softness of her hair and held her like that, rocking slightly. After a while, when he felt her arms come around him, it seemed to him the most incredible miracle.

"You're gonna have to forgive me," he said in a voice like sandpaper, muffled in her hair. "Apparently you don't know what it does to a man to hear something like that about the woman he—" He coughed and couldn't finish it.

"I didn't mean to shock you." She stirred a little, restive against him.

He drew her back in and enfolded her more completely. "It was a bit of a shock," he said, but didn't tell her the worst shock, for him, had been discovering in himself the powerful desire to kill someone. He hadn't known he was capable of such a thing. With the worrisome residuals of those primitive urges still percolating through him, he tilted Caitlyn's head back and stared down into her face. For a long moment her silver-glazed eyes seemed to gaze back at him, in a way that made his heart leap. And then her eyelids slowly closed.

"You do know," he said, husky and overfilled with emotions, "that I would never…that you don't ever have to worry… I mean, I would never, *ever* force you or even *ask* you—" He stumbled to a halt. Her lips had curved unexpectedly into a smile.

"I do know that," she said gently, and, standing on tiptoes, brushed his lips with hers. "C.J., you are the most honorable man I've ever met, besides my dad. You are, in fact, the very essence of Southern gentleman…hood. It's just that—" He would have been happy to contribute his part to that enticing mouth play, but she paused, rocked back on her heels and let out an exasperated breath. ''Dammit, C.J., sometimes a woman would like a little less Ashley Wilkes and a little more Rhett Butler.''

He frowned, his brain fuzzy with her nearness. ''Rhett Butler? Oh, yeah—that's *Gone with the Wind,* right?'' Dizzy from the scent of her, he mumbled, ''Sorry, never read the book, or saw the movie, either.''

Her hands lay on his chest, high up near the base of his throat, and her fingers were lightly stroking the place where his skin met the neck of his shirt. Her smile was slow, her voice a murmur. ''There's a scene—very famous—where Rhett scoops Scarlett—you do know who Scarlett O'Hara is?—anyway, he scoops her up in his arms and carries her up this great sweep of stairs to the bedroom. And...well...'' She paused, and he could feel his heartbeat tapping against her fingertips. His body—all of it—felt stretched and tight. His insides boiled sluggishly, like molten lava. ''The way I figure, you've had plenty of practice.''

''One problem—'' his lips were barely capable of movement ''—no stairs here.''

''Then that should make it easier, shouldn't it?''

Courage flooded through her. She felt lightened by it, buoyed up like a leaf in the wind. Catching her lower lip between her teeth to hold back laughter and excited breath, she stared intently at the indistinct blur where his smile would be, and then, impatient with her stubborn blindness, put her fingertips there and felt a shiver of happiness as it blossomed and grew beneath them. His lips were silky smooth, mobile and firm; her fingers tingled in the warm flow of his breath. And then, tilting his head slightly, he took them into his mouth, one by one. Desire fluttered in her belly. Her legs grew weak.

''I think,'' she whispered brokenly, ''you could do that Rhett Butler thing any time, now.''

His chuckle butted gently against her fingertips, and the

burgeoning confidence in it bolstered her own. When, with a sudden, fierce movement, he turned his head and pressed his mouth into her palm, she gasped aloud, then slowly drew her hand and his mouth down to hers. When his lips slid from her palm to her mouth, her awakening vision failed her. She saw golden showers and rainbows, and then her eyelids came down and there was only lavender darkness filled with sweet sensation…his silky-firm lips gently massaging the inside of hers…tingling darts of cold fire shooting from there straight into distant throbbing places.

His hand kneaded her back between her shoulder blades, gathering the fabric of her shirt so that the other, sweeping down her spine, met only naked skin where it dipped beneath the waistband of her jeans. His tongue, impatient with teasing, drove deep; her hand skidded along his jaw and her fingers pushed into his hair, wildly clutching. His hand, pressing hard on the lower part of her spine, brought her hips against his, and she remembered his lean, wiry strength and the taut and quivering muscles of his belly.

His hand slipped farther down, under her bottom, and with that same sudden, savage motion, like a movement in a passionate dance, a tango, perhaps, lifted her up and drew her legs around his hips, locking her to him. And through the supple fabric of his jeans and hers, she felt *him,* the very essence of him, and the essential feminine part of her body seemed to remember that, too, and giddily throbbed a welcome.

She felt a swaying, like the rocking of a boat, and knew that she was being carried. But there was something she wanted to say… Dizzy, she separated herself from the kiss, but before her swollen lips and passion-fogged mind could form words, C.J.'s voice came, raspy in her ear.

"Guess this probably isn't the way Rhett Butler did it.…"

Drunkenly she mumbled, "This is way better than

Rhett,'' but when she found his mouth again, for some reason she had begun to laugh.

And for some reason, so had he. Remembering how much she had wanted to laugh with him just this way, she clung to his shaking shoulders while he carried her to his bedroom, quivering and snickering and hiding spurting tears and breathless gusts in the warm hollow of his neck.

It's too much, she thought. Too much stimulation, too much emotion. She wondered if the laughter was a kind of safety valve, like the steam shooting out of a pressure cooker or the teakettle's whistle. Without it, maybe she would simply have to explode…fly apart in so many pieces, she would never find her way back together again.

"I've never been this way before," she told him, the words sticking to her swollen tongue. Her feet felt pins and needles where they touched the floor. Under her sweatshirt, where C.J.'s hands were stroking the sides of her waist, her skin was afire with goose bumps.

"This way…how?"

Excited…silly…scared…happy. She shrugged. Her hand lay under his shirt, fingers splayed across one hard, flat pectoral, gently kneading, greedily exploring. She felt his heart thumping against her palm, and deep in her belly, desire thumped a response. "I don't know—just…like this." *Wanting you…so much.*

He didn't say anything, not at first. Lowering his head until his forehead touched hers, he brought his hands from under her shirt and, warm and moist from her body, placed them on the sides of her neck. He moved them upward until they formed a basket for her head, and gently tipped it back, a little at a time, so that his lips touched her eyelids first…then her nose…and finally her mouth.

They barely touched her at first—lightly, delicately, like the brush of flower petals—caressing with feather strokes while she held herself in a rapt and breathless stillness. Then, as he had in the woods, increasing the pressure so slowly he seemed to become a part of her…come inside her and fill her so completely she couldn't imagine how it could ever end. And when it did end, she whimpered, as if a part of her had been wrested away.

"Neither have I…like this…" She felt his body tremble.

She understood, then, why he hadn't spoken after *her* declaration. Emotion filled her, a pool so vast it awed and overwhelmed her and left no room for words.

Her hands shook as she placed them on his sides and slowly, slowly lifted his shirt. Dazed, she thought how silky and fine his skin felt. She wanted it touching hers. Desire made her ache. Sick with it, she swayed forward and buried her face against his chest…her nose, first, then her mouth…her tongue. His skin smelled good, tasted good, felt good. It was smooth there, too; her exploring fingers found only a few hairs in the center of his chest and around his flat, hard nipples.

"You didn't turn the light on?" She wanted to, oh, how she wished she could *see* him.

"No." His hands were sliding upward along her back, raising her shirt with their slow, massaging progress. She lifted her arms and let him pull it over her head. Her chest rose and her breasts hardened as cool air sifted over her fevered skin.

"You can," she whispered. "I don't mind if you do."

"No," he said as he nested her breasts in his palms and gently kissed her, "it's not fair."

"Not…fair?"

"For me to see you when you can't see me."

Her breath caught; her heart stumbled. Mind and emotions reeled in hopeless disarray, caught up in the whirlwind created by the collision of those two opposing forces, joy and despair.

Because…in that moment she knew that she loved him, with all her heart and soul and mind and strength. And in that same moment knew that what she was about to do might cause her to lose him forever.

Chapter 14

Her cry, like that of a small, wounded animal, wrenched his heart. His tenderness for her was like a fine sweet down, softening the ruthless edges of his passion. His hands were gentle and certain; all sense of urgency and amazement fled.

"There are other ways to see," he murmured, smiling with his voice while his lips and fingertips traced smiles on her skin. "I can touch you...see you with my hands...."

At his first light touch her breasts felt small and virginal; his mind's eye saw them firm and perfect as a classic sculpture, ivory warmed with the delicate blush of desire. But...they filled his palms with unexpected voluptuousness, and his senses with sheer delight. By contrast, though slender enough to encircle with his hands, the muscles in her torso were taut and supple. And he remembered, with a little kick of excitement under his ribs, her unexpected strength.

She was "seeing" him, too; he could feel her hands skimming over his • ribs...his back. Everywhere they

touched they left a fever in his skin, as if he'd been too
long in the sun. His breathing grew choppy. His muscles
tensed and quivered. Enveloped in the glow of his love for
her, he could feel lust crouching like a tiger just beyond
the edges of the light. His ability to focus on his finer senses
was slipping away; the tiger's growl was louder, and he
needed all his concentration to keep it at bay.

He *had* to keep it at bay. He *had* to. Otherwise he might
not be able to hear her say no.

"Cait," he whispered. His hands were on her waist; he
slipped his fingers into the top of her jeans and felt her
belly quiver. "Caty, are you sure about this?"

"Yes...I'm sure." Her words gasped softly against the
base of his throat. Her fingertips were tucked into the waistband of *his* jeans, too, he realized then, and he groaned
when he felt them slide around to his back, warm on his
skin. "Are you?"

Laughing, groaning, he leaned to kiss her. Then drew
away with his hands still poised on the fastenings of her
jeans. "There's just one thing...."

"Yes?"

He didn't know how he managed to say the words. He
was hard...hurting for her, in a way he'd never hurt before,
his tongue glued to the roof of his mouth and his heart
pounding so it seemed a miracle he could even stand. But
he mumbled, "I didn't bring you here for this...."

And as he did the light came on. His conscience, shining
into the darkest reaches of his soul. And he knew it was
true, what he'd told himself and her. Because one thing he
knew—if he'd had seduction on his mind, he'd at least have
made damn sure he was ready for it.

At the moment, though, he didn't know whether to be
relieved that his motives were pure or ashamed for his un-
preparedness. Breath and nerves and heartbeat bumped
around inside him like birds in a cage as he kissed aside

her murmured assurances. "No—what I mean to say is, I don't know if I have anything. It's been a while…"

He felt her stillness…and deep inside, her shivering. After a moment she whispered, "Are you sure you don't—"

"No—I have to look. Just a sec…" It took only a little more than that, and he held his breath while he walked her the few steps to his dresser and opened the top drawer. While he rummaged blindly in the jumble of odds and ends and loosely folded underwear, he felt her hands on his back, felt her fingers drawing patterns up and down his spine. He laughed painfully. "You might not want to be doing that…just yet."

Her mouth was busy exploring his chest, kissing…laving…nibbling…tasting…but she murmured something indistinct and firmly shook her head.

Weak in the knees, his mind fogging, he wondered dazedly whether that meant she had confidence in him, or simply didn't care whether he had a condom or not. Which he couldn't see as being in keeping with her character; Caitlyn hadn't struck him as the reckless type. On the other hand, she was stubborn. He'd noticed that when she set her mind on doing something, she went ahead and did it, and didn't count the cost.

"Got one," he muttered, and his belly went hollow with relief as his fingers closed around the small foil packet.

I wonder, Caitlyn thought as tears of thankfulness squeezed between her eyelids, *what I would have done if he hadn't had one.…* Thank God she would never have to know.

Laughter woven with whimpers shook her body as she lifted her arms around his neck. He lowered his mouth over hers and she felt the button on her jeans give way. Denim scraped roughly over her hips, and his hands followed, a light but slightly catching caress, like satin. Where they touched, her skin sizzled and burned as if she'd passed through fire. Her heart thundered when she pulled away from his kiss; her breath staggered drunkenly while she wriggled the jeans down to her feet. Before she could step out of them, though, C.J. grasped her buttocks and pulled her hard against him, and her breath left her body in a gasp of utter shock…and purest joy.

Soaring, weightless, she threw her head back, and his mouth closed, hot and demanding, on her proffered throat. While he arched above her, his arms lifted her up and into him, and her legs parted and went around him as if they belonged *there,* just as they had before.

No—not as before. Now there was nothing between her and excruciating, overwhelming sensation—nothing at all. His hands stroked and molded the nerve-rich places on her buttocks and the back of her thighs. The hard ridge of his jeans abraded her swollen, tender places. Heat roiled in her belly and pulsed between her thighs. Darkness swirled around her like velvet.

She was sobbing when he laid her down. Frightened by that—she'd never made such sounds before—she writhed, bewildered and cold, until she felt his body stretch out alongside hers and his warmth flow over her like breath. She remembered the silkiness of his skin and wanted it touching her…all over. His mouth was hot and feverish on hers, but her breasts were cold, hard, aching. Her belly quivered. Her pulse pounded in places far distant from its source.

She reached for him, whimpering. His hands stroked, stinging, over her thighs, and moved them gently apart.

Prepared for his weight, wanting it so desperately, she knew a moment of surprise when she felt only the silky tickle of his hair instead. Briefly it feathered over her belly and thighs, like cool water on her parched skin…. Then his mouth touched her. Sensation drove through her like a shaft of steel.

She uttered a high, shocked cry. Her body bucked…arched…but his hands were firm and strong on her thighs and his mouth so incredibly, exquisitely gentle. Her body clenched—everything inside her seemed to buckle, collapse, fall apart like a house of cards. Great sobbing gasps tore through her chest, and as she reached for C.J.'s warm, comforting body in the darkness, she was whimpering incoherently, "Please…please…"

When she surfaced, she was lying on top of him, with her cheek on his sweat-damp chest and his heartbeat a muted drumming in her ear. Her body still throbbed and quivered, that terrible shaft of sensation only shards now…bright little stabs of pleasure-pain quietly twinging in far-off places.

She drew a long, shaken breath…and fury washed over her. Struggling to raise herself within the circle of his arms, she pounded on his chest with clenched fists. "Why did you— I wanted— You—"

His arms tightened around her. His chuckle gusted unevenly in her ear. "Easy…easy…"

"But I wanted—"

"You wanted…to be in control. Didn't you?"

Had she? Somehow, that seemed irrelevant to her now. She felt strangely bereft as she stared dumbly down at him in the darkness. Then she felt his hand curve around the back of her head. He drew her to him and kissed her deeply.

"I wanted that, too," he whispered. "And now you are. I'm all yours, sweetheart. Do with me what—"

She stopped him with her mouth, laughing, her nose bumping into his and her breasts brushing his chest, and he thought about how much he'd wanted to do just this—laugh with her in his arms. Now it seemed a gentle torment.

She lifted her head and made a happy, growling sound in her throat, then slowly, slowly eased her full weight onto him, bringing her knees up alongside his ribs and sliding her body over his in a lazy, all-over caress. She felt like the softest velvet…the lightest down.

He held himself still…except for his hands, which he

allowed to skim over her back from shoulders to buttocks, torturing himself some more. When they reached her bottom—he couldn't help it—they paused...asked...

But she denied him, chuckled softly and scooted backward, trailing kisses. He groaned, fearing what was coming. Her control was one thing; his was very much in doubt.

She must have known that, because after her lips had left kitten tracks across his abdomen, she moved quickly back astride him, nesting him excruciatingly in her damp feminine softness. He groaned again—he couldn't help it—and whispered, "Sweetheart—"

She leaned down to kiss him. "I want you, too...inside me. But I...don't know if I can...this way. It's been such a long time...."

And so, in the end, it was neither her control nor his, but a mutual joining...and not an easy one, nor painless—she was tight and he was hard. It had been a long time for him, too, but somehow the more satisfying for that.

As they laughed a little, dazed and giddy, he drew her down to him and raised his knees behind her to make of himself a cradle for her body, and holding her close, touching her everywhere he could, began to rock her, slowly at first, mindful of her tenderness.

His mind was full of her. Images of her, in all the ways he remembered: fairy princess, woodland sprite; pointing a gun at him; glaring silver-eyed from the back of a police car; lying bandaged and bruised in a hospital bed; sundusted and blind, picking wildflowers. But the memory that came to him most clearly—fierce and tender in his mind—was his own impression from way back then, almost at the beginning: *she's real*.

Yes...real. Her femininity warm and pulsating around him, her body strong and supple in his arms, her lips tender and soft under his...neither princess nor sprite, hijacker nor saint, just a woman—powerful, vulnerable...human.

And the codicil, lovely as a sonnet: *She's mine*.

The thought ignited in his mind, exploded and took off like a skyrocket…a shooting star. Soaring with it, he forgot to be tender and careful, slow and gentle. He forgot everything except how much he loved her, the joy and the certainty of that, and the miracle that she was here with him in his bed…warm, *real*…and that she'd come to him on her own. She'd come to *him*.

Dazed and enraptured, he opened wide his heart and mind, his body and soul, and returned the gift to her the only way he knew how.

C.J. Starr was a happy man as he babied his big blue Kenworth up the grade of the Blue Ridge Mountains, heading north. He had it all—clear weather, the road ahead dry and dusty, a sweet and powerful diesel engine humming along under him, reefer trailer loaded with North Carolina apples, and the woman he loved—the most beautiful woman he'd ever laid eyes on—waiting for him back home in Georgia. One day soon he'd take and pass that bar exam, find a nice little town somewhere in the South that could use another old-fashioned family-type lawyer, buy a big old house with a nice big staircase and plenty of bedrooms, and then he'd marry Caitlyn and they'd see about getting those bedrooms filled up with kids.

Kids. When he thought about kids, a face came into his mind, like a small shadow over his happiness: a thin, pale face with chin-length black hair with bangs cut straight across and great big black eyes—scared, hungry refugee eyes. Maybe, he thought, the first one of those kids could be adopted.

Yeah, he thought, smiling to himself, that's what we'll do. *When this is all over. When Vasily is put away. When Caitlyn is safe. We'll find Emma, Caty and I, and bring her home to live with us.*

The other little cloud in his blue sky wasn't as easy to

define or to banish. It had to do with the way things had ended with Caitlyn last night.

He'd wanted her to stay with him, of course. He'd have loved to spend the night sleeping with her body curled up next to his, the scent of her hair in his nostrils...wake up in the morning and see her face smiling at him across the rim of his coffee cup. But she'd insisted on having him drive her back to his mother's house. And hadn't that given him a weird feeling, to walk her into his momma's kitchen while his body still throbbed with hunger for her, his appetite for her in no way quenched.

Outside, in the glow of the yard light he'd held her and kissed her one more time, missing her already, but when he would have told her he loved her, she stopped him with fingertips pressed against his lips. Those silver eyes of hers had gazed for a long intense moment into his—he'd swear, it was almost as if she could *see* him—and then, just before she'd stood on her tiptoes to kiss him, she'd said, with a funny little break in her voice, "Thank you for this night."

Thank you for this night. As if, he thought, she didn't expect to have another.

The notion put a chill in his heart and a weakness in his knees, so the next truck stop he came to he pulled off the interstate. Most likely he was making something out of nothing. Most likely all he needed was a dinner break.

He was sitting in the driver's section of the restaurant having his usual on-the-road dinner of chicken-fried steak, mashed potatoes and gravy and coleslaw, keeping half an eye on the overhead television, which was once again tuned to CNN *Headline News.* He'd watched, without paying real close attention, the usual pentagon briefing on the military buildup in the Middle East and the war on terrorism, and pictures of the devastation caused by the latest hurricane down in Cuba. Then he saw something he didn't quite believe at first. When he did believe it his hands went numb and the bite of steak he'd just taken turned to grit in his mouth.

Caitlyn.

There she was, big as life, plain as day…talking to someone, looking, not at the camera, but at some interviewer off to the side. For an instant he dared to hope it was old footage, an update on the case, maybe. But no—the short, pale hair, cut in feathered layers like the petals of a chrysanthemum, couldn't quite hide the healing scar that slashed across her forehead.

The camera moved back, and he saw that she was sitting on a sofa in what looked like one of those made-up TV interview sets, with shelves full of books and a big vase of flowers behind her. Beside her on the sofa was C.J.'s sister-in-law, Charly—his own lawyer. And sitting in the chair facing those two was someone else he knew—Eve Waskowitz, the TV documentary filmmaker. Wife of Special Agent Jake Redfield of the FBI.

Caitlyn was speaking. Belatedly, C.J. tore his eyes from the women and focused on the closed captioning.

…nine o'clock tomorrow morning.

Interviewer: Will you be disclosing the whereabouts of Emma Vasily?

Caitlyn Brown: My position on that hasn't changed. I've said I don't know where she is. I still don't. And I will not disclose my contacts, so…

Interviewer: And are you prepared to go back to jail?

Caitlyn: I guess that will be up to the judge to decide.

Interviewer: Ms. Brown, what made you decide to turn yourself in? If you don't intend to obey Judge Calhoun's order—

Caitlyn: I never intended to spend the rest of my life as a fugitive. I just needed some time to heal…the shock of getting shot…Mary Kelly murdered…and then losing my eyesight. I didn't know whether I was going to be blind—

Interviewer: So, as I understand it your eyesight has returned.

Caitlyn: Yes, that's right. Not all the way yet—I see indistinctly and not really in color—sort of the way you see when there isn't much light. It's getting better all the time. The doctors said there was a chance it would come back as the swelling went down and it looks as though they were right.

Interviewer: I know you must be so happy.

Caitlyn: Well…relieved might be a better word. How can I be happy when Mary Kelly is still dead? She isn't ever going to get well.

Caitlyn's face disappeared. Now there was the anchorman again, and the white-on-black rectangles ticking across the screen: *You can catch the rest of Eve Redfield's exclusive interview tonight on…*

C.J. didn't see anything more. Next thing he knew he was on his feet with his dinner check in his hand, staring down at what might as well have been written in Chinese. He remembered throwing some money on the table and walking outside into a crisp autumn night. He remembered standing beside his truck, leaning his forehead against the cold steel door and waiting for the ground to stop heaving under his feet.

Déjà vu, that's what it is. This can't be happening again. It can't be.

He was about to climb into the cab when some sort of instinct—self-preservation, maybe—stopped him. He was in no condition to drive. He'd be an eighty-thousand-pound menace on the road if he did, a disaster looking for a place to happen.

He took deep breaths to steady himself, then walked slowly around the tractor-trailer, checking his lights and brake lines, plodding methodically through all the steps of a complete safety check, forcing himself to concentrate on that. Little by little his mind cleared, and the sense of shock and betrayal that had just about swamped him began to recede. And when it did, he realized he wasn't angry with her. He was barely even surprised. *Caty's stubborn. When she sets her mind to do something, she goes ahead and does it, and doesn't count the cost.*

Thank you for this night. He ought to have known, when she said that, the way she'd said it. The way she'd looked at him with that silver light in her eyes.

He wasn't angry or surprised, but he was disappointed. Disappointed she hadn't shared with him the incredible fact that her eyesight had come back. That hurt, way deep down inside, more than he wanted to admit or even think about. Disappointed, too, that she hadn't trusted him enough to let him in on what she was planning to do.

Trust you? a little voice way back in his mind mocked him. *Why should she trust you? Aren't you the one that turned her in to the cops the last time she did that? And be honest, Calvin James Starr, wouldn't you have tried to stop her this time, too?*

His answer to that was: *You're damn right I would.*

Because what he was most of all was scared to death. He knew exactly what Caitlyn was trying to do, with her television interview, announcing to the world her intention to turn herself in, even giving the exact time and place. She was staking herself out like a lamb in a clearing, to lure the tiger—Vasily—into the open. And it would probably work; he had an idea that most of the time in situations like this, the tiger ended up dead. Only thing is, most times the lamb did, too.

Nine o'clock tomorrow morning…

Cold washed over him and settled in the pit of his stomach. At nine o'clock tomorrow morning the woman he loved was going to walk into a killer's gunsight, and he was roughly six hundred miles away from being able to do anything to stop her. Six hundred miles. His only hope of getting there in time was to drive nonstop for ten hours and pray for good weather and no traffic tie-ups.

He took his cell phone out of its belt holster and punched in Charly's number. After five rings her voice mail picked up. He didn't leave a message. He didn't have Jake Redfield's number with him, so he called information and got the Bureau headquarters in Atlanta. After a couple of transfers and some waiting around he was told that Special Agent Redfield was on assignment. Was there someone else who could help him? Would he like to leave a message? C.J. said, "No, thank you," and disconnected.

His mind was clear and calm now, as he climbed into the cab of the idling Kenworth and turned on the running lights. A few minutes later he was roaring back onto the interstate, this time heading south.

The weather gods were against him. A cold front moving in from the west had, as usual, stalled out against the mountains and decided to dump its load of cold, sleety rain right there in the Virginias instead of saving it for the drought-stricken northeast. Between the nervous four-wheeler drivers poking along at fifty and the crazies trying to get around them, traffic was a zoo. Then there were the truck lane gear and speed restrictions on the grades, and a long slow crawl through construction outside Charlotte.… C.J. was tense enough to bite nails when he finally left the interstate at the Anderson exit and began to make his way down the stop-and-go main drag through town to the courthouse.

The way he remembered it, the designated truck route wouldn't let him go down Main Street, which had been subjected to one of those downtown renovation projects, including a lot of planter boxes and trees and the traffic flow restricted to one lane each way. He remembered the courthouse; the mall in front that was a patchwork of concrete and brick pavers, with more planters and shade trees and benches to sit on, and the stone steps that rose to the courthouse door. The steps Caitlyn had been making her way down, flanked by Mary Kelly and a platoon of police guards, that bright, sunshiny morning in September....

C.J.'s stomach flip-flopped as the TV news videos played over and over again in his mind. It's not going to happen, he told himself. *He won't shoot her. She's the only one who knows where Emma is. He won't shoot her...he won't shoot her....*

He repeated the words like a mantra. Or a prayer.

Before, when he'd dropped Caitlyn and her charges off at the police station, he'd taken the route on the east side of Main. This time he was on the west side, which was going to bring him into the parking lot directly behind the courthouse. Right on time, he thought, glancing at his watch just as he saw the light up ahead turn yellow.

Damn. He stomped on the brake and brought the truck to a creaking, hissing stop, then sat drumming his fingers on the steering wheel. Cold sweat trickled down the center of his chest. His leg, tense on the brake pedal, had developed a muscle twitch. Through the half-open window of the cab he could hear the clock on the bell tower across the street from the courthouse—the one from which the sniper had taken his shots—begin to strike the hour.

Come on, come on, dammit. Turn green....

And then he saw her. Them. Caitlyn and Charly. There they were, crossing the street from the parking lot about a block and a half in front of him. Caitlyn was wearing a light-gray tailored business-type suit she must have borrowed from Charly—he couldn't imagine where else she'd have come by such a thing—but he'd have known that chrysanthemum cap of pale-gold hair...that graceful, light-as-a-fairy walk anywhere.

His heart just about shot through the roof of his mouth. Heart hammering, wired and helpless, he gripped the steering wheel hard enough to break it off in his hands, while his mind shouted futilely, *Caitlyn, wait!*

He was so focused on the two women he failed to notice right away the long white sedan with dark tinted windows that was moving slowly toward them from the opposite direction. Not until it stopped, and the passenger side door opened, and a man got out. Even though he'd been half expecting it, C.J. was so frozen with shock it was a second or two before he realized the man was wearing a ski mask.

It happened so quickly. The man didn't hesitate, but rushed straight at the two women, grabbed Caitlyn's arms from behind and at the same time kicked Charly savagely in the back of her legs. As she crumpled to the pavement, he was already turning, half dragging, half carrying Caitlyn toward the waiting car.

But by that time C.J. had the Kenworth in gear and, as truckers used to say, the pedal to the metal. He hadn't thought about it, didn't know he was going to do it, he just reacted. Caitlyn was in trouble, and in the best hero fashion he went charging to her rescue with the only weapon he had.

Had the light changed? He didn't know nor care. Horns blared as the powerful diesel engine roared and roughly eighty thousand pounds of eighteen wheeler rolled through the intersection. Through a red fog of rage C.J. saw the ski mask swivel toward him, as if in slow motion. He saw the mouth form a round black *O* of astonishment. He had one brief glimpse of Caitlyn's face, bleached white with shock, and then, with a hideous screeching, grinding, breaking sound, his Kenworth's front bumper plowed into the hood of the white sedan.

For a moment he sat frozen, staring down at the wreckage through the windshield of the cab. Truth was, he was pretty shocked at himself, now that the deed was done, even though the driver of the sedan didn't seem to be hurt much. C.J. could see him flailing around inside the car, trying to untangle himself from the airbag and at the same time get the door open—it had apparently been jammed shut by the collision.

What he didn't see was Caitlyn, or the guy in the ski mask. Not until the door on the passenger side of his cab suddenly opened and Caitlyn came hurtling through, propelled by a powerful shove. Right behind her was the ski mask—and something else. For the second time in his life, C.J. found himself staring at the barrel of a gun.

Chapter 15

"Drive," the man in the ski mask snarled, slamming the door behind him. *"Now."*

Hijacked. I don't believe this, C.J. thought. This can't be happening to me *again*.

This time there was no sense of déjà vu. The individual pointing the gun at him now was a long way from a girl with silver eyes trying to save the lives of a woman and her child and no other way to do it except to try a desperate bluff. This guy wasn't bluffing. How, he didn't know—it sure wasn't from experience—but C.J. knew a cold-blooded killer when he saw one.

"I'm drivin', I'm drivin'," he muttered. He already had the truck in reverse.

As the big Kenworth shuddered and separated itself from the wrecked white sedan with another shriek of mangled metal, C.J. glanced over at Caitlyn and was all set to ask her if she was okay when he saw her eyes widen and her head move just slightly. A tiny, almost imperceptible shake. *No!*

"I'm sorry about your truck, mister," she said in a small, frightened voice. A stranger's voice.

Ski Mask cut her off with a savage, "Shut up! Get down!" and shoved her roughly until she was on her knees on the floor between his feet and the center console. The gun in his hand was pressed against her head now, its ugly gray barrel buried in the soft petals of her hair.

A strange prickly rush, like a shower of ice particles, swept C.J. from his scalp to his toes. Ice formed a great lump in the center of his chest.

Outside the windows of the cab, howling sirens and blaring air horns announced the arrival of a whole array of police and emergency vehicles. The light mid-morning traffic was beginning to snarl.

"Get on your radio," Ski Mask growled. "Tell 'em they better clear us out. Otherwise I'm gonna start putting bullets into people, and since I need you to drive, it looks like it'll have to be blondie, here."

C.J. nodded and picked up his CB mike. His mind was clear and calm, and he was pretty sure the guy in the ski mask wasn't going to kill Caitlyn—not yet, anyway. Considering he'd been paid to bring her back alive and in a fit condition to tell what she knew about the whereabouts of Vasily's daughter, Emma, and that the last hired hand to put Caitlyn's life in danger had wound up dead a short time later. So, it was a fairly safe bet that if Ski Mask did put a bullet in her it wouldn't be in a critical place. Not that that made a big difference to C.J.

Dialing in channel nine, he thumbed on the mike and spoke into it. "Uh…channel nine emergency, this is Blue Starr Transport driver requesting assistance…over."

After a tense pause, a woman's voice, calm and professional but at the same time typically, informally Southern, replied, "Yes, Blue Starr, we read you. How's ever'body doin' in there?"

"Doin' okay so far." C.J. glanced over at Caitlyn. Her gaze was fastened on him with that strange silvery intensity, as if she were trying to talk to him with her eyes. Ski Mask made an impatient gesture, and, heart pounding, he turned back to the mike. "We have a, uh…situation here, though. I have a, uh…couple passengers, guy with a hostage. He has a gun, which he says he's gonna use if he doesn't get clear road outa here. Any chance you could, uh…help me out on that?"

There was another pause, longer and even more tense. C.J. waited, his heart thumping against the constriction of his seat belt. Finally, "Okay, Blue Starr, which way you headed?"

C.J. glanced at Ski Mask this time, and chuckled darkly. "Quickest way outa town, would be my guess. I'm thinkin' the interstate?" He looked at Ski Mask, who nodded confirmation.

"Tell 'em they better not follow us, either," he added in a low growl. "I so much as see a cop I'm gonna start shootin'."

"They're never gonna go for that. You think they're gonna let us just drive away?" C.J. said in an incredulous hiss.

"You better hope they do" was Ski Mask's reply.

Grinding his teeth, C.J. passed on the demand and the threat. After the usual pause the calm voice responded, "Okay, Blue Starr, we're gonna give you some room." Another, gentler pause. "You be careful, now…." And then silence.

With a grunt of surprise C.J. hung the mike on its hook and gave his full attention to driving.

Cramped and uncomfortable, wedged unpleasantly against the gunman's legs, Caitlyn closed her eyes and listened to C.J.'s voice, talking in that drawling monotone truckers use on their CB radios…the police dispatcher's voice calmly answering. As the truck growled in stops and starts, twists and turns, the gunman took out a cell phone and punched in a number. She listened to his low-voiced conversation and felt cold, clammy relief wash over her. He was talking to his boss, obviously, telling him about the glitch in their plans…the change of getaway car. Something about a rendezvous point. Everything else, it seemed, was still on track.

For her, too. It's going to be all right, she told herself, riding on the crest of a wave of improbable optimism. It can still work. And then, plunging into a trough of utter despair: *Oh, C.J.—why couldn't you have stayed out of this?*

The FBI's plan had taken everything into account—except this. Maybe it had been a mistake, after all, not to tell him. He would have tried to keep her from taking part in it, of course he would have, but at least he wouldn't have stumbled—no, not stumbled—come charging into the middle of things, magnificently, heroically, like some gallant knight on his great blue and silver steed. *Oh, C.J., how wonderful, how magnificent you were. And how I wish you hadn't done it!*

Vasily wouldn't kill her, she was sure of that, not until he had Emma back in his clutches. And long before that happened, the FBI would have him in theirs. But C.J. Oh, God, they wouldn't hesitate to—and almost certainly would—kill him once they had no more need of him and his truck. How she would stop them, she didn't know; she only knew she had to. *She had to.*

The images of her nightmare came back to her…the people she loved most in the world lying dead in pools of blood.

Once he'd made it to the interstate, C.J. began to breathe easier. The cops were evidently taking Ski Mask's threat seriously. The way through town had been wide-open, and he hadn't seen any overt signs of pursuit in his mirrors so far—not that that meant the cops weren't out there somewhere, following at a safe distance, waiting to see what developed. In fact, C.J. had been wondering what Ski Mask hoped to accomplish with what had undoubtedly been a spur-of-the-moment desperation gambit. Surely he didn't think the cops were just going to stand by and let them drive off into the sunset, free and clear!

That was before he'd heard part of that cell-phone conversation with the bossman. After that he'd understood—especially when Ski Mask instructed him to take the exit for the scenic highway that ran north up into the mountains. They were heading for a "rendezvous," probably with another vehicle. Which meant all they needed was to get far enough ahead of the nearest pursuer to make the switch unseen. The way those little roads wound around up there in the mountains and met themselves coming and going, the cops wouldn't have any way of knowing what vehicle they were in or which way they'd gone.

More important to C.J., with a new car and a new driver, they weren't going to have any further use of the driver they now had—namely him. He didn't have any illusions about what that meant in terms of his future.

Which meant, since he didn't have any way of knowing exactly where this rendezvous was supposed to take place, that he was going to have to make his move as soon as possible. All he had to do was figure out what move to make—preferably one that wasn't going to get him or Caitlyn killed in the execution.

As the Kenworth churned along the two-lane highway through rolling pastureland dotted with farmhouses and cattle grazing in the chilly drizzle, C.J.'s mind was churning, as well, spinning as fast as those eighteen wheels; discarded scenarios hurtling off the vortex of his consciousness like chunks of mud flung from the truck's tires. His heart pounded and the steering wheel grew slick in his hands. The closer to the looming blue haze of the mountains they came, the faster his mind whirled. They were running out of time. He had to do something. *But what?*

They passed sedately through a small town, and shortly after that the road began to curve and climb. That quickly they were in the mountains. And most likely out of time.

It was raining harder now; the cold front lay draped along the shoulders of the Blue Ridge like a feather boa. The road was shiny in the truck's headlights, and wisps of fog sifted through the tops of trees still thick with yellow leaves. The road twisted and turned and climbed steadily higher…and higher. There were few other cars; the rain had evidently deterred the sight-seers who would normally have clogged the mountains roads this time of year.

Any minute now, C.J. thought. Around the next bend we could come to that rendezvous.…

He could feel his heart beating, like the ticking of a clock counting down the final seconds of his life. And Caitlyn's. What would become of her after they killed him? Vasily would have her then. Would the FBI rescue her in time? Had they figured *this* into their plans?

His mind careened backward to the first moment he'd laid eyes on Caitlyn Brown, there in that rainy interstate rest stop. He remembered the fist-in-the-belly shock when she'd pulled that gun out of her pocket. How could he ever have imagined that six months later he'd be fighting to save her life—and the future lives of his unborn children?

Who'd have thought, when she pointed that gun at me and hijacked—

Adrenaline hit him, jolting him so hard he almost let go of the steering wheel. *This has happened to me before. I took a gun away from a hijacker once. I can do it again.*

Calm settled over him. A glance at his passengers, dis-

guised as a check of his right-hand mirror, confirmed what
he'd already observed without realizing it: whether he'd
forgotten in his haste to get himself and his prisoner into
the truck, or hadn't wanted to risk restricting his gun hand,
Ski Mask had neglected to fasten his seat belt. And Caitlyn
was wedged securely into the space between the seat and
the dash, her head resting on folded arms. Snug as a babe
in a car seat.

He could do it. Just like before. If he could get up some
more speed…

"That next turnoff up there, take a right," Ski Mask said.

C.J.'s heart pounded harder. "Right," he said.

Caitlyn lifted her head. Her eyes swiveled toward him
like searchlights, silver beacons in the murky twilight inside
the cab. He gave her a long, intent look as he took the turn,
and a barely perceptible nod.

The side road was paved but narrow. It wound steeply
down between banks thick with ferns, rhododendron and
mountain laurel. Trees rising high on both sides of the road
blocked the light.

"Take it easy," Ski Mask growled, glaring over at him,
"you tryin' to get us killed?"

"Sorry," C.J. muttered. Up ahead he could see a straight
downhill stretch of road, just before it disappeared in a
sharp turn to the left. *Perfect.* He ran it over one more time
in his mind, then hauled in a breath and sent up a prayer.
Then he hit his brakes.

The sound was like a boiler letting go—a giant hiss,
creaks and groans and thumps—as everything in the cab
and the sleeper compartment that wasn't fastened down
hurtled forward at roughly twenty-five miles per hour. One
of the loudest thumps was caused by Ski Mask's forehead
hitting the windshield. C.J. tried not to think too hard about
that sound; it was one he hoped to go the rest of his life
without ever hearing again.

Anyway, for the next few minutes he had enough to do to keep him from dwelling on the fact that he might have just killed somebody. He'd never jackknifed a tractor-trailer before, and that was another experience he'd just as soon never repeat. The ride was bumpy and *loud*. His stomach cringed at the hideous noises his rig was making and the thought of what must be happening to the shiny blue Kenworth and that trailer load of North Carolina apples.

But at last there was stillness, both of sound and of motion. C.J. sat gripping the wheel, thinking for one dazed moment that he must be dizzy, that his internal axis was off plumb. But it was only the cab, which had come to rest canted at an odd angle, with the driver's side higher than the passenger side. Fear clutched at his heart as he looked over at his passengers. It released him, wrung out, drained, limp with relief, when he saw Caitlyn slowly unfolding herself from her cubbyhole, moving stiffly, as if she wasn't sure everything was going to work the way it should.

Ski Mask was slumped against the passenger door; no way to tell if he was breathing or not. His gun was in Caitlyn's hands.

"You okay?" his voice felt sandy in his throat.

She nodded. Her eyes skidded sideways, toward the inert figure by the door. "Is he—?"

"I don't know. I don't think we ought to wait around to find out, though. Whoever he was planning on hooking up with—"

"Your truck—"

"Isn't going anywhere anytime soon," he said dryly. "It's jackknifed. Come on, we have to get—" He was shoving at his door, which seemed to be jammed. "No dice. It'll have to be this way." He shoehorned himself out from under the steering wheel and stretched across the center console.

Caitlyn cringed back out of his way. "Oh God, you're not—"

Trying not to notice her horrified expression, C.J. reached across the gunman's body and opened the door. In an awful sort of slow motion, Ski Mask began to lean…then all at once, tumbled out of the truck. C.J. felt as sick as Caitlyn looked when they heard him hit the pavement with a slithery thud.

"Now you," C.J. said grimly, half lifting, half shoving her toward the door. "I'm right behind you."

He tried not to think about the body lying crumpled on the ground as he stepped over it.

He found Caitlyn waiting for him on the other side of the trailer, as far from Ski Mask as she could get. She was standing in the middle of wet, leaf-littered pavement, hugging herself and looking first up the road, then down, like a lost traveler. He went to her and without a word, folded her into his arms.

He held her for a while, not nearly as long as he wanted to, feeling the tremors she tried to hide. Until she drew away from him with a reluctant sniff.

"I guess you had to do that," she said huskily. "I think he was going to kill you as soon as we got to— Oh, C.J.—" her voice broke "—why did you have to come back? Why couldn't you just—stop…trying…to *help* me, dammit!"

She pounded him once on his chest, then slipped away from him. Eluding him when he reached for her, she put a hand over her eyes. Her vision was still blurry, but she didn't need detail to recognize the shock and bewilderment in his face. She felt awful. Her heart hurt as though it were being torn in two.

"You set it up," he said in a flat voice. "You and Jake Redfield. Right? You were hoping Vasily would make his move. You were hoping to be kidnapped.'' His laugh was a whisper without amusement. "And I...messed things up.''

Pain lanced through her; she cried out with it. "Oh, no! C.J., you were brilliant. Absolutely...complete-ly...magnificent. I couldn't have imagined a more spectac-ular—'' And she was crying, but laughing, too.

Then she was back where she wanted to be, in his arms again, and he was kissing her, wildly, recklessly, smearing both their mouths with her tears. She held him tightly, with all her strength, and felt the tremors he tried so valiantly to hide.

"It's just," she whispered brokenly, "that now I have to worry about keeping you alive. I don't know what I'd do if—''

"Yeah, well, this wouldn't have happened if you hadn't tried to keep me out of it. If you hadn't lied—''

"I know, I know. I'm sorry. I swear I'll never do it again. It's just that you're so damn protective—''

"You damn right I'm protective. I *love* you, dammit!''

"Oh, C.J.," she whispered. She pulled back from him and gazed, unfocused, into his face. "What are we going to do now?''

"Good question.'' Looking past her, over her head, he added grimly, "This might be a good time to let me in on the plan.''

Caitlyn let out a slow breath. Her teeth had begun to chatter. It had stopped raining, but water and leaves fell with a noisy patter as the wind stirred the tops of the trees. "It's simple, really. We figured Vasily would try to kidnap me—he still thinks I know where his daughter is.''

"You mean...you don't?''

"No.'' Her laugh was scared and breathy. "I don't. I know how to get in touch with the people who know, but I can't just...take him to where she is.''

"Oh, God."

"It doesn't matter," Caitlyn said quickly, over his ago-nized groan. "The plan was for me to pretend to know and then lead him into a trap—a fake safe house—where FBI agents would be waiting. C.J.—" At his angry hiss, she caught at his arms, and felt a strange thrill go through her at the strength, the coiled-spring tension in them. "C.J., listen—it would have been all right. Vasily wouldn't risk harming me as long as Emma's in hiding. I'm still his only hope of getting her back."

"Yeah, well—" he cleared his throat with a low growl-ing sound "—right now we have to worry about getting *us* back. I don't suppose you know where the cavalry is, right about now?"

"Staying well back out of the way, I should imagine. They're not going to risk scaring Vasily away."

"Yeah…and speaking of Vasily…" He was once again directing his nervous and searching gaze beyond her. "I don't know how far away the rendezvous point was, but that truck made a good bit of noise jacking itself up like that. If they were anywhere nearby, there's a good possi-bility they heard it. No telling how much time we have before somebody comes to investigate. Do you have any way of contacting those FBI guys? No…guess not." He sighed grimly. "Then I'd say—" He froze. So did she.

They both heard it at the same time: the roar of a pow-erful engine making its way toward them up the steep, winding road.

They took off running instinctively, like flushed quail. Caitlyn's thick-heeled dress shoes making scraping, clump-ing noises on the wet pavement. After a few steps they halted, clutching each other's arms, both talking at once, in panting gusts.

"Where's the gun?" C.J. wheezed.

At the same time Caitlyn was saying, "*You* go—it's me they want."

There was a shocked pause. Caitlyn said, "Oh, no—I left it in the truck."

And C.J. was yelling, "Are you *crazy?*"

They both halted again, breathing hard. Then C.J. said evenly, "I'm not leaving you here. Don't even think about it."

Caitlyn was sobbing. "C.J., you're the one they'll kill!"

"Then I guess we'd better both get the hell out of here, hadn't we?" He gave her a halfhearted smile as he grabbed for her hand. She made a whimpering sound and resisted, only for an instant. "Cheer up," he panted, "maybe it's the Feds."

It wasn't. She knew it wouldn't be, even before she saw the hood of a gray sedan inching its way past the cab of the jackknifed truck, dark tinted windows reflecting jigsaw puzzle pieces of a pearly sky.

"We can't outrun them," C.J. gasped. "If we can make it to the woods—"

But the laurel- and fern-covered banks rose high on both sides of the road, and it was at least fifty yards to a place where they might have been able to leave the road and lose themselves in the undergrowth. It might as well have been miles. C.J. could probably have made it, but he wouldn't leave her, and in her short skirt and clumsy, hard-soled shoes she didn't have a prayer.

The gray sedan throbbed softly and puffed out its warm breath like some great beast, its unhurried pace making it seem almost benign as it came up behind them. Accepting the inevitable, Caitlyn slowed to a limping walk, and after a moment C.J. did, too. The big car glided past them and halted just beyond. The rear door opened and a man stepped out and gestured silently to them with one hand.

In the other was a gun, held with the relaxed competence of one entirely comfortable with its use.

"I'm really starting to hate those things," C.J. muttered as he ducked his head to climb into the back seat.

Caitlyn followed, groping involuntarily, her vision failing in the car's shadowy interior. She felt C.J.'s hand envelop hers, and the sick terror in her heart subsided…just a little.

That small comfort was short-lived. The gunman motioned her impatiently to move over, then wedged himself between her and C.J. She felt the barrel of the gun dig into her ribs as he reached across her to close the door.

Silence settled around the five people inside the car. Cold to the bone, C.J. found that his eyes were riveted on the man in the front passenger seat, the same way they'd have kept track of a coiled rattlesnake.

The man had turned in his seat and was observing them with a tight-lipped smile. Now he favored Caitlyn with a slight nod and said softly, "I am delighted to finally meet you, Miss Brown." His voice, C.J. noted, was slightly accented, something vaguely Eastern European, he guessed. He would probably be considered a handsome man, with even, deeply tanned features and silver hair, thick, wavy and expensively groomed. For some reason he had on sunglasses with mirror lenses, in spite of the heavily overcast day.

He signaled the driver with a hand gesture, and the car began to glide forward. "As you probably have guessed, I am Ari Vasily. I have waited for this moment for…quite a long time. You have something that belongs to me, I believe. Or…perhaps I should say, you know where it may be found." His lips parted to reveal rather large and very white teeth. "But before we get to that—might I ask what you have done with Lorenzo?"

"If you mean the guy who hijacked me," C.J. said, "he didn't fare too well in the...accident."

Vasily's sunglasses swiveled toward C.J., as if until that moment he'd considered him of little consequence. After an interminable moment, his mouth gave a twitch of vexation. "Ah, I see. A pity. Reliable employees are hard to find. Well—" the sunglasses shifted back to Caitlyn "—then we will get immediately to business. My dear Miss Brown—Caitlyn—you will, of course, tell me where they have been keeping my daughter. And quickly—I am certain the authorities will not be far away." He sounded faintly amused by that, C.J. thought, as someone might observing the antics of a clumsy child.

Cold inside, Caitlyn stared at the shiny blur that was Ari Vasily's eyes. This was it—the moment she had been preparing herself for. Everything—*everything*—depended on whether or not she could carry it off.

She took a deep breath and did not have to try very hard to make her voice sound timid and afraid. "But I don't know where Emma is. I swear—"

A slight movement of Vasily's head interrupted her. He made a mild shame-on-you sound with his tongue. "Caitlyn...Caitlyn. Please don't waste our time. If you do not know precisely where my daughter is, you most certainly know how to contact those who do. I want that information, and will do whatever is necessary to obtain it—as quickly as possible. Do you understand?"

She couldn't answer. Her heart was beating too fast, and her tongue seemed to have stuck to the roof of her mouth.

After regarding her for a moment, Vasily shook his head and sighed. "You are correct in thinking I will not kill you, since that would defeat my purpose. There are, of course, numerous ways in which I can induce you to tell me what I want to know, without ever harming one hair of your pretty head. For example..." His voice was a thoughtful purr. Caitlyn's skin shivered as if something unspeakable had crawled over it. "I know that you are a person who cares about other people…very much. You no doubt even care for this unfortunate fellow here—this truck driver who has had the bad judgment to interfere in my affairs."

The sunglasses flicked toward the gunman sitting beside Caitlyn. With the casual indifference of one brushing at a fly, Vasily said, "Shoot him."

Chapter 16

Caitlyn jerked as though she felt the impact of a bullet in her own flesh; her throat contracted in a high, sharp cry. "No—*wait*—please—" She didn't have to pretend the violent shudders that racked her body.

Vasily's hand flicked, and beside her she felt the gunman's body relax slightly. "Yes, Caitlyn?" Vasily purred. "You have changed your mind, perhaps? There is, after all, something you wish to tell me?"

"I...there is a safe house...." She could barely whisper. Her throat felt scoured and peppery. Her heart lumbered in her chest like a stampede, making it hard to breathe. "They would probably take her there. With everybody looking for her...it's the closest place. It's...not far from here, I think. Off the Blue Ridge Parkway. I don't know if I can find it...I was only there once...." Her babbling died for lack of air.

There was a thoughtful silence. Then Vasily turned back to the front of the car with a soft grunt. "For your trucker-friend's sake, I pray that you will find it. Dominic, if you please—"

Clammy and sick to her stomach, Caitlyn closed her eyes and let her head fall back against the seat. She couldn't bring herself to look at C.J. Her mind cried out to him in anguish. *Oh, C.J., I'm so sorry for getting you into this...please forgive me...I love you...I'm so sorry...forgive me....*

The car wound steadily through the mountains, uphill then down, around hairpin curves and along breathless ridges. Ten more miles, maybe fifteen, Caitlyn told herself...the FBI would be ready...waiting. They'd take Vasily down. It would be all over. *It's going to be all right.*

There was only one thing wrong with that reasoning. The agents lying in wait at the safe house would be expecting only one hostage, one Vasily had good reason not to harm. They hadn't counted on C.J.

C.J., I'm sorry...I love you....

"Turn here." The voice was a whip-crack in the silent car.

Caitlyn sat bolt upright. Adrenaline surged through her body as the car swerved sharply to the right onto a paved crossroad. "Why are we turning here?" she gasped. "The parkway—"

"Is a trap, of course," Vasily said in a chillingly conversational tone as the car sped along the gently winding road. He turned in his seat, the sunglasses homing in on her like the eyes of some great predatory insect. "Isn't it, Caitlyn? Did you really think I would fall for such an obvious plot? I have not gotten to where I am by being stupid. Now—let us go back to the beginning and try this again. Sean—your gun, please."

Her mouth opened. Words froze in her throat as the man beside her silently handed his gun to Vasily. She watched in horror as it swung in a short, efficient arc until it was pointing at C.J.

"Now then, Caitlyn—one more time. Where is my daughter?"

"I don't know!" Caitlyn sobbed. "It's the truth. I don't—"

The explosion in that enclosed space was shocking. On its echoes, Caitlyn's scream merged in awful harmony with the agonized sound C.J. made as he doubled over, clutching at his thigh. Numb in mind and body, Caitlyn reached for him, throwing herself across the gunman—Sean's—lap. A hand grabbed her by the hair and jerked her roughly back.

"Now, then," Vasily said softly. "The next bullet will, I assure you, be in a more important spot. So, I ask you again—where are you keeping my daughter?"

"I'll tell you. I *will*," said Caitlyn hoarsely, lifting a shaking hand to her nose. "But you're going to have to turn around. You're going the wrong way."

Funny thing—except for her concern for C.J., she no longer felt the slightest bit afraid. Rage had wiped her mind clear. She knew she had to stall for time, make Vasily believe she really was taking him to Emma's hiding place. All she needed was enough time to allow the agents monitoring the tracking device in her belt buckle to realize, since they were now going in the wrong direction, that the plan had gone awry, and to move in.

Yes. All she needed was time. But how much time did C.J. have? Vasily wouldn't hesitate to kill him—in an instant. But even without another bullet, he was bleeding badly. In utter silence, he lay slumped against the far door, still clutching his thigh with both hands, while blood welled in an unstoppable flood between his fingers. His face was the color of the clouds outside the windows of the car.

After the first glance, she couldn't bring herself to look at him again.

The car lurched and jerked in a clumsy U-turn, then accelerated, careening back down the mountain road at a stomach-churning speed. A low groan came from C.J.'s side of the car.

"I'm going to be sick," Caitlyn announced in a tight voice. She wasn't kidding; she'd always had a tendency to get carsick. At the same time, a desperate plan was forming in the back of her mind. "I mean it—I have to throw up. Pull over—*pull over!*"

The authenticity of her plea was unmistakable, even to Vasily. He made a small hand gesture, and the car rolled to a stop. Caitlyn pounded on the door with her fists until she heard the lock release. Then, grasping the door handle she gave it a mighty push and lunged just in the nick of time into open air.

Empty, drained…she felt weak in the vicinity of her middle, but oddly, at the same time, stronger in mind and body than she'd ever been in her life.

As though from a distance, she heard herself say with utter calm, "I'll be all right if I can just walk around a little. Is it okay if I get out for a minute?"

Vasily jerked his head toward Sean. "Go with her." His voice was tight with disgust.

As though from a distance, she saw herself standing near the car. Her back was to it, as she drew in long breaths of cool, damp air. Behind her, Sean was stooped over as he emerged from the open door. The gun was back in his hand.

From that same great distance she saw herself whirl, and the gun go spinning through the air. She didn't feel the impact of her foot against the side of Sean's head, but she heard it—a wet, sickening *smack.*

As she lunged for the gun, as she picked it up from the ground and felt the still-warm weight of it in her hand, distance suddenly telescoped. Back in her body again, dazed and shaking, she heard confusing and alarming sounds coming from inside the car.

"Calvin!" she screamed, and was lurching toward the open door when he came tumbling headfirst through it, half crawling, half falling. Beyond him through the open door she could see, silhouetted against the driver's-side window, the head of the driver, Dominic, slumped forward over the steering wheel. She realized then that one of the alarming sounds she'd been hearing was the blaring of the car's horn.

"Come on out, Vasily," she yelled, gripping the gun with both hands as she aimed it at the tinted window. "It's over. The FBI is on its way."

Then she watched, openmouthed, as the driver's-side door suddenly opened. Dominic's body rolled sideways and disappeared. The car leaped forward, slamming both open doors with its forward momentum. It roared away down the winding road, leaving Caitlyn standing, swaying, among three inert bodies.

Sobbing, she dropped to her knees beside one of them. "C.J., you idiot," she whispered as she gathered his head into her lap. "What did you have to go and do that for? Why are you always trying to help me? If you bleed to death, what am I going to do? Huh? Answer me that…you…you… What will I ever do without you?"

C.J. looked up through patches of blackness and saw silver eyes gazing down into his. Silver eyes…shining with tears.

"Oh, Lord…if you're crying, I guess I must be dying," he said in a thickened croak. "Either that or you must love me."

"Well, you're not dying!" Caitlyn shouted.

Smiling the famous Starr smile, complete with dimples, C.J. closed his eyes. In the distance, sirens were wailing.

Mid-November—Grand Central Station, New York City

"It's almost two," C.J. said. His voice was tight and gruff with nervousness. "The e-mail said two o'clock. I don't see her. You don't think—"

"She'll be here," Caitlyn said, glancing at him. "Are you okay? Maybe you ought to sit down—"

"I'm *okay*." He shifted irritably. He hadn't been out of the hospital all that long, but he was already sick and tired of people fussing over him. He'd be glad when he could throw away the damn cane—that would help. He gave it a defiant little wave to demonstrate that he was only using it to please her, but the truth was, he still had to lean on it a lot more than he liked.

"This place is huge," he muttered, glancing superstitiously over his shoulder at the two women following at a discreet distance behind them—his lawyer, Charly, and the tall, gaunt black woman with her, Mrs. Gibson, from Florida Social Services. This moment seemed a miracle to him already, but he couldn't get rid of the fear in his heart. So much had happened to get him to this place, and so much still had to happen before he would consider the people he loved safe again. Vasily was being held without bail, his empire was being dismantled and unraveled piece by piece…but still.

"There she is," Caitlyn said softly. She gave his hand a squeeze and began to move toward the child sitting all by herself in a long row of seats.

He didn't recognize her at first. Not until she looked up to see who it was that was stopping to speak to her, calling her by a half-forgotten name. Her hair was brown, not black, and long on her shoulders, the bangs pulled to one side and fastened with a plastic clip. But there was no mistaking those eyes. Frightened eyes…dark as pools. Refugee eyes. He felt an odd little kick in his heart. A remembered tremor under his ribs.

"Hello, Emma," Caitlyn said, as she sat on the edge of the seat next to her. "I'm Caitlyn—remember me?"

The little girl nodded. Her eyes slid past Caitlyn. She

glanced fearfully at C.J., then asked in a small voice, "Where's Myrna? She told me to wait right here. She said we were going to Disney World."

"That's right. C.J. and I are going to take you to Disney World. But Myrna can't come, sweetie—I'm sorry."

"Why not?" The big eyes shimmered with impending tears.

"She has to go away, Emma," Caitlyn said gently. "She can't be with you anymore."

"Like my mommy?"

Caitlyn hesitated, then nodded. "Sort of, yeah."

Emma sniffed. Her bewildered eyes lifted again. "Then who's going to take care of me?"

"We are," Caitlyn said. "C.J. and me." Her groping hand found C.J.'s and drew him closer. "You remember C.J., don't you?" Emma gazed up at him in unblinking silence.

He looked back at her, hollow with nervousness and a kind of fear he'd never felt before. Then he shifted the cane to his other hand so he could open the plastic shopping bag he'd been carrying. The bag had the name FAO Schwarz printed on it. He opened it and took something out—a small figure of a little girl with superpowers and huge black eyes. He heard a tiny hitch of indrawn breath. "I don't know which one this is," he said gruffly. "Guess you're gonna have to tell me."

A small hand reached slowly. The black eyes widened, then lifted once more to C.J.'s. He nodded, and with a sudden, swift movement, she took the toy from him and clasped it to her narrow chest. She hitched herself forward in the chair and stood up, at the same time reaching for his hand.

C.J.'s heart trembled when he felt the warm little hand burrow into his, like a baby animal into its nest.

"Did you hurt yourself?" Emma was looking at his cane.

C.J. cleared his throat and managed to mutter, "Yeah…a little bit."

"Are you going to get well?"

"Oh, yeah," said C.J. He was still looking into Caitlyn's eyes. "I'm going to be fine."

"Then I guess it'll be okay," said Emma. She looked up at him, and for the first time ever, he saw her smile. "You have to walk an awful lot at Disney World, you know."

C.J. didn't think of himself as macho, but he wasn't all that crazy about the idea of weeping in public, either. Panic-stricken, he looked over at Caitlyn. She was smiling at him, her eyes silvery and overflowing with all the love a man could ever wish for.

"We'd better be going, then," she said, picking it up from there. "It's a long way to Disney World."

"After that where will we go?" Emma asked, uncertain again.

"Home," C.J. said gruffly, still looking at Caitlyn. He was thinking of his wish, his impossible dream, and the miracle that had granted it to him. *Or…Providence?*

Caitlyn's eyes softened, and so did her smile. "Yes, home," she said. "You've got those bar exams to study for. And…we've got a wedding to plan."

*   *   *   *   *

Coming in August 2003

Back by popular demand!

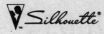 *Silhouette*®

INTIMATE MOMENTS™

proudly presents RITA® Award-winning
and RWA Hall of Fame author

KATHLEEN KORBEL

Enjoy her latest Kendall Family title

Some Men's Dreams
(IM #1237)

Genevieve Kendall had devoted her entire
life to caring for others, all the while hiding
the pain of her own childhood. Now, to help
single father Dr. Jack O'Neill's little girl, she
must finally reveal her most personal secret.
But if she risks herself to save his daughter,
will Jack be there to mend Gen's broken heart?

*Don't miss the other emotional Kendall Family titles,
available only from Silhouette Books.*

JAKE'S WAY IM #413
SIMPLE GIFTS IM #571

Silhouette®

Where love comes alive™

Three men of mystery, three riveting classics from
the incomparable mistress of romantic suspense

#1 *New York Times* bestselling author

NORA ROBERTS

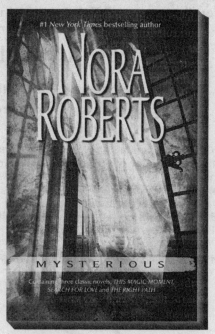

Available at your favorite retail outlet.

Where love comes alive™

If you enjoyed what you just read,
then we've got an offer you can't resist!

Take 2 bestselling
love stories FREE!
Plus get a FREE surprise gift!

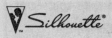
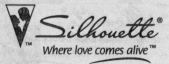